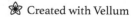 Created with Vellum

REAPER'S ORDER

Founders Series Book One

MARI DIETZ

CONTENTS

For my brother, Stephen.
You gave me a notebook and told me to write. That's the best
writing advice anyone can give.
Even though you aren't on Earth anymore, I hold you in my
heart.

❦ I ❦
VIC

Time to hunt.

Vic cracked her neck and shuffled through the black clothing on the floor. After a few failed sniff tests, she deemed a pair of jeans and hooded sweatshirt passable, detecting only the slight smell of mildew. Cold wetness dripped onto her bare back as she dressed. Vic shivered and ducked out of the way of the ceiling leak in her apartment. With her foot, she slid the bucket back into place and ignored the fresh puddle. It wasn't like a little more water would damage the floor.

The floorboards bent under her weight as she padded to her fridge. Even though she'd grown bone thin from her lack of food, the rotted floor still complained.

She opened the fridge, and a cockroach skittered out, fleeing the light. She crunched it under her heel. "Scraps, you missed one."

The gray cat blinked his yellow eyes at her from the bed, then ignored her once more.

Vic grinned. This one-room apartment's moldy walls

could fall down around them and Scraps would sleep through it. The rent for this trash heap was next to nothing, and Vic didn't mind its shabby state. During the first few weeks after moving in, she hadn't been able to sleep, but in a way, she'd found a peace here that she'd never had while living with her family. For that price, she could live with a leaky ceiling and unwanted critters until she fell through the floors.

A jar of pickles sat at the back of her fridge. Vic didn't remember buying them. Better this than nothing while she hunted. Her fingers dug into the jar, grabbing the sadly floating pickle, then she tipped back the container and drank the liquid. She gagged at the vinegary taste. Not that it mattered, but pickles went on her list of things she never wanted to eat again. To wash down the brine on her tongue, she turned on the rusty faucet. The pipes groaned, but no water came out.

"Blight, I didn't pay the gic bill." GicCorp monitored the use of water, and everything ran on magic, aka gic. Monitoring was supposed to help combat the magic pollution called blight.

As if on cue, the lights flickered and plunged her into darkness. The freedom of living on her own had come at a steeper price than she'd realized. She blinked as her vision adjusted to the streetlight shining through her grimy windows.

Her scythe felt out of place leaning in the corner of her studio apartment. Its slender, polished wooden handle shone from use. The silver blade gleamed in the bleak lighting. The weapon was the only thing from her past life that mattered.

She pressed the top of the staff, and with a loud click, her scythe folded in on itself, the blade tucked into the handle. She shrugged on her leather harness, slid the relic into place on her back, pulled up her hood, and tucked her braided red hair under it. She pulled down the sleeves to cover her pale skin. Her sister, Emilia, joked that her skin reflected all light, even at night, which was ironic since she was as pale as Vic. Tonight, she needed to be invisible.

"Keep an eye on the apartment, Scraps. If you hunt, be careful." Not that she had anything of value to steal. Her scythe stayed with her, and if any thieves wanted a pile of dirty clothing, they could have at it. Still, she clicked the lock into place behind her. A small hole to the side of the door with a flap allowed Scraps in and out of the apartment. He might have plenty of rats to catch inside, though.

Her booted feet hit the rough stone of the narrow street. The constant sound of the canal water bubbled in the night. Vic took a deep breath of the wonderfully humid air, thick with the smell of rot and mildew. Most might find it hard to breathe here, in the so-called slums of Verrin, but Vic found the cleaner air in the center of town more stifling.

Instead of going to the unowned territory to hunt like the other freelancers, Vic headed toward the land of an Order. Scratching her neck nervously, she stayed in the shadows. If the Order's reapers caught her, they would take her relic away, but if she didn't get paid, she might as well dig through the trash for food.

She could imagine the headline in the tabloid *Verrin Daily*: "Glass Heiress Eats Trash."

This time, her mother might actually faint over her disgraced daughter's escapades. Vic had already left her family home; she didn't need to provide her father with a reason to drag her back by the hair.

She jogged across the low bridge over the canal. Boreus territory was her best bet to hunt in. If they caught her, they would be the most merciful—maybe. In these last few weeks, too much competition from other freelancers had left her gicgauge empty. All she had to look forward to were some packaged noodles. Yum.

"Get the blight, get out, get paid. That's all I need."

Her breath evened out as she ran.

After sunset, corrupted souls roamed the city, their minds decaying from the blight. Magic powered everything in Verrin, but it also corrupted the citizens. The blight resulted from the overuse of magic. As a reaper, it was her job to collect it.

Vic glanced up at the bright streaks of colorful blight swirling in the night sky. The infected air might be beautiful if only it would stay in the sky and not cling to humans, mutating them into monsters called *mogs,* which enjoyed feasting on uncorrupted humans.

A low gateway appeared ahead, and she vaulted over it. She ducked into a dark and narrow alley and drew her scythe. In the cold night air, the magic hummed through the scythe, warming her hands. She slid on her eyepiece and winced as her right eye adjusted to the light. Her nose wrinkled at the hint of human waste coming from her hiding place.

There'd be nothing flashy about tonight. Reap the blight from humans and stay hidden. Vic crouched in wait, letting the darkness of the alley absorb her.

A foot skidded against stone to her left, and Vic took in the distant form. The figure gave off a bluish hue through her eyepiece. Only mildly corrupted, but she needed to start filling her scythe's gicgauge with blight.

The woman shuffled past Vic's hiding place, her hair hanging limply in the humid air and her eyes glazed over. The blight had already taken over her mind.

Vic kicked the back of the woman's knees. The woman jerked and fell to the ground. Vic pounced and planted her foot on the woman's lower back. She pressed the scythe blade to the exposed skin of the woman's arm, and with a jolt, the scythe absorbed the blight from her.

The woman thrashed, but Vic leaned into her lower hip to pin her, and after only a few moments, the woman stilled. When the hot flow of magic stopped, Vic gently stood, not wanting to hurt her.

She eyed the gicgauge on her scythe. The glass attachment showed what percentage of blight the stone in the relic could hold. The tiny amount of blight she'd gathered had barely made a blip. She massaged her temples and sighed heavily. This would be a long night.

Vic mentally groaned. She might not be able to gather enough blight to pay the bills. Plans for a hot meal faded, but she focused on the woman. Nudging her with her hand, she asked, "Are you okay?"

A noise escaped the woman, and she turned over. The whites of her eyes reflected the moonlight. Her hair fanned out and clung to the muck on the street. "What happened?"

Vic held out her hand. "You had the blight."

There was no need to elaborate. She should be safe —for now.

The woman shot up, ignoring Vic's proffered hand. "What?" She touched her neck. "Didn't I get charged?"

To prevent getting infected with blight, the citizens of Verrin all had a gicorb implanted in their necks. Only a raised section of skin gave away the implanted orb. However, if they didn't keep up the charge, the blight could enter their bodies. "I don't know, but you should be good to go. Make sure you charge when you need it. Do you need help getting home?" Vic didn't have time to help her, but the woman was more out of it than usual. Sometimes, even if you monitored your charge, you could get corrupted. In Verrin, you needed a bit of luck.

The woman placed her hand on the wall to steady herself. "No, I'm fine. Thank you, reaper. Which Order are you from?"

None of them. "Boreus."

Vic had already broken the law by hunting outside the freelance territory, so lying to this person hardly mattered.

The woman nodded. "I will direct my thanks to them."

Vic walked down the edge of the canal and away from her. No need to stick around for her to notice how her neck lacked the brand of an Order. She pulled her hood tighter around her neck. A quick glance at her gicgauge caused her skin to itch. Worrying about her hunger could wait. Charging her gicorb was more important.

To put her mind at ease, Vic navigated to the nearest charging station. A green box sat on the street corner, and she folded the doors aside and got inside. The lights in the charging station hummed softly. It figured these would be worn down. Nothing like not giving the people in the poorer sections of town a nice charging station.

The bright panel, attached to the wall, glowed with three different lighter green circles for gicgauges. Vic clamped her gicgauge to the far right circle. With a hiss, a bright light surrounded the gicgauge, and a clacking sound rose as it drained the blight she'd gathered. A ping told her it had finished. After that, the station gave her two options: she could slide her card in and get credits, or she could raise the pole to recharge her gicorb directly.

Her neck burned from her scratching it, but she needed to charge her gicorb. Blight couldn't enter their bodies if they stayed charged. From her frantic itching all night, she knew she'd let her orb run low too long. She held the pole up to her neck where the orb was implanted. It pulsed, and instant relief filled her as the itching went away. Vic placed the pole back down and grabbed her scythe. One worry down and only a hundred more to go. She let out a laugh. If she turned into a mog, there would be no more bills to pay. She could live in the sewers free of charge and feed on rats and humans. What a life that would be.

She stuck to the shadows and headed toward the parts of the lower district where it would be darker. Mogs would be out hunting for food soon; she needed to find them before the Order did. The mogs in the city would be recently turned and have less blight. The gicgauge had one drawback: once full, it couldn't gather any more blight until emptied at a charging station. Older mogs required a group of reapers to drain all the blight.

The pickle juice gurgled inside her stomach as she darted through the shadows. She passed by a stone bridge crumbling into the canal below. The city didn't bother maintaining the slums of Verrin. Stone crumbled into the canal from the cobbled streets, and the air practically felt like water in her lungs. A pattering of footsteps sounded to her right. She ducked to avoid detection as a group of hooded figures ran past her. Reapers.

Not that way, then.

Vic turned down the alley, and the overhangs on the buildings blocked out the moonlight. Then a low groan filled the silent alley. Vic's vision flicked to the side, and vivid, putrid crimson flashed in her eyepiece. She rolled, the clawed hand missing her by mere inches.

There's my mog.

With no time to think, Vic jumped up and backed away from the looming figure. Black, shiny skin hung in globs off large, misshapen bones, and the scent of rotting flesh filled her nose. From its wide head, two reddish eyes pulsated mindlessly. The thing had once been human, but with the blight going unchecked, it had mutated into something that knew only endless hunger. There would be no pinning this thing down like the woman, but she couldn't leave the alley and risk someone spotting her. The cramped space wasn't ideal for dealing with a mog this size.

Vic drew her scythe, and it unfolded with a click that echoed in the night. The mog rose onto its haunches. Liquid, which looked red in her eyepiece, dripped in thick rivulets, leaving a trail of blighted skin chunks behind. There was no way to tell who the mog used to be. The blight didn't care who you were, and all humans who couldn't get charged mutated.

Another groan filled her ears, and its jaws widened to show squat, stubby teeth good for grinding bones. Vic lowered the blade between her and the mog. Hitting it early would be her best chance. The mog swung its burly arms at her and met her blade. The blight scorched as it tore through her scythe. The mog screeched and withdrew its arm. Its eyes burned through the globs of blighted skin dripping down its face. It quickly learned to avoid the blade, but some of its energy would be depleted.

Vic stepped forward on the offensive and slashed at the creature. Its heavy form dodged backward, avoiding the blade of her scythe. As she pushed it back, the cobblestones grew slippery from the mog's skin. Just her luck to get a slimy mog; it had to live in the water. Finding footing in the dark was difficult, and the mog backed out onto the main road near the canal. Her chances of discovery would rise if she fought it out in the open.

This mog cared more about getting sliced than its hunger, so Vic stood still and lowered her blade to her side.

"Come on, swamp breath. Are you hungry?" Vic raised her hand at the creature, palm up, and flicked her fingers toward herself. "Come and get it. I may taste stringy, but I'll be the best snack you've ever eaten. I'm even marinated in pickle juice."

A groan rumbled from its throat. It shook its massive body, and clumps of skin flew all over her and the alley. In the quarter of a second that Vic blinked, a massive force slammed into her ribs. She gasped as she was thrown back. Her body hit the wall, and she slid down, coughing. As the mog's fist flashed forward to crush her head, she flattened herself to the ground. It must like ground meat.

Vic flinched at the sharp pain in her side. Getting out of the alley now seemed like a smart option. She rolled to the side, getting covered in bits of its mutated body, jumped to her feet, and ran out into the open area of the main canal. The mog loped after her on its fists. She turned and slashed the blade across its face. The energy drained, and the mog flung its arms up, knocking the scythe upward and tipping her back on her heels. She placed her foot back to catch herself but only found air.

With a yelp, she fell backward and splashed into the cold water. Her clothes stuck to her skin and grew heavier as water saturated them. After a bit of flailing, she found her footing. The water was up to her neck. The smooth walls offered no way out of the water. A wave hit her in the face, and she spat out putrid canal water. A glance to the side revealed the mog had joined her in the canal. It had lumbered on land, but in the water, it swam with quick, sure strokes.

Vic let the current take her as the mog followed. She floated backward, kicking her legs to gain speed. With no time to look for a ladder out of the water, she tried to stay ahead, but the mog was gaining on her. Over the sound of the water, she could hear herself gasping in short, shallow breaths as she swam away from the monster.

It dipped under the water, and she lost sight of it. She flitted her gaze across the surface of the dark water, but she was in the mog's domain now. Something brushed against her leg, and she kicked. Wrong move. It seized her ankle and pulled her up. The mog rose, dangling Vic in front of its stumpy teeth.

Its rotten breath flowed over her face, and her stomach ejected the pickle juice. Blood rushed to her head as she struggled in the mog's grip. Her ankle screamed as her weight tried to pull it apart from her leg. She desperately clutched her relic, shaking.

Jaws looming open, it lowered Vic into its mouth, but in its hunger, it had forgotten about the scythe. She grabbed the staff in both hands and swung the point of the blade through its throat, spearing the mog's neck.

The mog gurgled, its airway cut off. It thrashed, dropping Vic, but she hung on to the end of the scythe, the weapon still lodged in its neck. Energy poured out of the mog, and globs of flesh melted off its frame. When the only thing left was its mutated skeleton, which crumbled in the current, the scythe dropped and Vic splashed into the water. Her relic burned in her hands. The gicgauge was more than full enough for food credits. Blight, maybe she could go crazy and pay the gic bill and get the water turned back on. Since her gicgauge had been empty, she'd been able to drain the mog on her own. Her lack of successful hunting had helped her survive tonight.

She tried to walk in the canal, but when she put pressure on her ankle, pain burned in her leg. She went back to floating. The bridge ahead had small steps built into the wall, and Vic used her arms and one leg to guide herself toward it. She took off her eyepiece and tucked it into her harness.

As she reached for the steps, a low voice sounded from the other side. "Quite the show you put on."

Vic's hand froze on the first algae-covered step, and she turned around to see four figures dressed in black—reapers. In an Order, reapers always hunted in groups of four or more.

"Thanks." She took her time pulling herself up the steps, pretending to be calm. They didn't know she didn't have a brand. She sat on the edge of the canal, feet dangling over the side. The scythe, still warm in her hands, folded up with a click, and she tucked it back in her harness. Once she had her breathing under control, she pushed herself up and rested her weight on her right foot.

If she needed to run, it wouldn't be fun. Four reapers against a Limpy Lou. Vic didn't like her odds. Her mind raced on how to get out of this situation. She willed her face to stay neutral. Her ankle wasn't broken, but it also couldn't bear her weight.

Vic made sure her hood covered her bare neck. She shivered in her wet clothes.

The tallest figure walked to the bridge. He glided, with no movement wasted. A fighter and a good one.

Vic controlled her urge to gulp at his approach. He took his time. A patient hunter. She couldn't help but feel like trapped prey. The canal's water lapped against the walls, and Vic's heart pounded.

He stood in the middle of the bridge, and to the untrained eye, he'd seem relaxed, but Vic could see his body was ready to spring forward and attack.

"I don't know you. Do you hunt alone?" His tone sounded casual, and he practically purred with confidence. He pushed back his hood, and in the lamplight, his skin glowed a golden sepia. His russet hair was tied back in a smooth bun. Reapers didn't like having hair in their face while they hunted. He flashed his teeth in a simple smile. This man could have been talking about the color of the blight that day he was so relaxed. If she hadn't been in horrible trouble, she would have found his voice soothing.

Vic rubbed her tongue against her teeth and tried to discern where she'd ended up in the city. The buildings all looked the same at night, and there were no signs around. The bridge was uncovered, but most of them were in Verrin.

"I got separated when I fell in the canal." Vic waved downstream. "I need to head back and let them know I'm okay." She smiled and hoped it looked convincingly innocent. "Taking a mog on by myself is something I wouldn't attempt. I got lucky." She tested her ankle again, and pain shot through her leg. She groaned. So much for running away.

He nodded, but she couldn't see his expression very well in the darkness. His eyes remained two dark pools in the night. "What territory did you come from? You aren't one of mine."

His stance shifted, and he rested his hands on the bridge. Each movement was careful and precise.

All the luck in the world must have gone to someone else tonight. Of course she would run into a commander. He deliberately hadn't mentioned where he was from. If she said the wrong Order, he would know she was lying right away. If she'd started in Boreus, then the current must have taken her into another territory. Vic braced herself and choked out a name: "Boreus."

He ambled forward, not in any rush. "I see. And this canal carried you here?"

She couldn't read anything from his tone, but she would have to be blind not to notice how his hand inched behind his back. To get restraints, perhaps?

"If it's okay, I should get back to my group. I got turned around in the chase." Vic edged backward before he got any closer. From that distance, he could jump over the bridge railing and land next to her. Time to leave. Couldn't he just believe her?

"You're injured. Let us at least help you back to your team. Don't worry, we're well aware of what happens in a chase. In that case, there's no worry about crossing territory lines. Let us offer hospitality."

The words offered kindness, but her skin crawled with foreboding at his tone. A sinking feeling filled her as she thought of which territory she'd ended up in.

She raised her hands. "It isn't bad. I don't want you to lose time."

She willed the pushy man to back off. She couldn't lose her relic. It was her only ticket to freedom.

"The night's young." His white teeth caught the lamp-light again as he grinned.

Vic smiled tightly. "No need, really. I'll be off."

She limped to the sidewalk next to the canal and headed back in the direction she'd come from.

He raised his voice over the echo of the water, saying, "You see, there's one small problem."

Vic froze but didn't turn around. Her skin prickled along her spine. "Yes?"

"Boreus territory isn't in that direction. That's Nyx territory, so I will need you to let me see your brand or lack thereof."

Vic bit her lip and turned her head. "Oh, that's not a problem," she said and promptly jumped back into the water.

The icy water didn't feel as brutal the second time around. Actually, it felt warm. Maybe she was hypothermic. Remaining under the water, Vic let the current push her away from the man. Blight take her, she'd ended up in the number one Order. She might as well gift-wrap her scythe and hand it over to the officers. The pressure in her lungs warned that she needed to breathe soon. Vic used her arms to propel herself downstream. Her mind spun.

How am I going to get out of this? Think.

The main canals all led to the center of Verrin. The side paths and alleys were wider and not as winding as the poorer sections of town. Some buildings stood over two stories tall, so she couldn't scale them, even with two good ankles. Brighter lamps left little to no shadows. There was nowhere to hide.

No longer able to hold her breath, she broke through the surface and gasped. She tipped her head to the side and kept swimming, but she also tried to see if anyone was pursuing her. The sound of running footsteps made her heart sink. She rotated onto her back, and in the glow of the streetlights, she saw one figure keeping pace with her. Apparently, there was no need for the others; he could apprehend the injured trespasser by himself. Cocky jerk. He jogged with the ease of a practiced runner in no rush.

The lamplight shone down on them as they arrived at the center of town.

She met his eyes.

He smiled.

Vic gritted her teeth.

"Nice night for a swim?" he asked. He didn't even sound a little out of breath.

"Why don't you come in and join me?" Canal water entered her mouth, making her sputter.

He barked out a laugh and skirted a lamppost with ease. "I have a feeling you'll make me fish you out, but I'd appreciate it if you came out. I don't want to freeze off certain body parts I'm rather attached to."

"Blight take your balls," Vic spat. She paddled downstream and searched for any hopeful escape routes. Why did the center of town have to be so structured?

"What's the plan? Get caught in a grate downtown?"

"No, I have a better plan than that." *Not.*

Yelling at each other wasn't working very well, so no plan there.

"Can't wait to see it, Sparks." His voice remained steady as he ran. Now that he could run on smoother cobbles, he wouldn't have the decency to trip.

The cold seeped into her skin. Her fingers stiffened, and gripping anything at the moment would be problematic.

"How about you let me get out, then we can fight?"

"So, that's the big plan?"

"Or you could go away?"

"Not a chance."

Was that a hint of laughter in his voice? Vic planted her feet and faced her mysterious stalker. The water lapped against her waist, and as the cold night air wove through her wet clothing, she tried to stop shaking.

The man stopped and crossed his arms. "Give up?"

"Just waiting for you to come in here." Her gaze wandered in search of anything that could help her.

He snorted. "All right, Sparks." In measured movements, he removed his long-sleeved black shirt. The shirt had hidden the defined muscles now very much on display as he undressed under a tall streetlight. Vic couldn't help herself. She swallowed.

He neatly folded his shirt, placed it at the edge of the canal, and winked at her. "Like the view?"

"Yes, very nice for a man about to ruin my life." Vic hopped on her foot, trying to stay upright as the current pushed against her.

He pulled off his boots and placed them next to his shirt. "Did I miss something where I made you break the law?"

Heat flooded through Vic as she clutched her waist. "Yeah, like starving people don't concern you."

His face smoothed, then he jumped into the canal. With a steady gait, he waded to where she stood. Even in the water, he moved gracefully.

He reached for her arm, but Vic hopped aside and lifted her feet to let the current carry her out of his reach.

With a sigh, he lunged forward and knocked her off balance from her right leg. Her left foot came down, and she yelped in pain.

"Can you just get out of the water?" He splashed water at her.

"I made that offer earlier."

"I have zero desire to fight an injured person."

She returned the splash, and the water hit his face. "Oh, how gentlemanly of you."

As he brushed away the water, she forced herself to stand on both feet. She bit the inside of her cheek when the pain hit her. With all the force she could muster, she swung her left leg through the water and smashed it against his legs. The surprise caused him to slip, and losing his footing, he dipped under the water.

Vic took her chance to swim toward the ladder on the side wall. Her numb fingers slipped on the stone, but she scrambled up to the edge and rolled onto the street. The sound of splashing behind her told her he wasn't far behind.

"Come on, body, move." Her order fueled her. She pushed herself onto her hands and knees and got her feet under her. Her whole body shook.

She limped away at a sad pace.

The man walking next to her only added insult to injury.

"This is going well," he said, mirth tainting his voice.

Vic glared at him and continued to limp along the road. Water ran in rivulets down his bare skin. She forced herself to look away. "You lost your shirt."

"At this rate, I'll have time to go get it and come back. Twice."

Hysterical laugher fell out of Vic. She dropped to her knees, not caring that the stone bit through her jeans. The pain returned some feeling to her limbs. She crossed her arms and sat back on the ground, laughing. This was it. With her body frozen and ankle useless, this man could run circles around her.

He stood over her, eyebrows raised. "Sparks, you okay?"

"Just give me a second and I'll grab my scythe and fight you from my knees." She gasped with laughter. A puddle of water pooled around her.

He disappeared, and when he came back, she felt something dry on her head. She reached up, and her numb fingers held his shirt. Her eyes met his, and for the first time, she saw they were a deep brown. How odd that they felt kind. She wrapped the dry shirt around her shoulders.

He held out a hand. "Let's go."

She ignored it and pushed herself up.

"Do you need me to carry you?"

"No." Despite her years of training, she couldn't put up a decent fight. She raised her hand to hit him, and he grasped her wrist, his grip like an iron band.

He turned and tugged on her to follow. "Do I need to tie you up, or are you done?"

She didn't respond. She'd rather go in for her sentencing on her own two feet. If she continued her pathetic attempts to escape, he would sling her over his shoulder like a gutted goat. She jerked her wrist away and wrapped her arms around her waist. Maybe she'd have another opportunity. It couldn't be over yet. Her father had taught her that when all was lost, there would always be a chance to escape. Vic bit her cheek and shook her head. What would that coward know? He'd given up already.

"I suppose if you weren't already injured, you would give me more of a fight." His warm voice washed over her.

Or she could've run. "It doesn't matter."

Her boots grew heavier as she walked, the left one now uncomfortably tight.

"How long have you been freelancing?"

"It doesn't matter."

What did he care? Did he want to know the person he'd doomed? Living in Verrin without a relic—be it a scythe, wand, or ring—was impossible. Those who lost theirs soon became mogs. Now she would have to crawl back to her family, relicless, and watch her sister leave for Haven. The place where the chosen few, called vitals, purified magic.

He paused and faced her. "Pouting?"

"Why does it matter? We both know what happens next."

He walked beside her. "Humor me."

Why did his tone sound like he cared? For a man about to take her to trial, she couldn't hate him. "For the last six months, I've been on my own. I planned to join the trials for the Dei Order next week, but I was hungry." She wanted to join Nyx, but she didn't tell him that. Somehow, she thought it would be more embarrassing since a commander from Nyx had caught her breaking the law.

"Dei? You took out a mog solo. Why not Nyx?" He waited for her to limp onto the narrow bridge first.

"'Cause you're there." Nyx, the top Order, made the most money and had the most prestige. If she got in, she might convince her sister that being a vital was a stupid tradition and she could leave Glass.

Every generation of founders gave one of their children to Haven, and they became vitals. At Haven, the vitals purified the blighted magic by connecting to an ancient relic and producing magic that the citizens of Verrin used to charge their gicorb and stay safe. The kicker? The vitals could never leave Haven. Once connected to the relic, they would die if they left. They lived in a walled-off area, and no one was allowed in or out. Even those who cared for them stayed inside. No one knew what happened to the vitals behind the walls of Haven, and most were too afraid to ask. If they did ask, they were fed the usual rhetoric about the vitals saving Verrin and the connection to the relic. Nothing specific was ever given.

If a founder chose not to be a vital, the family would be ordered to surrender the vital's wand and kick them from the home. If Vic joined an Order, her sister she wouldn't need to disappear to save the world. She could live with Vic. Who cared if there might be a small amount of shame attached? Okay, maybe a large amount of shame.

"Hmm ..." He led her to an alley.

Vic paused at the entrance. The alley, though well lit, didn't lead to the holding cells. "Where are we going?"

"Someplace warm."

"Not the holding cells?"

He gestured to the well-lit main road. "Do you want to go there?"

"No."

"Then come on, Sparks."

"I get it, my hair's red. You can call me Vic. What should I call you? Numb Nuts?"

He stopped in front of a green wooden door. "Kai is fine, but I think you might be more numb than I am."

Kai pushed the door open and turned on the lights.

Vic followed him inside the home. Though it was made of stone, the smell of cedar filled the space. The living area contained a well-used plush couch and two cushy sitting chairs. Though their warm tones didn't match, they somehow looked good together. Different rugs covered the stone floor, making the room cozy. Vic paused in the doorway before she dripped dirty water all over the clean home.

Kai noticed her hesitation. "Don't worry about it. Come in." He went to another room, and she could hear him shuffling around. He came back with more black clothing. "Take a shower and put these on."

Why was he treating her so nicely? He must want something, and Vic felt strange trusting someone she'd just met.

"I won't peek at you. Just get warm. There's a towel under the sink."

Accepting the clothing with stiff fingers, she went to the bathroom. There wasn't much in there, but the smell of cedar grew stronger. A comb lay perfectly in line with a bar of soap on the sink top. She poked the comb to make it crooked, enjoying her petty revenge. She peeled off her wet clothing and harness, and placed her scythe in the bathroom corner close to the shower.

She turned the water as hot as she could handle and stepped under the spray. She kept her weight off her left ankle. Warmth covered her skin as the hot water pelted her. As feeling returned to her limbs, they burned. Vic combed her fingers through her hair, undoing what was left of her braid.

Vic helped herself to the shampoo, and the crisp scent of cedar intensified in the room. What was the point of bringing her here? An ache that wasn't hunger filled her stomach. Nyx always came down the hardest on trespassers. Kai had to be up to something. She shivered but not from the cold. What did he want? She washed the canal water off her skin. What lengths would she go to to make sure her sister didn't go to Haven?

She turned off the water. Steam hung in the air, and she swiftly wrapped her naked body in a towel to get all the moisture off her. Now dry, she put on his clothes. Thankfully, the pants had a drawstring to tighten them, and they hung off her boney hips. Due to a lack of food and weeks spent hunting at night, her skin looked translucent.

With a slight tremor, she opened the door. His home wrapped her in heat. Kai stood next to a wooden table behind the sofa. The smell of vegetable stew hit her, and she closed her eyelids. Saliva filled her mouth, and she swallowed.

"Eat." He gestured at the table. "I'll shower, and if I have to run after you naked, I will, so stay put." He glanced at her. "Or should I tie you?"

"The night air might be refreshing on your skin." She grinned and stayed by the bathroom door.

He sucked in his cheeks, grabbed her by the arms, and pushed her onto the chair. "I have a feeling I should tie you."

As he stood over her, his breath tickled her stray hairs around her temples.

She blushed and blinked at him, her face only inches from his. "I'll be good."

He trailed his hand down her arm, heating her skin. Nothing like finding your captor attractive.

Kai went into the side room again and returned with handcuffs. He bent over, took her uninjured ankle, and cuffed it to a hook in the wall.

Vic raised her brows at the hook. "Just how many women have you brought here and chained up?"

"So many I've lost count." He leaned over and tested the cuffs, making sure they were locked.

Vic shifted back. "Glad I'm important."

"Quiet, Number Forty-Three."

"Thought you'd lost count."

He quirked his lips and went to the bathroom.

When the shower started again, Vic grabbed the spoon and shoveled the stew into her mouth. The vegetables burst on her tongue, along with generous pieces of fish. Moaning, she gulped down the best food she'd eaten in the last month. There was no time to chew. Blight and stone, he didn't have to chain her to the wall. She would have stayed for the food. It could have tasted like the rotted skin from a mog and she still would have eaten it. Warmth spread inside her as her belly filled, and she slowed to savor the stew. When was the last time she'd had meat?

She put the spoon down. The temptation to keep eating nagged at her, but if she ate any more, it would come up again. Vic ran her fingers over the hook and tested how well it was anchored into the wall by trying to twist it. It didn't even rattle a little. He'd joked about it, but worry filled her. Why did he need a hook in the wall?

The bathroom door banged open behind her, and she turned to see Kai wrapped in a towel. His shirtless torso was all hard lines and planes. He winked at her staring at him and went into his room. It only took a moment for him to come out dressed in the normal reaper black.

He sat across from her. "Done?"

"Yes." Vic's heart pounded as she waited for him to tell her what he wanted.

"Why haven't you gone through the trials yet?"

"My parents didn't see the need for a reaper." Her parents expected her to marry an imb, someone who could imbue and form objects with magic, unlike her, and continue the Glass line. Imbs had built the city, and reapers protected it. Her sister, the vital, would be gone soon, and Vic was the only heir. Founders didn't have time to run around after mogs, risking their lives.

"Yet you have an impressive relic?"

Relics like her scythe were passed down in families, unless the officers took them as punishment for committing certain crimes. The more important the family, the more relics they owned. Every member of her family had a first-generation relic. First generations were the most powerful relics and found mostly in Founder homes. A person could either bond with a scythe or a wand. The radiant rings were the exception, apparently anyone could use them if they really wanted to be the pariahs of Verrin. It didn't matter what a person wanted to be, there was never a choice to be an imb or a reaper. Only a choice in the generation level of relic you inherited or bought. The wands hadn't bonded Vic, so she'd taken the only scythe left to her family.

Some tried to control whether they gave birth to a reaper versus an imb, but it was always random. Both of Vic's parents had been born imbs, but she'd turned out to be a reaper. Since she was the only heir, that was a problem for all the Glass factories. She would have to marry an imb who could manage all the Glass holdings.

"I was meant to do other things." Her teeth clenched at the reality that her only purpose in life was to make babies. Nothing could make a woman feel more special than that. Stupid founders.

"What happens once your little rebellion is over? You go back home?" he asked.

Vic pressed her hands to the wooden table. "Excuse me, but you know nothing about me. I fought every day to become a reaper. I'm going to join an Order and stay away from my family."

She would also get her sister away, even if she had to drag her.

"Sometimes, independence isn't everything." Kai gazed off, lost in thought.

She plopped back against the chair. "My life may not be great, but at least I chose it. I have the freedom to do what I want."

Once those words had left her mouth, she realized how selfish they sounded.

His lips formed a thin line. "Noble for someone about to join a group where members depend on each other."

Vic tugged on her damp hair. "I know ... I just mean that ... ugh. I want to be a reaper. This is something I want to be part of rather than have my path in life chosen for me because of the family I was born into. Or a sister forced to purify magic."

Kai studied her as they sat in silence. He knew she was referring to Haven. The founders might be rich, but some didn't have a choice. "Reapers can't join Haven."

She tapped her finger on the table. He was nice, but she shouldn't spill her life problems to him. Also, he might not see them as problems. It was considered an honor to be a vital—so the city said. A vital's duty was to sacrifice a normal life and leave behind everyone they knew. Her heart ached at the thought of her sister.

He sighed. "I'm the second in command in the Nyx Order."

She gaped at him. "Oh." He was the commander of his group, but being a second, he should've taken her in right away.

"It's my job to take you in. However, I think you'd add value to our Order."

She didn't want to hope, but it grew inside her anyway.

"You should be in the best Order. Dei resides on the outskirts of the city and is ranked third." He tilted his head. "You might also have a chance to help someone out." He placed a hand on the table. "If you were hoping to avoid something like Haven."

She pressed her fingers into her thighs. One shouldn't talk about trying to get out of being a vital.

She doubted her sister would join her, but other than throwing her over her shoulder and fleeing to the swamps outside the city, she had no other option but to use persuasion against years of indoctrination. He must have guessed her plan to support her sister financially, even though they would live in shame.

Kai side-eyed her. "Put in for Nyx when you join the trials, or I'll turn you in and you'll lose your relic."

Vic shifted away.

He huffed a laugh. "That was your plan, right?" He leaned in, his eyes dancing with laughter. "You wanted Nyx all along, didn't you?"

"Are you going to pull strings to get me in?"

Nyx only took one reaper per quarter. If he helped her, she might have a better chance of joining, but she didn't want to get in that way.

He shook his head. "If you do your best in the trials, I won't need to mention that you took on a mog by yourself or that you're a Glass."

Vic's throat went dry. "You know?"

"Your family's falling out is quite famous. You might want to keep your hair under a hood when you go to the trials. It might make you a target." He casually tugged her hair. "They might gang up on you."

He dropped the strand of hair, and her face warmed.

"I'll keep that in mind." Rumors had already spread that the Glass heirs were trying to get out of being vitals when Vic had run away from home. It didn't matter for Vic. Reapers couldn't be vitals. People enjoyed spreading foolish rumors no matter if they made any sense.

He put out his hand. "Deal?"

There wasn't much choice. She clasped his hand, his rough calluses brushing her skin. "Deal." She pointed to her chained foot. "Can you let me go now?"

"In a moment." He stood, went into the bathroom, and came out with a medical kit. "Let me see your ankle."

Vic lifted the leg that was chained to the wall. "You don't have to leave me chained up for this."

"I don't want to take any chances." He pulled the wooden chair next to hers.

"Power trip," Vic huffed but lifted her injured ankle.

He gently took it and sat down. He ran his fingers along her ankle. Vic flinched as he probed. It had turned into a swollen mass that would soon form bruises.

"How did you walk on this?" He clicked his tongue and took out softly glowing white bandages from the medical kit.

"You don't need to waste those on me." Magic-imbued bandages were expensive, but the healing would be quicker with them.

"Just let me do this. I want you at your best next week."

Vic crossed her arms. "Fine."

He quickly wrapped her ankle. "I'll take you home. You shouldn't put any weight on this."

"I don't need you to."

He shut the box. "I guess I could leave you chained until the trial."

"You know what? I think I'll take that help home." He made her nervous, though an easy trust had formed between them. "Don't you live in the Order?"

He glanced around the small room. "This is in case I need to make a deal."

Deal? Had he tried to get others to join Nyx by chaining them up too? "Okay, then. Can you unhook me now?"

He laughed and took a key out of his pocket to unhook her. Then, before she could try to stand, he scooped her up in his arms.

"Excuse me?" Vic yelped.

Without responding, he opened the door while cradling her in one arm. Before he shut the door, he grabbed both of their folded-up scythes by their harness straps. Vic's eyepiece was tucked inside her still-wet harness.

Vic's face grew hot, her body pressed against his hard muscles. "This isn't necessary."

He walked to the main canal. "Where're we going?"

"It won't take me long to get home on my own."

Kai stopped. "Do I need to stand here all night holding you?" He tipped his face over hers. "Or do you like this?" He leaned in, and the overwhelming scent of cedar filled her nose, setting her skin on fire.

"Ha. I'm down in the lower district. Scrum Creek." She wriggled in his grip.

He didn't comment on the location but headed to a water-taxi stop. He pressed a button to summon a water taxi. In the night hours, some automated, imbued boats still took those unlucky enough to be out after dark. A water taxi floated into view.

Kai carried her onto the boat, pressed the location for Scum Creek, then placed his credits card to the reader to pay the fee.

With a slight pulse, the boat pulled away from the dock and puttered through the water toward her home.

Vic whispered, "You can put me down."

Kai ignored her and stared at the side streets. He wasn't wearing an eyepiece, but Vic had a feeling he was on the lookout for corrupted souls. They would have been easier to see with the imbued eyewear, but corrupted souls, even new ones, showed signs of corruption, which included black or red veins in their eyes and lack of eye contact. In the darker streets, those signs were harder to see.

She relaxed against him. Holding her couldn't be comfortable. She'd lost a lot of weight since leaving her parents' house, and sometimes, she felt like a walking skeleton.

The farther they went, the more rundown the streets and houses grew—missing roof pieces, crumbling stairways, and overgrown vines. Many items weren't imbued too well on the outskirts to hold things together or keep them protected. The Stone founders had imbs to maintain the streets. Vic figured they didn't waste their time on the slums. If the founders didn't come down here, why bother? They reached her stop, and Kai needed to take a large step since the first step wasn't there anymore.

Vic pointed him down the turns in the narrow walkways until they arrived at her small apartment.

"This is it. Will you let me walk this far?" With the imbued bandages, her ankle was already feeling much better.

Kai scanned the derelict building. "You chose this?"

Vic elbowed him, and he hissed in a breath but placed her down on the ground. "See you next week."

As she waved goodbye, his hand shot out and caught her wrist.

"Do you need food until next week?" His low tone was filled with worry.

She clenched her jaw. "I have food."

Scraps came up to her, brushed against her legs, and dropped a dead rat at her feet.

They stared down at the shaggy cat's offering.

Kai's mouth parted. "Blight take me, you don't eat rats, do you?"

"No!" Vic gestured wildly. "This is just my cat. He eats the rats."

Kai swallowed and looked her up and down. "Sparks, you can pay me back."

"See you next week," Vic repeated.

She took her scythe from him and turned.

Vic slowly took the steps up to her apartment. Scraps followed behind her after he'd picked up his dinner. She could feel Kai watching her, but she didn't turn around. She unlocked her apartment door, went inside, and shut it behind her and Scraps.

Only then did she let out a deep breath and slid down the door. Her gicgauge was full, but now she had to contend with the second of Nyx. After next week, she would find out if she would see him again. The thought that she might not make it into Nyx saddened her, but for a different reason.

✿ 3 ✿
VIC

The arena contained all the reaper freelancers. White stone spires rose from the gravel-covered ground to support a second floor for spectators. A huge waste of space in a walled city, but since they held other sporting events here, that was how they justified it. The scent of dirt and sweat permeated the thick air, forcing Vic to breathe through her mouth. Even though three Orders—Dei, Boreus, and Nyx—took in new recruits, not everyone had a powerful enough relic to cut it past freelancing.

Her boots scuffed against the gravel as she kicked a stray pebble. A drop of sweat trailed down Vic's neck as she waited on the arena floor. Her hair remained hidden under her hood, making her hotter among the press of bodies. If the other freelancers recognized her as the daughter of a founder, they might come after her in the trials. Her first-generation relic would be noticeable enough without pairing it with her hair. They might be able to recognize her by her face—it had been in the newspaper often enough after she'd left home. She didn't blame them. She had an advantage over most with her training, not to mention her relic.

The trials never repeated the same task, so no one knew what awaited them. Her scythe remained in its harness, but some freelancers showed off for each other. A tall, muscular blond with a permanent smirk on his face stood along the outer edge, proudly displaying his scythe. It looked nice as it caught the light. The blade had a decent reach, but that wasn't a predictor of how much magic it could wield or how much blight the stone could hold.

From the sea of black-clad bodies, Vic glanced up at the stands. The leaders sat in front of their Order's flag, which displayed each Order symbol proudly. A stocky brown-haired man sat before a cerulean banner with two waves in the center. He leaned back in his chair and drank deeply from a stone goblet. He must have thought the whole trial was a show. In a way, it was, but if he was meant to pick reapers, drinking on the job was a bit careless. Boreus would be an okay Order to join, though the commander seemed less than impressive.

If Vic wanted to push herself further from her family, Dei was her ticket. The ragged flag of Dei stood out with its blood-red color and large black X in the center. A thin, scrappy woman sat back with her dirty boots on the ledge. Dei reapers lived on the western outskirts. They had plenty of blight available to collect, but few reapers wanted to live as roughly. Most people would rather go through the trials again than join them. The thought appealed to her, but joining Nyx would come with a certain nobility that she needed. If she didn't get into an Order, she would be right back where she'd been last week: starving.

The gray banner with the two crossed scythes had no one in front of it. The Nyx Order commander had yet to arrive.

"Probably why we're all waiting," Vic muttered.

The commanders' sense of self-importance matched the founders'.

The crowd hushed, and Xiona, leader of Nyx, walked onto the platform and gazed out over the arena. Her hair hung in dark, thick braids that disappeared behind her back. She stood away from the freelancers, taking in everything around her. The harsh angles of her face showed no delicacy, but on Xiona, the features looked striking and highlighted her tawny skin. Her frame was small and wiry, every movement calculated. Vic didn't want to face her in a fight; she'd sneak in behind you at night and slit your throat before you could scream.

"Welcome. You're here to take on the noble task of clearing the city of blight and supplying us with magic to purify and protect." A hint of boredom hung in Xiona's voice as she spoke, like she was reciting lines from a play.

Vic stopped herself from rolling her eyes. She bet everyone here already reaped blight, but with less payment. And the vitals gave up everything to purify it after it was collected. She couldn't get distracted by her sister's plight today. She needed to get into an Order.

"There will be three tasks, but do not worry. If you fail one, that does not mean an Order won't ask you to join them."

"Just not you." Vic snorted, and those around her shifted away in case their proximity to the negative person hurt their chances of getting into the "best" Order.

"In the first task, only one of you will remain standing, then we will decide who will compete in the second task."

Vic reached under her hood to itch her scalp. The mood of the crowd shifted.

A group of people dressed in white, unlike the black clothing of the reapers, came to stand around them.

"Are those radiant?" a slender male next to her whispered to a girl next to him.

Vic could see why he'd think so, since only radiant wore white daily. The radiant were those who purified blight by taking away the ability to use magic. After a person got purified, they didn't act the same anymore. They wandered around the radiant land with vague smiles and performed monotonous tasks for their new community. Magic users claimed the radiant sucked out your soul. It was safe to say radiant and magic users didn't get along.

"Just imbs," the girl replied. "They need to stand out, probably."

The imbs held on to a long white rope and formed a circle around the freelancers. Then they took their wands, and magic flowed into the rope, making it glow. When they finished imbuing the rope, they lowered it onto the ground and backed away.

Xiona spoke again. "This rope will shrink and you'll be marked as you're cast out of the circle. We will announce the meaning of the mark once there's only one person left. You must push others out of the circle using only your strength. No killing."

"That had to be specified?" Vic grimaced. It was her first trial, but she'd never heard of anyone dying before. Maybe they just didn't advertise it?

"Begin."

They all paused. Then the tall blond shoved two people out. They fell on their backs with a thud, and the ring got smaller. Those who still hadn't registered that the trial had started ended up on the other side of the rope because they hadn't moved. With the elimination of the stand abouts, the rope shot forward, and Vic found herself in a crush of free-lancers rushing to the center of the arena. Thankful for once that she had a thin body, she darted among the rush in search of a place to make her stand.

A loud crack filled the air, but in the chaos, she couldn't see what had happened.

"It finally stopped!" someone shouted, and Vic discerned her location to the rope.

Then someone grabbed her and lifted her above their head. Vic couldn't see the person.

"Not today," she huffed.

She twisted, and her skin burned where they gripped her arms, but their fingers had loosened around her. She flung her arms wide, and they dropped her to the ground. She rolled onto her feet, facing her attacker.

The blond smirked, then went on to easier prey.

Vic dashed after him and kicked the back of his legs, bringing him down. Before he could get up, she darted into the pile of freelancers. She had a feeling she would see him later.

Her basic plan was to push toward the center of the circle. Reapers were clustered in the middle, where everyone wanted to be.

If she climbed the swarming freelancers, it wouldn't work. She would have to pull them away by force. Taking a lesson from the blond, she searched for the weak links.

A young boy struggled at the edge of the circle with a

woman twice his size. It would be nothing to push them both out. Vic ran forward and grabbed the back of the woman's shirt. The force threw the woman off the boy. As he fell back, Vic whirled around, reaching for him. Shocked, he took her hand. He didn't have a choice.

His hand gripped hers as she pulled him toward her. Then she wrapped him in her arms, using the momentum to push the woman out of the circle.

"Blight take you! Why did you save him?" The woman cursed.

The young boy trembled in her arms.

Vic let him go, and he backed out of reach. "I guess I don't like an unfair fight," she replied.

The boy crossed his arms. "I could've taken her."

"Sorry, little man. I guess I shouldn't have interrupted." Vic smiled and edged away. "Careful out there!"

"That's right. You better run!"

Vic laughed and called out, "See ya next round."

Poor kid would probably get kicked out soon, but she liked the fight in him and didn't want to see him thrown out too early. After all, he might need to work for his family. Most families in Verrin, who weren't founders, only have one relic to their names.

The circle closed in again, and the reapers packed into the center. Those around the edge gripped other freelancers and threw them out of the circle. The number of people left grew smaller. A husky man approached her, and Vic squared off against him. She had the advantage since he stood closer to the rope, but she couldn't watch her back. That was the main problem. Though the reapers would need to work together after they joined an Order, this task required them to look out for themselves.

He flexed his fingers and dove for her. He wanted to tackle her, apparently. Good strategy—if she didn't move. She slid right and kicked out her foot to trip him. He didn't fall, but he lost control of his movement. Vic used his momentum and shoved him, directing his blunder to the rope. He fell out with an angry shout.

Someone landed a hit to her back. Vic stepped back and thrust her arm out to catch herself on a tall woman who'd tried to shove her out after hitting her back. She stopped Vic's fall but stumbled out of the circle herself.

"Sorry about that." Vic laughed. Served her right for attacking Vic's back.

She answered Vic with an obscene gesture.

Vic turned her back to the rope. Only five people were left inside the circle.

The tall blond grinned at her. "We meet again." He tilted his head toward the others. "I think we can take on those three."

The rope's shrinking paused, letting them take in the last ones standing. A light coating of dust covered them all. Vic wiped her forehead, yearning to rip off the itchy hood.

"I don't trust you." Could she blame him for attacking the weak, though? Didn't they all go after the weak ones in this game?

The look in his eye said he'd do anything to get what he wanted.

"Better to be second place than fifth."

She scoffed over his assumption that she'd come in second place.

The other three—two women and one man—had wide stances. One woman had a wiry build and tired eyes. The other shifted her weight from side to side, ready to pounce in any direction. The man stood taller than the blond, and his tree-trunk arms flexed.

"Fine," she replied.

The blond would betray her; she would need to take care of them fast and then face him. Her muscles tensed as she faced the other freelancers.

The blond stood beside her, and Vic shifted. He could shove her out of the circle.

The tired one glanced at the others. "We can take them." She pointed at Vic. "I got the scrawny one."

Vic blanched. "Hey now!"

She shrugged. "Let's get this over with."

Tree Trunk growled. "No. I'm alone." He charged at the blond, maybe seeing him as the biggest threat.

The blond skirted wide, then rolled under the man's grab. Vic hooked her leg around his ankle. Tree Trunk grunted but didn't fall.

"Not an original move, Sticks." The blond bounced away from the larger man.

"Worked on you," she retorted.

Vic flanked the large man. If he hit her directly, she would be done for. While they took on Tree Trunk, the two women approached them.

The blond nodded toward the women. Vic got the hint: keep them away so he could keep fighting.

Tired Eyes swung at Vic's face. Vic easily blocked the punch, grabbed her arm, and pulled the woman toward her. The woman shouted in surprise, and Vic kneed her in the stomach. The bouncy one rushed in with a kick to Vic's hip. Vic didn't have time to dodge, so she tackled Tired Eyes to the gravel. The woman gasped as she hit the ground. Bouncy's kick landed on Vic's rear.

From the ground, Vic pushed away from Tired Eyes and swung her legs at Bouncy's feet. Their shins connected, making Vic flinch, and the woman fell back onto the rope.

Vic let out a breath and pushed herself up, the rope only inches from her head. *Lucky.*

"Behind you!" someone shouted.

Vic turned. Only the blond stood there.

They were the last two standing. The circle shrank, and they had about five feet to move. It continued to inch forward but at a slower pace.

"Nice working with you, but I'm sorry, it's time for me to throw you out of the ring." He cracked his neck and smiled.

"Do you think we'll need to save our strength for the next two trials?" She brushed the dirt off her clothes.

The man paced in the circle. "What of it?"

"What if I told you we could both win and save our strength?"

He raised his eyebrows.

"Lift me on your shoulders."

"You plan on making me that tired?"

Vic slid her foot across the gravel, ready in case he attacked. "I don't fight fair."

The rope contracted, and they stepped closer.

He extended his hand. "Get up, then."

Vic thought he might grab her and shove her out, but she wanted to keep up her stamina for the next two trials. She didn't know whether they would see this as cheating or clever. She took his hand carefully, and he pulled her toward him. He bent his leg, and Vic used his thigh as a step to swing onto his shoulders.

The white rope snapped in, and a number appeared on the back of her hand.

I.

She glanced at the blond's hand. He also had a one. Vic unhooked her legs, but he grabbed them.

"What's your hurry?" He saw their matching numbers. "Looks like your plan worked. I don't mind sharing with a cutie like you."

Vic sighed. "Just let me down."

He shifted under her but didn't stop her this time when she unhooked her legs and jumped down.

"Name's Yaris. You?"

"Vic. Thanks for the teamwork. I think." She understood the need to look out for oneself. Everyone did that daily in Verrin. If she got in the same Order as him, she would have to trust him to watch her back.

Before he could reply, Xiona stood. "This ends the first trial. If you are numbered one to twenty, you may stay. The rest of you leave. Try again next quarter."

As the reapers left, Vic faced their glares. She didn't blame the freelancers for fighting for a better life. Unless you were an imb, your only other option was to freelance, and that didn't pay well.

A hand tugged at her sleeve. "Thanks, lady."

She recognized the boy from earlier. "You too." She smiled. "I hope you try again."

"I have to." He pulled on his harness, the folded scythe still too big for his small frame.

Vic nodded, and he left. He didn't need to spell it out. She wished he would have made it further, but joining an Order that young would have been more dangerous. She hoped he didn't hunt alone.

Twenty-one dusty reapers stood in the arena and held out their hands to be checked by an imb dressed in white.

Xiona didn't react when she realized they had double ones. "It makes no difference." Her gaze rested longer on Vic. "We will move to the next trial. Come to the front."

They all stood under the balcony where the different leaders stayed. The side doors opened, and a flood of people dressed in white wandered into the arena. They stilled with their backs to the freelancers. The imbs placed blindfolds over their eyes and turned around.

"We scored you on your last round. After all the rounds, we will combine your scores. In this round, be the first to claim a low-level corrupted soul. You must find them without any eye gear." Xiona gestured to a man wearing white in the corner of the arena. "Time starts now."

With his wand, the man flipped a large hourglass.

Vic supposed she could use her scythe to nick them and see if it picked up any blight, but that might fill the gicgauge on her scythe too soon. She might need every bit of it for the final trial.

A person dressed in white jumped as a reaper drew blood. Guess she wasn't the only one with that idea. With a low-level corruption, they might feel cold. Vic rubbed her hands together. Her hands might not tell her much if they were too cold.

"Better than nothing."

Starting with the first line, she grabbed the strangers' hands. They each jerked in surprise, then calmed when they realized she wouldn't stab at them like some of the other reapers. She avoided the ones who were already bleeding since they likely weren't corrupted.

Cold. Cold. Cold.

Vic snorted. This wasn't going well, it was cold in the arena without the pack of freelancers. She hoped her score from the first round helped her out. New to the field, she didn't recognize all the signs of corruption. Mogs were easy. They were beasts and beyond saving. The sand in the hourglass dwindled, and she felt the skin of all the imbs. She tried to think of something clever, but her brain offered no clues. Her stomach growled.

"That isn't helpful," she whispered.

No other reaper had found a corrupted soul yet either.

Vic paused. *No one else has found one.*

She glanced at the blindfolded faces. Surely it couldn't be that easy. She continued to touch hands so as not to give away her theory. The sand trickled lower. Some reapers pulled forward a random person and stood in front of the commanders.

The last grains of sand fell, and an alarm sounded. Vic came to the front without a person. The blond didn't have one either. His brow was furrowed, and his arms were crossed. He must not have liked this trial. Although he perked up when he saw she was empty-handed too.

Xiona glanced down the line. "Remove your blindfolds. Now tell us, reapers, why did you choose them?"

They gave various reasons. Those who didn't have a person gave excuses, such as, "I didn't have enough time."

From the pull of Xiona's lips, that excuse didn't go over well.

Xiona looked at Vic. "What is your excuse?"

Vic gave a showy bow. "There are no corrupted souls here in the arena."

"Really? How did you come to that conclusion?"

"This was a test of personality, not skill. If you cared about us spotting the corrupted soul, you wouldn't have covered their eyes. You wanted to see who would lie or make excuses."

"Interesting theory," Xiona responded.

She went down the rest of the line. "There will be a short break. Find a door that leads into the arena and wait outside until it opens again. Only one person per door."

Vic sighed.

"Clever excuse," Yaris said, standing over her.

"I went with my gut. Excuse me."

She felt his gaze boring into her back as she strode out of the arena and to a doorway with no other freelancers. Outside the door, she leaned against the shaded wall, thin stone pillars held up the small overhang next to the cobbled street. Verrin citizens chatted as they walked down the road or stepped into a water taxi. After a moment, the arena door shut behind her. The outside air refreshed her, and she blinked against the afternoon sun, though she stood in the shade.

"Proud of yourself?" a harsh voice asked from behind her.

She flexed her fingers and turned. The man in front of her wore an expensive tailored suit. His crimson hair was combed neatly to the side, and his wand peeked out from under his suit coat. Founders liked to show off the gems at the end of their wands as some sort of status symbol that said, "Look here, I have a first-generation relic." The sneer on his face had become familiar during this last year.

"Why hello, Father."

❧ 4 ❧
WILLIAM

William brushed an invisible piece of dirt from his white uniform. Waiting outside the holding cells on a purification day had him grinding his teeth. Instead of preparing to help the souls lost to this sick world of magic, he'd been tasked with babysitting. Every muscle in his body clenched, and he twirled the ring relic around his finger.

If this makes me late...

He sighed. Nothing would happen. His mother and father had raised him to protect the reputation of the radiant, and so he would. The officer finally came out with a young man who could have been William's mirror, if that mirror had been covered in grime. The light brown hair was unkempt, and the smell of vomit and sour alcohol reeked from the young man. Dark circles lined his bloodshot eyes, which squinted at William in the daylight. Served him right for overdrinking.

William sighed again. "Really, Sammy? Why do you do this?"

Samuel flinched at the nickname, but his light blue eyes met his. "I can't take it, Brother. All we do is sit in the dark without magic. If I could get a wand, I could at least live some sort of life. What you do isn't normal, Will. Even if our family had another ring for a relic, I wouldn't want it."

Nothing new with this argument. They didn't need to have another spat in front of the officers. They both shifted, and Samuel faced away from him, a glob of something stuck in his hair.

William backed away from his filthy brother. "Let's go. We have to get you cleaned up if we want to make it to the ceremony on time." William walked to the door.

"Yeah, it would be horrible if we missed the soul-sucking ceremony." Samuel groaned but followed William to the door, only staggering slightly as they left.

William eyed his brother. His nose scrunched at the yellow fleck of what could only be vomit on Samuel's shirt. "You know that we purify them." He raised his hands in frustration over the old fight. "Why do I bother? Once they're purified, they can no longer get corrupted or turned into mogs. We're saving our city, but they won't accept it! There are monsters out there that eat humans, but we keep using magic and adding to the blight." Despite being in public, William couldn't stop his voice from rising.

Samuel walked next to him. "Whatever you say, but you can clearly see those afflicted aren't normal after you *purify* them."

William sighed. "We aren't normal. One day, we too may be purified, once we save them all. Then we'll discover the mysterious plane they exist on."

To no longer have to worry about money, or being eaten

by a mog, or getting the blight... it would be wonderful to exist in such a place.

His brother laughed and kicked a stray stone in the road. It skidded into the canal and fell in with a plunk. "You don't see the irony that you need magic to *save* them?"

It was time to change the subject. People in the street were giving the brothers lingering looks.

"What led you astray this time? You promised you wouldn't go around violating the radiant life." They weren't purified yet and still needed to live up to the radiant's honor.

"I lied." Samuel poked his brother's arm. "You have a small stain."

William thrust his arm forward and studied the white fabric. When he couldn't find a stain, he shot his brother another glare. "Really? Are you this petty?"

William resisted the urge to smack his brother in the head. Who knew what coated his dirty mop of hair after a drunken night?

Samuel laughed. "Come on. You used to be fun."

"You can't have fun your whole life. People need to be led to the way of the radiant."

William remembered the night, a year ago, when his father had given him the ring. His face grim, he'd informed him that it was time to grow up and take care of the radiant. William held back a sad smile. That night, he'd stopped running around with his brother. One day, his brother would understand the responsibility he faced.

"Yeah, it's super great living without magic. You wouldn't believe some of the things women do with their relics—"

William slapped his hand over Samuel's mouth. "Enough. Maybe we shouldn't talk." William felt something wet on his hand and yanked it back. "Gross, Samuel."

"Heh." Samuel stuck out his tongue but said nothing else.

They walked in silence down the roadways. The smooth rock of the road grew rougher the closer they got to radiant land. The canal's water got muddier. No imbs came out to keep things nice where the radiant lived. The magic users would be chased off by the radiant if they did. The people of this city had been led astray by magic, letting it turn them into mutants. They wanted to inject themselves with more magic so they could continue to live their easy lives. William shook his head and touched the implant in his neck. Soon, he could take it out. Once his father passed on, it would be his job to lead the radiant and save the population from themselves. He adjusted his cuffs and picked up the pace. It wouldn't do for the future leader of the radiant to be late.

William ignored the constant sighs behind him as they walked briskly through the narrow alleys. He avoided the grimy walls of buildings. Mold and algae were a problem in Verrin that magic would have cleaned up, but clean walls weren't worth one's sanity.

A modest home appeared in front of them, and William directed his brother to go in first. Sunlight came in from the wide windows. They wouldn't need candles at this time of day. The plain furniture had been hand-carved from wood. Sometimes, they would have to get magic-made items, but the radiant tried their best to make everything themselves. Stones in the floor, placed by hand, got replaced more often. The home always had the scent of fresh dirt, which was an improvement over the mildew smell of Verrin. Samuel went into the bathroom, where a drawn bath awaited him. William heard a gasp from the other side of the door.

"Blight, it's cold!"

"It would have been warm had you not been taken in for disorderly conduct." William smiled at the small revenge.

His mother had asked before he left if she should warm the water. William had told her no. He smiled; it would make Samuel bathe faster and also make William feel better. It might be childish, but sometimes, he didn't understand his brother or how to help him. The bitterness at having to babysit ate at him.

More loud gasps came from the bathroom. "You know the rest of the city is connected to the pipelines and can get hot water whenever they want?"

"I know, and I don't care. Is hot water worth the mutation of your body and soul?" How many times would he have to repeat himself to his brother? He annoyed himself at this point.

William pumped water into the large sink and rinsed off the hand that Samuel had licked.

"Probably," Samuel muttered.

"Just hurry."

"You don't have to stand guard." His voice trembled from the cold water as he splashed, cleaning himself.

William crossed his arms and chose not to lean against the wall. The house was extremely clean, but while wearing white, one had to be careful. "Oh, I think I have to. Who knows where you will run off to or what you'll pee on next?"

A short laugh echoed from the other side. "They told you I peed in the canal?" Samuel sounded pleased with himself. "It's not like it did any harm."

"No, it's just against the rules of the city."

"And we all know how much you love rules, Will."

The splashing on the other side quieted, and William heard him getting out of the tub.

William took in the tiny living space. He had to share a room with his brother, but he would soon be on his own and perhaps married. His father thought he should marry a founder to help with the cause. Since he was the future leader, some founders wanted his pull within the radiant community. His father had said he might have to accept that she would still use magic, so it would expose him to some danger. It was a matter of finding the right woman, preferably a calm and submissive one. Soon, he would have his own family and not have to take care of his brother. He loved him, but fetching him from the holding cells every morning was tiring him.

His brother appeared, his hair sticking up in every direction, and made his way toward the bedroom.

"If you're so cold, why don't you have any clothes on?"

He opened the bedroom door. "They were dirty, and I'm already numb, so who cares?"

"It wasn't that cold. Now hurry."

"Yeah, yeah." Samuel shut the door behind him to dress.

Thankfully, it didn't take long to get ready. William again directed Samuel to go ahead of him out the door.

Samuel saluted him and marched out. "So how many souls are we stealing today?"

They walked down the narrow alley toward the canal. They'd gotten permission to hold a purification ceremony in the center of town, something that rarely happened. All the radiant who had a relic would be there to help purify those who'd chosen life over magic.

"We'll give the message and see who's moved. That's all we can do."

They waved down a water taxi.

Samuel eyed the boat that floated with magic. "Isn't it wrong taking these?"

William stepped into the boat. "Well, we're late."

The radiant land was closer to the center of the city than other sections of town, and without water transportation, it could take a day to travel from one side of the city to the other.

"Isn't magic convenient?" Samuel sat down in the water taxi.

"No." William got out of the water taxi, ignoring Samuel's laughter. His brother loved it when he slipped up.

Samuel wrapped an arm around his shoulders. "Hey, don't worry so much, Will. You can't be perfect all the time." Samuel leaned in. "You don't have it easy. I get it."

"If you get it, then why make my life harder?"

Samuel stepped back, letting William go. He stared at the ground as they walked down the stone roads. "I'm trying to save you."

William jerked. "Save me? You can't be serious." He still couldn't believe his brother thought becoming a mog was preferable to joining the elevated plane of a full radiant.

His expression softened. "Yeah. We should have run off when you first got that relic. But it's too late. Maybe if I make you see... just maybe you'll come back."

William's lips parted. "I didn't go anywhere. And where would we run to? How would we get credits?" The appeal of a carefree life was evident, but eventually, everyone needed to accept their responsibilities in life.

Samuel stared up at the sky. "Don't you think there's more out there than Verrin?"

"I suppose, but what's the point?"

People had tried to get past the swamps. Only one had

ever returned. His journal told tales of how his whole group had slowly turned into mogs, with only more swamp ahead of them. Out in the middle of the swamp, they'd had no way of getting purified magic into their orbs to keep them charged.

Samuel smiled. "Don't worry about it, Brother. Let's get you to the ceremony."

Run off. William's shoulders tensed. There was nowhere to run to, and it was Samuel who needed saving, not William.

The roadways widened and smoothed closer to the center of town. A road car drove past them. From the backseat, the imb directed the car down the street while using magic to make it move. The cars only worked inside the center of Verrin because of the size of the canals in the city, and they needed magic to function. The large statue in the center of town showed a person holding a wand in the air. It towered above everyone, and on special occasions, illusions of fire would come out of the wand.

The sounds of people chattering increased. From here, William could see the brilliant white of the radiant. Those with relics stood at the back, while others fanned out in the crowd to bring more people in to hear the message.

Many times, the radiant would get those who'd recently lost a loved one to corruption. The choice became their own, and only those who'd reached adulthood could choose to get purified. Parents would beg to have their children purified, but the radiant refused. Some feared that the radiant would purify them by force, but they followed a strict moral code: the person had the right of choice.

William made eye contact with his father, who stood

directly under the large statue, and nodded. His father narrowed his eyes to look past him at Samuel.

"Old man is pissed that I pissed?"

William groaned. "Please don't let him hear you say that."

"Maybe I will. Maybe I won't." Samuel grinned at the pained look on William's face. "All right, where do we set up camp?"

William found an empty spot, greeting other radiant with a smile and grasping their hands as he walked by. He stood and waited with what he hoped was a pleasant expression. His brother stayed back a few feet. He never tried to recruit anyone. Their father had lectured Samuel on their cause, but they'd only come to the compromise that Samuel would stand quietly.

He didn't dwell long before a smiling radiant approached with a young woman trailing behind him. After nodding respectfully, the radiant left the girl in William's care. Only an unpurified radiant could use the ring.

"Welcome. I'm William. I'm glad you're here. What's your name, and do you have questions?"

The young woman twisted her boney fingers and stared at the ground. Her ragged hair hung in greasy clumps. "Jamie. Do we get shelter after it's over?"

"As a radiant, food and shelter are provided as a community effort, but you shouldn't join because you're hungry. Do you desire to keep the blight out of your life?"

She nodded. "Oh yes. My friend Tona turned into"—she shuddered—"a mog. She tried to eat me." Tears leaked from her eyes. "We couldn't get charged, and I-I think I'm already corrupted."

She didn't want him to look at her for fear he'd see the

corruption. She was lucky to still have the presence of mind to come to the ceremony.

"Don't worry, you can be saved. But you understand you'll no longer be able to use magic?"

Her red-rimmed eyes glanced up. The red was from more than tears. "I don't have a relic. I'd rather learn to live without it."

"Kneel in acceptance of your new life."

Her frail frame knelt, and William placed his hands on her head. He opened himself up to the relic on his finger. Through the ring, he could feel the magic in her body. A slippery feeling confirmed the blight had settled inside her.

William pulled all the blight out of her. He felt it slide through his hands. When it hit him, it broke down into nothing. Through his relic, he poured in a bit of white light, only a little, to flush out her body. William removed his hands.

Jamie, still on her knees, looked up at him. The redness had left her eyes. A faint white glow showed around her brown irises, then faded away. A calm smile appeared on her face.

"Now go to the radiant land. You will be greeted and told your new place in this world."

Her gaze filled with easy contentment. They would sort her according to her talents. She might return here to help save more souls.

"It's the best part, seeing the life leave their eyes, isn't it?" Bitterness flowed from Samuel's voice. He kicked his heels at the wall he sat on.

William resisted wiping his hands on his white pants. "You're not supposed to talk." He checked the gicgauge on the side of his ring. Jamie had come just in time; she'd had quite a lot of blight in her.

"Oh yeah, it's almost like I'm a full radiant."

"I could make you one." William flexed his fingers repeatedly. "And the radiant can talk."

Samuel tilted his head. "You would do that to me?"

William turned. "You aren't ready."

Samuel touched his shoulder. "But would you do that to me?"

He shrugged off his brother's hand. "I don't purify the unwilling, Sam. Please go back to standing quietly."

If they purified his brother, he would be saved, and William would no longer have to babysit him. William squashed that thought, guilt filling him. Though it would save him, Samuel needed to give his permission.

"I see it's going about as well as expected over here." Their father stood before them, his thick eyebrows furrowed. He'd likely heard Samuel's comments.

William swallowed. "It's going well. I purified a young woman."

"Come with me, William."

His father walked toward the perimeter, and William trailed behind, leaving his brother. His father breezed through the crowd, his broad shoulders easy to follow. His gray hair shone, the blighted sun giving it a reddish cast. Everyone made way for the radiant leader, but his father nodded respectfully as he passed by. William had always admired how calm his father remained in public. William always let Samuel get under his skin.

He stopped in front of a man in a perfectly tailored dark suit. William spotted the wand strapped in its harness. A bright red stone glowed on the end. This wasn't like most relics; it screamed first-generation privilege.

"William, this is Conrad, a founder."

Each founder owned a powerful relic that imbued the materials in their factories' assembly lines. They refined the raw materials since they had more magic, then the materials would be passed to other imbs to form other products. The founders controlled the city's resources, but GicCorp kept them in check.

William nodded. "A pleasure to meet you."

Conrad looked him up and down. "You're looking for a match for your son?"

The statement hung in the air.

"In speaking with the head of GicCorp, we thought it best to make relations between us and magic users more friendly."

Conrad's lip twitched. "Interesting. My youngest is a vital, and all I can offer you is a meeting with my eldest."

William's father frowned. "My understanding was that we were to meet with Emilia?"

The other man fluttered his fingers in the air. "There must have been a misunderstanding. Emilia's spoken for. You may meet my eldest today, but I'm not sure about any potential there. She's my only heir."

"Fine." William's father glowered. "I don't think it should be our job to tame your daughter. Other houses will take the GicCorp deal."

Conrad looked down at them. He glanced toward where Samuel loitered. "I think you understand how it is to have an unruly child."

William's father balked, but he'd gotten the message: *don't judge us when you have one of your own.* "I will be busy with the purification ceremony. My son will go with you to meet your daughter."

Conrad turned as if he'd dismissed them and walked on the smooth stone road to a shiny black car parked beside the large canal.

William glanced between his father and the car. His father shooed him, so William followed the stuffy founder to the car.

He carefully got in and sat down. The driver started the car, and they drove down the street.

Conrad tapped his fingers against the car door. "Your first time on a marriage meeting?"

"Yes." William wasn't sure where to look, so he focused on the seat in front of him.

Conrad stared out the window. His tone sounded flat as he asked, "You must know the scandal with my daughter?"

"I pay little attention to gossip." A scandal? What was his father thinking? How would getting mixed up in a scandal help the radiant cause?

"Well, don't get your hopes up. I only have so much leverage with her. She prefers starvation over her family obligations."

Founders tended to marry each other, believing they had the strongest magic for their relics. William mused that there had never been any proof that the wielder of the relic mattered. It came down to the relic's power. If they gave Conrad's wand to an unbound imb, they might imbue as well as he could.

The car veered right. "May I ask where we're going, sir?"

Conrad sneered. "To the reaper trials, where my daughter's competing."

"**A**re you still planning to join an Order and leave your family?" Her father's thin lips turned downward at his disgraced daughter.

Vic glared at the man who'd had a part in bringing her into the world. "You know what, Father? I don't think they have little balls or tea parties. I guess I'll have to make do without all those fun social parties you're so fond of."

His stance was stiff as he faced her down. The sun was shining in the open hallway, but it still felt dark. "Do you want to see your sister?"

A frozen vein of pain lanced through Vic's chest. He needed something, and he didn't have time to mess around. "Are you saying I won't see her again unless I give up being a reaper and take over as the heir?"

Time with her sister was limited already. She didn't want to believe her father would take away her last days with her.

"And we have a matchmaking meeting."

Vic blinked. "Dang, you've been busy. Also, you don't have the right to keep me away from her. We both know it's only a matter of time before either of us sees her again." Her throat tightened.

If she could trade her powers for anyone, it would be her sister. Only imbs could become vitals. Vic was a reaper, and her sister was an imb.

Her father stepped closer, and his eyes glowed as they looked down at her. "You have no rights. You left your family, Victoria. You left Emilia, the same as you left your mother and me. Do you think we don't know about your little visits? Those will end. Now."

Her insides burned. The idea of leaving her sister pained her. At the moment, she could sneak out to see her every so often. Now he threatened to take that away. "This will hurt Em too. Do you really want to take away any joy she has in her last days of freedom?"

He smirked. "She's used to her disappointment of a sister and understands the duty of being born into the privileged life of a founder and the honor of being chosen as a vital. What you've been given is a gift, and she will keep the whole city safe."

"And I'm not?"

Her father didn't answer.

"If I give up my position as heir to collect blight, won't I be helping Verrin?" In that way, her sister wouldn't need to be ashamed of her anymore. Reapers were heroes in their own right. Maybe not as revered as the mysterious vitals in Haven but still regarded with respect.

He didn't deny it.

"You chose to let her go, and you don't want to lose me too." As the words left her mouth, she knew she was being unfair. These past months had been a harsh reality check. As younger girls, they'd ignored the fact that Em would be the vital and Vic would be the heir. Their father had changed as the date for the vital ceremony approached. He'd become harsh, and Vic had become angry. Neither of them was handling the pending loss of Emilia very well. Their relationship had become a battle of who could hurt the other more. Vic no longer recognized the man she'd once loved as her father, and he probably could say the same about her.

"What did you expect? You nearly ruined our family by being born a reaper. I thank magic I had another daughter to give to Haven." His cool green eyes pierced her. "You should consider yourself lucky to have a sister to sacrifice in your place. Otherwise, you never would have gotten these six months of rebellion. Come back and all will be well."

Vic bit the insides of her cheeks and let the twinge of pain calm her down. His words cut through her, but she schooled her face to remain impassive. He knew Vic would trade places with Emilia if she could. She didn't want her sister to go away, even though it was an honor. Call Vic silly, but she wanted her sister to keep living and creating her glass art. Her heart told her Emilia deserved to be so much more than a vital. The vitals were heroes. But could they be heroes if the choice had been forced on them?

"Yes, so lucky that you have these humans to sell off." She clapped her hands slowly. He knew no one could control whether they were born a reaper or an imb, yet he blamed her. "Congratulations on your sperm donation."

He smoothed back his already perfectly styled hair. "I guess you have another choice to make, Victoria."

"Right, you will keep my sister from me if I don't become the heir or meet with my future husband. Choose one, Father. At least give me a piece of fake freedom."

He studied her. "I'll introduce you later." He bowed

slightly. "I'll enjoy the show." With only a scuff of his shoes against the gravel, he walked along the shaded overhang.

Vic leaned against the cool stone wall. She should have known there wouldn't be any freedom from that man. She reached for her harness and pulled out her scythe. The relic burned with magic. She unfolded her scythe and held it to her body. The magic warmed her, giving her comfort. If she gave in to this marriage meeting, she'd have a better chance of seeing Em. She could be the heir and a reaper, but staying in the Glass house represented everything she hated about Verrin. Her father was so adamant she couldn't do both. Soon, he would have no choice.

It had started out as small changes in her father. First, he'd spend longer hours in his office. Then he would be out, sometimes all night, at what he'd say were meetings. When he'd pushed the GicCorp founders' son, Tristan, on Vic, she'd balked. Over the last year, they'd battled over Vic marrying Tristan. Vic had won, and the GicCorp founders had withdrawn their proposal for her to marry Tristan, the heir. After that night, her father had told them that Emilia's vital ceremony would happen this year. Vitals went to Haven after their twentieth birthday, but they could stay in Verrin until they were twenty-five. Emilia, only twenty-two, could spend more time with her family. He was taking away three years. Vic had accused him of punishing Emilia because she wouldn't marry Tristan. Part of her feared that this was also retaliation from GicCorp for her refusal. Too scared of the answer, she'd never asked.

Vic had wondered if she only hated Haven because of her father sending Emilia there so soon. But then, as she got older, she'd realized she didn't really understand Haven. She didn't want her sister to go somewhere with so many unknowns. It didn't make sense. But GicCorp ran the city, providing them with gicorbs and purified magic from Haven. Questioning them might be dangerous for Verrin. The people were in a position where GicCorp could cut them off from power, charging, and orbs. Founders should have had equal power and say with GicCorp, but before Vic's time, there must have been a shift in power.

A loud creak and the scraping of stone on wood jarred her attention to the doorway. It opened on its own. The other side now looked like a long hallway instead of an open arena.

A voice sounded over the walls. "Enter."

Vic stepped over the threshold, her stomach twisting, and the gate shut behind her. Only a dim light shone from the arena ceiling, casting the new walls in thick shadows.

"The maze contains a mog that has been grown for over a year," Xiona said. "One relic cannot drain it. Inside it, you will find a clear stone. If you want to win this round, you must claim the stone." Xiona cleared her throat. "We have reapers on standby to get you out should you get injured or reach the limit of your gicgauge and want to withdraw. There is some danger, and we can't promise you will come out alive. If you no longer want to participate, raise your scythe now and you'll be let out."

Vic listened but didn't hear any doors opening. They needed to work together, but there could only be one winner. Nothing like pitting them against each other in round one, then having them work together in round three. Maybe reapers needed to learn forgiveness.

"Ready, reapers."

A loud but slow *clack clack clack* rose from somewhere in the maze. She gripped her scythe.

"It's loose. Go."

A raspy howl filled her ears, and she didn't know if she wanted to head in that direction. No scuffing sounds, only her breathing and the lone howl that continued until it dropped off in a final note.

Vic rolled her shoulders and set off at a jog. The settling dust tickled her nose and made her want to sneeze. Right now, she could only go forward. She didn't know if she preferred the sound of the mog or the isolated sounds of her heartbeat mixed with the thuds of her feet.

The path ahead forked. A shriek shattered the silence. Then nothing. Vic swallowed. First, she needed to find other reapers. She didn't need the stone; without each other, they would die. She didn't want to assume, but ranking high in the previous two trials should win her a spot in an Order. If it wasn't Nyx, another Order would still be support away from her family.

As if summoned by her thoughts, Yaris skidded into view. He jumped at her sudden appearance.

"Ah, it's the smart one." He grinned.

Vic held up her hands. "We can't survive this unless we all drain it."

"Yes, but don't you think the top two should separate? Our scores are the closest." He twirled his scythe in his hands.

"Won't matter if we're dead. You can have the stone."

He paused his overly fancy movements with his relic. "You don't want to get into Nyx?"

"Yes, but there is no one else to work with at the moment." As much as he gave her a bad feeling, he was a good fighter. Surviving mattered more than winning.

Vic knew he didn't trust her. She didn't trust him either,

but when she picked the next fork to run down, he stayed next to her.

He snorted as he ran. "Don't think I'm a fool to trust you."

"Back at you."

As they ran through the maze, they didn't see anyone else. "We might not even find the mog."

A shout sounded to their right. Vic couldn't make out what they'd said.

"Are they crying for help?" he asked.

"Could be." It was hard to hear anything with the thick stone walls. Only echoes came over the top of the maze.

At the next fork, they picked the right, but after a while, they came across more and more forks. Everything was the same.

She sighed. "We're running in circles."

"Most likely. Whoever needed help, it's too late now." Yaris was unfazed by the thought of others getting hurt.

Two other reapers ran out of the dim light, startling them.

"Thank magic we found you!" the thin man gasped.

The other man glanced over his shoulder. "We don't know if we lost it or not, but with four of us ... maybe we'll stand a chance."

Yaris stepped closer. "You saw it?"

The thin man bobbed his head. "Unfortunately. It can climb over walls and pick us off like snacks."

Vic turned to Yaris. "Should we find a place to make a stand or keep running?"

Yaris glanced up. "If it comes from above, we can't guard our backs. The best we can do is find a more open space.

With too many people, we'll get in each other's way, unless we can flank it."

"Flank it," Vic muttered. "We can stand on opposite ends of a pathway, and if it drops in the middle and faces one team, the others can come around from behind."

Yaris glanced at the two men. "Yes, as long as they come."

The thin man puffed out his chest. "I'm here to fight, but I'm not stupid. Two people against an old mog isn't enough." He nudged the silent man, who nodded.

"We should split up," Yaris whispered to Vic, "and each take one of them. I think I trust you more than them."

"They won't go for that," Vic replied. These two men had formed a partnership like her and Yaris. They would trust each other more. "Let's keep moving until we find a spot we all like."

They took a path away from where the others said they'd lost the mog. Their pathway widened.

"This is the best place to make a stand," Yaris said. "We can still see each other, but we won't be in each other's way. If you see anyone run by, ask if they'll join us. Go down to the end of the path."

The two men ran off, and Vic could still see their outlines in the dark maze.

"Now we wait." Vic stood with her back to the wall and faced Yaris, who also had his back to the wall. This way, they could watch the wall above each other in case the mog showed up above them.

A rhythmic thud started to their left, and it sounded like scales scraping on stone. Two large hands grasped the edge of the wall on Vic's side. Foot-long fingers bent over the top of the wall. Sharp claws tipped each finger and dripped blood.

"Ready," Vic said.

She heard the rush of feet as they all ran in to surround the area before the mog dropped over. Then its maw cleared the top of the wall. Elongated teeth overlapped its jaw so that it couldn't close its mouth completely. Any of those teeth could spear them through their body. Vic imagined herself dangling from its tooth like a sad piece of leftover food.

She swallowed as the large creature climbed over the wall. The scraping sound of its scales made her ears twitch. The fingers and head dwarfed them, and its arms and legs were too short for its frame. Thick scales covered the mog. It landed on its massive feet with a loud thunk. She wished for another slimy mog. These scales would be a pain to penetrate. The smell of the mog's rotting flesh filled the air.

It turned, smacking its large maw as it took in the four reapers.

"Go!" Yaris darted forward, Vic close on his heels. Thankfully, the other two also came toward the mog.

The mog slashed at them with its long fingers. Vic searched for a piece of exposed flesh to thrust her blade into. Yaris attempted to breach its scales, but his scythe bounced off, and he almost lost his grip.

"Flesh flesh flesh," Vic muttered. The only flesh was on its head. "Perfect. The head! Hit it there!" Vic ran to the front of the mog. "Hey! Hey!" She clicked her tongue and yelled until it looked at her. She gripped her scythe and swung at its fingers. Yaris and the thin man flanked it, aiming for the flesh of its head. They could drain more blight if they hit it at the same time.

She paced in front of it, keeping its focus on her. Its claws were its primary weapons. She skidded on the gravel as it swiped at her middle. Between the maze walls, there wasn't much room to maneuver. It lunged at Vic, all its fingers aimed at her, leaving an opening for the men. They struck its head with their blades.

The mog howled, and as it tried to turn around, the men stayed with it to keep their blades connected with its flesh. Their scythes glowed with energy. Then the mog gave up searching for them and lunged for Vic again. Light on her feet, she danced back and slammed against the wall.

The air left her lungs, and the long fingers slashed at her. Vic had no choice but to drop to the ground. The claws caught her down her side, and a burning sensation bloomed from her head to her waist. She gasped and rolled out of the way.

"Hit it again!" Yaris ordered.

The low howl told her they'd been successful, and she squeezed out from under the creature. It rambled at the men, Yaris distracting it, and Vic pushed the point of her scythe into the back of its neck. Magic burned in her relic and flowed through it, filling her gicgauge to the brim before the mog thrashed out its arms, dislodging the blade from its neck.

The thing had slowed down but was still intact.

"I'm almost full," Vic shouted.

"Same," Yaris answered.

The silent man limped forward, his leg damp with blood. He nodded to them, and they dove in, screaming at the mog to get its attention.

Vic, Yaris, and the thin man clanged their scythes against the mog's scales. The thin man tripped as the mog slammed its fingers against his relic. It threw them aside, and they landed in a pile. Before the mog could hit them, the silent partner struck it in the neck and his relic flared. The mog fell back, close to crushing the man. Globs of rotted flesh fell from its frame.

"This is it. We need to use whatever we have left." Vic pushed herself up from the pile, and they all surrounded the mog, stabbing its fleshy head.

The mog flailed erratically, making it harder to avoid its long fingers. Vic's vision blurred. She'd lost too much blood.

When it swung at Yaris, she dove in and connected her blade with its flesh. A final flash. The gicgauge was full. The scales dripped off the mog, and the thin man dashed forward, his shoulders squared, but he didn't notice the mog's still-grasping fingers.

"Wait!" Vic tried to block the sharp claws with her scythe, but she was too late. The fingers speared the man, the scales coated in his blood. The silent man came up and stabbed the mog with a final burst. The mog disintegrated.

In the mess of fleshy scales, Vic spotted a gleaming stone. She kicked it to Yaris. He heard the thunk and glanced at her, eyebrows raised. Vic rushed to the thin man to help plug his bleeding wounds. She'd considered grabbing the stone, but the commanders were watching. The stone meant nothing if this lesson was about teamwork. The trials might be straight-forward:

1. Can you fight?
2. Can you tell the truth?
3. Can you work as a team?

In her gut, she felt that many overthought the trials. Kai had mentioned that reapers had each other's backs. Vic had given her word to Yaris that he could have the stone, and it was more important to keep her word than win.

Vic called out to reapers with a blue healer armband. "Over here!"

The thin man still took in breaths, but they were shallow.

A distant clang sounded, and the maze walls lowered into the ground. A group of reapers dashed forward to carry out the thin man. Another reaper with a blue armband came up to her and wrapped up her long cut.

Vic's hair framed her face in a sweaty mess. She pushed it back and twisted it into a makeshift knot. She'd put her name in the application for Orders without her surname, but the distinctive Glass hair could be seen for miles. It wasn't like they were the only redheads in Verrin.

"These bandages should hold until after the announcement of invitations." The reaper went to help others.

Vic walked to the overhang of the arena. She was surprised they hadn't called in imb healers. Some reapers trained in battle healing, but they couldn't make imbued bandages, only buy them, so maybe they wanted to make it more realistic to life in an Order. Only a handful of freelance reapers remained. Yaris clutched the stone, his gaze on the leader of Nyx.

Xiona stood, and she scanned the remaining reapers. "This is the final part of the trial. Everyone who took part in the maze will be granted a spot." Xiona's gaze flicked to the Dei commander. "You will now decide if you accept. Maybe becoming a reaper in an Order is something you no longer desire. The battle you faced today is nothing compared to the growing number of mogs in the city or those trying to come in over the walls." The great breach, when mogs had broken through a weakened part of the wall, had happened recently. "Think carefully. Once you're branded, you belong to that Order, and there's no leaving to join another."

Three banners fell down from under the overhang in the

colors of the Orders. On them, the names of the reapers who were accepted were already scrawled in black.

The others rushed forward, most biting their lips and nodding in acceptance. If Dei wasn't their first choice, Dei Order was better than the streets, especially if they couldn't afford to wait until next quarter to try again. Some of them had their names on two banners, so they would get a choice. The excited voices filled the arena, then an angry shout boomed, and everyone went still.

"Is this a joke?" Yaris yelled up at Xiona.

Xiona tilted her head. "What do you mean?"

His chest heaved, and he pointed at Vic, who hadn't even looked yet. "How did she get into Nyx? I have the stone. Shouldn't the third trial be worth the most points?"

"Points?" Xiona's asked blankly.

Yaris threw down the stone. "The points from each trial!"

Xiona laughed, and all the reapers backed away from the mocking tone. "Young one, we see what we like, and we claim it." She pointed a finger at him as though she were aiming an arrow at his throat. "You were found lacking compared to her. Did you think getting the stone meant something? Working together, thinking, sacrifice—these traits matter, not some silly rock. If I ever need to pave a new walkway, I'll find you."

Yaris's face burned, and his gaze rested on Vic.

Oh Blight, she thought.

"A Glass? You hid your hair and shadowed your face in a hood to make us all into fools? It didn't matter who came here today, not when there's a founder. They will always get top choice. Skill doesn't matter, only your privilege." He took a step closer, and other reapers closed in but didn't stop him.

"Yes, I had more training, but you can't say I don't have any skill. I'm sorry you didn't get what you wanted."

The other reapers watched the two in silence.

"Is that why you gave me the stone? You wanted my help? Then like a bitch in heat, you used me and shoved me aside."

"Just because I'm a woman doesn't mean I want you. Also, I didn't need you. It made sense to work together so, you know, we wouldn't die." Vic widened her stance, subtly preparing to fight him. Her wounds hurt, but he wanted to lash out at someone, and she was the closest.

Yaris's fingers curled into his palm. He must have regained some sense, since he took a deep breath and glanced at the overhang. He bowed sharply and stalked out of the arena.

Vic sighed. "I wonder where else I got in."

She saw her name on all three banners. Relief filled her. Maybe she could make enough and convince her sister that being a vital didn't matter. The Glass founders would still provide the city with a hero.

"Report to your Order of choice tomorrow morning." Xiona dipped her chin, and with that, all the leaders left.

Vic spotted a man dressed in white in the stands. At first she thought he was an imb from the trial. His stiff stature and judgmental gaze, gave him away as a radiant. What was a radiant doing here? They hated magic. Now that Vic's identity had become clear to the other reapers, she felt like she was on display. With no reason to stick around, she headed to the door. To her dismay, it took her a long time to leave as other reapers congratulated her. Apparently, they all didn't have the same resentment as Yaris. She finally reached the outside of the area. Her father stood there with the man in white she'd seen earlier.

This couldn't be good. Vic debated walking past but figured it would only hurt Em if she did. She leaned against the wall, arms crossed. "Why are you with a nightlight?"

The radiant's narrowed eyes took in her disheveled appearance.

Her father smiled lazily. "Oh, this is your future husband."

❄ 6 ❄

VIC

"Ha!" Vic bent over and gasped for air, her wounds throbbing. "What could you possibly gain by marrying me off to one of those Sally Sunshines?"

If her father wanted to continue the Glass line, it made no sense for her to marry a radiant. What in blight was he thinking?

The man stood next to her father, appalled by Vic's dirty state.

Vic grimaced. She was covered in blood and dirt, and that man looked like he didn't even know what dirt was. His white uniform didn't have a speck of dust on it. How tiring was it to keep it clean? It would be funny if she brushed up against him. Would he freak out? This person probably loved rules and cleaning.

The man glanced between Vic and her father, his full lips pressed into a thin line. "I think you may have spoken too soon, sir."

"That remains to be seen." He regarded Vic. "Today, you

are to join this young man at their purification ceremony, then for dinner at our house tomorrow night."

She raised her eyebrow. "Am I missing something? I don't live under your roof anymore."

Her father's eyes emptied of emotion and became flat. The green irises dulled, and Vic's throat constricted. The feeling of razors tickled along her skin. No loving father appeared here.

"Victoria," he intoned, "do you want to go into this with company present?" His fingers gripped his left arm. The bright sun contracted with the chill in the air.

Vic focused on the feel of the air coming in through her nose. The way it brushed her upper lip. The way it tickled the inside of her nose to the back of her throat. She needed to calm down.

"Fine." The single word burst out, and Vic felt ashamed over how he could still control her. So much for leaving the family. Her victory in getting into the Nyx Order dampened under her father's gaze.

"William, please look after her today." Her father bowed and strolled away.

Vic stared at the space her father had left.

"Do you need to treat those wounds?"

"Huh? Oh, yeah. I'll be a moment, William." She squinted. Blight, his uniform was bright.

Blood had already leaked through the patch job the reaper had given her. Her flustered gaze caught his eyes. He shifted on his feet. Vic guessed he was as caught up in this as she was.

She sat down at the temporary tents set up outside the arena and let the reapers clean her wounds and bandage them. Her clothing was shredded on one side but still covered her.

"Would you like something to wear?" a reaper offered.

She smiled at the thought of showing up in rags to a purification ceremony. "Nah, I'm good."

If her father wanted her to meet the future in-laws, it was on him for throwing this at her last minute.

William stood right where she'd left him, easy to spot in his bright white clothing. She had to admit he was handsome, in an orderly way. His light brown hair caught the sun and became streaked with gold. The blinding whiteness of his uniform accented his tan. This was someone who worked outside during the day. His shoulders were broad, and he had a tapered waist. He didn't have the same build as a reaper, but radiant worked hard to live without magic. His angular face was alluring, but the fact he was a radiant closed off any attraction. She could only imagine what had gone through her father's head to make this arrangement. Whatever he plotted was way beyond her, and she didn't have the energy to figure out his goal. For now, she just had to go to the ceremony and maybe dinner.

Vic knew she had a chance to win this battle with her father. Once her sister left for Haven, what would her father have to hold over her anymore? He wouldn't stoop so low as to take her scythe—maybe.

"What Order will you choose?" William asked, interrupting her thoughts. The disapproval had left his eyes, and he might be kind. The radiant weren't bad people. Mostly, they judged magic users harshly. The thought of losing their magic made most people nervous around them.

"The one that will give me the most freedom."

If the statement shocked him, he didn't show it. "I see."

His tone softened. "I think I understand." The last part he spoke so quietly Vic barely heard it.

They followed the canal. Other reaper hopefuls trailed down the pathways, going home with smiles or tear-streaked faces.

Vic let William take the lead. She'd never been to a purification ceremony, so she didn't know where they purified others.

She felt an odd kinship with this stranger. "What brought you out to see the reaper trials? Had a craving to see what magic turns us into?"

He also seemed like a good target to tease.

He glanced at her sideways. "I'm well aware of what we turn into if we don't charge ourselves with magic. I wish for a world where we don't have to depend on this broken economy."

Vic chewed on her bottom lip. He had a point. They needed blighted magic to purify in order to charge and keep the blight away. If the cycle broke, they would all turn into mogs. If everyone stopped using magic, how long would it take for the blight to go away? That was something everyone was too afraid to test.

"It isn't perfect, but I think being a walking automaton would be worse?"

William stiffened. "Everyone is still in control of themselves."

"Hmm, the glassy-eyed ones are great at making choices." They responded, but their answers were simple, and they always did what they were told. She shivered at having that kind of power over another human life. How could they trust that the radiant wouldn't abuse that power? It didn't feel right. Only the radiant who purified kept their magic.

Apparently, once everyone was purified, they would join the rest.

His jaw twitched. "They're happy and uncorrupted."

"If you say so."

"If you would rather go home ..." William paused and straightened his cuffs.

Her father's eyes flashed in her mind's eye. "No. I guess I need to be respectful. I'll try." She glanced at him. "But you have to understand that I think what you do is wrong."

He ran his tongue over his teeth. "The feeling is mutual."

"Wow, this will be a great marriage, don't ya think?"

Blight help her that his show of attitude made her like this orderly light lover.

"If the blight doesn't kill us, we'll likely kill each other," William responded dryly.

Vic lightly punched his shoulder. "Look at that! A joke!"

"You know, I am human." A flicker of a smile twitched at the corner of his mouth, his stance relaxing.

Vic wished she could see him really smile. "Good to know."

They neared the center of town, and Vic saw the sea of people wearing white. Radiant led the unpurified to the center, where the few radiant with rings waited. After a moment, the new radiant would be led away smiling.

"So creepy," she whispered. What went on in a radiant's mind? Was it just filled with happiness?

William looked at her sharply.

"Fine, fine. Tell me where to stand, and I'll shut up and be good." She needed to sit down. She had the urge to take a nap on the ground.

"Why do I always have to babysit?" he muttered under his breath.

He led her away from the others, and she noticed another man who was like the happier version of William. He flashed his teeth in a wide grin.

"Whoa, Brother, I didn't know you could leave the ceremony to pick up women. Nice score!" He smiled brilliantly and stuck out his hand. "I'm Samuel." He pointed his thumb at William. "This one's better-looking brother."

He mirrored William in appearance, with slight differences. His light brown hair was ruffled, and his clothing had wrinkles. Samuel's tan was a smidge darker, and he had more smile lines around his mouth. His blue eyes were the biggest difference. Where William's were cool and maybe tired, Samuel's danced with mischief. He stood back from the purification. Was he not wanted here?

Vic grasped his hand. "Nice to meet you, I think."

Her gaze wandered around the center of town and over all those gathered. Other citizens of Verrin still shopped around the purification ceremony. Those who didn't want to get purified gave the radiant a wide berth.

"Yeah, this isn't a great place to meet people. What brings you here? Don't tell me you're getting purified?" Samuel grimaced.

William cleared his throat at his younger brother.

Vic laughed. "No, and you make quite the sales pitch. Are you sure you should be here?" She let her guard down. Something about these brothers made her relax. She'd spent the last few months mostly in isolation. How long had it been since she'd sat down and spoken with other people? She'd grown tired of games and walls. Her instincts told her Samuel was good people and she would go with it.

"I could ask the same of you." He took in her torn black

clothing and the scythe holstered on her back. Bandages covered the exposed skin on her waist.

William broke in, saying, "Okay, we get it. Will both of you stop talking? There are desperate people coming to be cleansed, and you're making a mockery of it."

Vic sat on the ledge next to the statue. Samuel sat next to her, and they watched in silence as William purified those who came to him.

"I don't think I understand what all this means," Vic whispered. She felt something strange as she watched those broken people who couldn't afford to charge or eat leave with a vacant look and a smile. It couldn't be right, could it?

"You're telling me," Samuel answered. "Try growing up around it and watching your friends turn into smiling radiant who're happy at their little jobs and only talk about purity without magic." He scuffed his foot against the stone. "William's all I have left of my group of friends, and he spends most of his time telling me how wonderful it is to be a radiant."

Vic shuddered. "Why are you normal?" She caught herself. "I mean, not normal, but you don't buy into what they're selling." She understood the feeling of having everyone believe something different from her. If it wasn't for her sister, would she think people should leave their families to become vitals and save the city?

Samuel nearly laughed but stopped himself. "Thanks? William and I used to run around town." He winked at Vic. "He actually got in more trouble than I did. Then one night, he changed." He gripped the ledge. "And here we are. He's the future leader of the radiant, and I'm the odd brother who won't step in line and purify people."

"Were you supposed to?" Vic leaned in, wanting his answer to match her own rebellion at leaving her family.

Samuel nodded. "I turned down my relic. I may have a way to get a third-generation wand, though. I have a little money. I hope I can be an imb instead of a reaper castoff without a scythe. I wasn't tested to see what I could be." He waved his hand toward the ceremony. "But I don't want to leave him." His gaze shifted to the swirls of blight above them. "Wow, I told you our life story."

Vic snorted. "Not wary of strangers, are you?"

His face tilted, and he looked thoughtful. "Usually, yes, but I don't know. I have a strange feeling William will need you."

Vic scrunched her face. "I'm not sure about that. We'll likely be at each other's throats."

Samuel nudged her. "Now you spill. It's only fair."

It wasn't like the town didn't already know the gossip about the Glass founders. "I'm a rich brat from Glass, and I don't agree with the founders or Haven, so I ran off to be a reaper in a lone protest. I got to live alone for a while, but now it looks like I'm right back where I started."

Samuel stared at his brother. "Blight take us. It's easier to fall in line than mess with the system, isn't it?" His blue eyes studied her. "But that isn't it, is it?"

Vic flexed her fingers and noted how thin they were. "I have a sister, and she's an imb."

"Vital?"

"Vital. She was supposed to leave with me, but she didn't." In one heated argument, Vic had thrown away everything she'd known. She'd thought her sister would follow her. She had a strange feeling he understood the broken system they lived in.

He cracked a smile. "I don't suppose you'll bring her around?" He waggled his eyebrows, breaking the somber mood.

"Not a chance, lover boy." Emilia would have liked him, but it was pointless. Vitals didn't have long relationships.

His face grew thoughtful. "I wonder if our parents had two children to use one to blackmail the other."

The dull green of her father's eyes came to mind. She'd left her sister with him. Her sister claimed she wanted to fulfill her duty to the city. Emilia didn't share Vic's doubts. It's not like Vic had proof that Haven was bad. She could be honest and admit she didn't want to lose her sister, so it was easy to make Haven the villain.

"I wouldn't put it past them. Reputation is more important than our choices."

"You two must be having a serious conversation." William stood over them, the setting sun haloing him from behind.

Samuel jumped and put his arm around William, who immediately shrugged him off. "You wanted us to be serious, dear brother. We merely complied with your wishes."

Vic stood with Samuel. "Is it over?"

William nodded. "I will take you home now." He glared at his brother. "You are to go home. Straight home."

Samuel saluted. "Yes, sir." He winked at Vic. "I hope you stick around. We have a lot of work to do with this one." He launched himself at William and hugged him. Before William could do anything, Samuel let go and ran off.

She watched Samuel leave with the other radiant. They left the center of Verrin, their white uniforms ghostlike in the growing darkness. It surprised her that they wanted to be out this late. Mogs still ate the purified.

William stared after his brother, his brow furrowed.

"You're worried?" Vic asked.

"Let's go."

Apparently, William didn't like to share as much as Samuel. It was strange, but she understood him. William might want to purify her, but they seemed to be in a similar situation. She wondered if, like her sister, he didn't have a choice. Samuel had said he'd changed in one night, just like her father.

Vic's muscles ached, and her feet throbbed, even though she'd gotten to sit down. She wistfully eyed the water-taxi drivers docking their boats for the night in the canal. Some of them used the last of their magic to automate their boats. They steered those next to the call button on the dock. "Are we walking the whole way?"

William stopped and folded his hands behind his back. "Why would we need a boat? Isn't the Glass property ahead?" He tapped his foot impatiently at her perceived laziness.

"I don't live with them." Her tone came out sharper than she'd meant.

"That's right. Where are we headed?"

"I don't need you to walk me home. I'm sure I can take on anything that comes after me." *I might be the one protecting you.*

He didn't leave; he just waited.

"Scrum Creek."

This situation mirrored the one with Kai before the trial. At least Kai could fight. What would William do? Tell the mog it needed purification?

He peered at her bandaged wounds. "In that case, it would be better to take a water taxi."

"I would hate for you to break any vows or become impure." Vic blinked at him. She bit her lip to keep from smiling at the radiant.

"I'll worry about my soul. Thanks for your concern." He headed to the canal.

Vic selected the destination and paid for the ride. She stepped onto the boat after William. His clean white clothing stood out more in the canal. The darker it grew, the more he glowed.

"Did you have a good day?" Vic needed to fill the silence. In all her life, she'd never thought she'd be stuck in a water taxi with a radiant escorting her home.

"Yes. You?" He sat straight.

"A great day. Found out I'm still under my father's thumb, so there's that." Nothing like trying to get out on your own. Well, he'd let her be a reaper if she married. It still didn't make sense that he'd chosen a radiant. William for sure couldn't run the factories.

He faced her. "I'm not sure what my loose-lipped brother has shared with you, but I'm sure he exaggerated. Our family is fine, and he has no business sharing personal things with a stranger."

"Um, okay? I was just sharing." Talk about an overreaction. She leaned back in the wooden boat. "You're worried about what your brother told me?" Vic wrinkled her nose. Couldn't he lighten up? She didn't want to marry him either, but he didn't have to be so closed off.

"You pity me."

"What now?" Vic jolted and shook the water taxi with her movement. The canal water lapped against the wood.

William leaned away from the water, even though it

didn't enter the boat. "After you talked to him, you pitied me. For what, I don't know."

"Okay. I'm sorry I did whatever you said I did. I'm confused. Your brother's worried about you. I didn't get your life story." *Sort of.*

William paused, and quietness filled the air.

"He doesn't need to worry."

"Fine." If he didn't want to get to know her, that was all right with her. It wasn't like she would go through with the marriage. What would her father do? Tie her up? She clutched the side of the boat. Probably.

William swallowed. "Sorry."

Vic shook her head. "It's fine. I like your brother. He was fun." *Unlike you.*

"And I'm not." His features remained stiff and closed off. Nothing like the relaxed Samuel.

"You said it, not me." Vic rolled her neck. She wanted to go home. She hadn't expected this sudden drama. "You don't have to be fun or like your brother. I don't even know if it matters. This thing"—Vic waved her finger between them —"may not even last. Your father may find another founder's daughter, and mine's always coming up with something new. So this may be a really random blip in our lives, where we briefly cross paths."

They might not want to attach their name to the disgraced Glass house.

"Perhaps. I'm honestly not sure what to do with you."

"I wouldn't worry too much about it."

She let the silence fall without filling it. The puttering sound of the boat and the bubbling canal could take that job.

"What are you doing? Help!" The voice shattered the awkward silence, and she scanned the shore.

The sky was already dark, and the canal water reflected the lamplight.

Vic slammed her hand down on the emergency stop and stood, rocking the boat.

"What are you doing?" William steadied himself.

"My job is to help people. You can wait here if you want."

"What are you going to do?" He reached for her as if to stop her.

Vic rolled her eyes and bent her legs. When the water taxi got close, she pushed off the boat, nearly tipping it. She landed and slid on the moss-covered stone.

"Stop!" the voice sounded again.

Vic ran in the direction of the voice. She couldn't see anyone, but she pulled out her eyepiece in case it was a corrupted soul.

William's footsteps were catching up with her. Then to her left, she heard a thud. She ran around the bend of a narrow alley. One-story houses with their lights out stood guard. She took her scythe out of the halter and flicked it open.

She skidded to a halt when she came upon two black-clothed people attacking someone. Her eyepiece told her that neither of them contained the blue glow of mild corruption. She ran forward and slammed her body into the side of one of the attackers.

The attackers clawed at the young man's bleeding neck, but he clasped his hands over the wound.

"Help me!" he gasped.

The black-clad figure still holding him down tried to get the young man's hands away from his neck.

The one she'd body slammed jumped to their feet. Only dark eyes showed behind a cloth mask. She lunged and swung at them, but their arms blocked it. They returned the punch. Vic danced to the side and kicked at the back of his leg. They spun away and faked to the right. Vic stepped back and caught their arm. Her hands locked onto their arm, and as she pulled them to her, she kneed them in their stomach.

The person gasped and jerked away. Vic scrabbled to hold on to their shirt. Their pale skin stood out in the moonlight that glowed behind the colorful blight. It revealed the black brand on their neck. Vic paused as she stared at the image. They pulled away.

William came up behind them, and the two in black scattered, leaving their victim bleeding on the ground. Vic stood there on the road, frozen.

"What was that? Blight? Are they corrupted souls?" He paced as if to go after them.

Vic took off her eyepiece. She knelt next to the young man. "What were they doing?"

The young man clasped his neck. "They were trying to cut out my gicorb."

Vic rocked back on her heels. She had to have misunderstood. "What?"

"They take them so we can't charge." He kept his hand over the orb as he eyed her black clothing. He made it sound like this had been going on for a while.

"They do?"

The man nodded. "They dress all in black like reapers so no one will know who they are."

Only Vic had seen the brand and knew what the young man didn't. "Why hasn't this been reported to the officers?" Vic's hands clenched.

"We have, but the witness turns into a mog faster than normal. Or nothing is done."

Vic eyed the blood between his fingers. "Did they get yours?"

If they had, she would only have bad news for him. The orb protected them, but if damaged or removed, it couldn't be replaced or fixed. Everyone only got one, and once it was gone, it was gone.

He shook his head. "No, thank you, miss. I better get home. My family will worry."

Vic stood and stared after the man as he took off in a different direction from the two black figures.

"What happened?" William asked. He'd heard the conversation, but he didn't seem to understand.

Vic shivered. "They tried to take out his gicorb and corrupt him." She folded her scythe and tucked it back into her harness. "You do that with your radiant."

William gaped. "We would never do that to an unpurified soul! The orb is only removed after they are purified. When did this start happening?"

Vic rubbed her hands down her arms. "This is the first I've heard of it."

William peered toward where the figures in black had disappeared. "What happened when you were fighting? I'm surprised you didn't go after them."

"Me too. I wasn't expecting that."

"What?"

The shadows from the alley felt like they were watching them in the night. "They had the brand of Nyx on their necks. They were reapers."

7
VIC

Vic stared at a web of cracks in her apartment ceiling. She supposed she should pack. She regarded the empty apartment. *Well, that's done.*

The few items of clothing she owned were stuffed in her bag. The image of the two crossed scythes on the person's neck glared in her mind. The brand hadn't been damaged. If an Order removed a reaper, they blacked out the brand. It meant active members of an Order were corrupting souls on purpose.

She moaned. "Perfect. This is just what I needed—to join an Order that hurts others."

Vic frowned and sat on the edge of her bed. Kai didn't look like the type who would do something like this.

"It's not like I know him," she said to the empty room.

Scraps blinked at her. In a few hours, she would need to go to the Order of her choice. Vic wasn't sure what she was getting into.

Part of her wondered how deep this went—if the whole

Order knew about it or only a small faction was responsible. If so, had Kai or Xiona sanctioned it? Vic shook her head.

How was this her responsibility? She had enough to worry about with trying to convince her sister to betray the whole city.

Vic groaned and pushed herself off the bed. With mechanical movements, she folded her blanket and fit it into the top of her bag with room to spare. She scratched the top of Scraps's head. "Ready to go to our new home?"

He purred and sat inside her bag. She smiled and clipped the bag, leaving his head to poke out. She wasn't sure if animals could live there, but she wouldn't leave him behind. She took in the apartment, her home for the last six months. It had given her freedom, but it had no trace of her. She held her folded scythe and carefully shouldered her bag. The vibrations of Scraps's purrs rumbled against her back.

"Time to go, buddy."

She picked her way down the steps and dropped off her key in the landlord's box. She planted her feet on the stone walkway. To the right, she could go to Dei, take the challenge, and not deal with whatever drama awaited at Nyx. To the left, she could go to Nyx, the top Order. With slow movements, she went left. She couldn't be sure how far the corruption went. The freedom she'd thought she had locked down, and she felt a pull back to the center of Verrin. Today, she didn't bother with a water taxi. Even if she'd had the money for one, she wanted to walk. When the doors of Nyx closed behind her, she would have money but not a sense of ease. After all, it was for her sister.

"I guess it'll be my problem."

Nothing was without some sort of corruption. How could she have been so naïve?

The blight swirled in the sky and covered the sun, making it a vibrant shade of green. The streets widened, and a few store owners on the roadside opened their shops. The smell of baked bread mixed with the musty smell of the canal. Vic hadn't eaten today since she'd run out of food again. It didn't matter. She had a job, and it would put food on the table. She didn't have to live with her father.

The sun warmed the back of her neck, and the gray stone walls of the Nyx Order rose in the distance. The stone roadway smoothed out. In Verrin, only those who lived in the center of the city deserved smooth roads. She reached the iron gate, which had two scythes crossed on the front, and the gateway opened. She was taken aback when Kai appeared.

He took in her single bag and the cat head sticking out of it.

"Brought a friend?" He smiled and reached around to scratch Scraps's head.

Scraps's purrs hit the maximum level as Kai scratched his ears. The vibrations massaged her back through her bag.

"Yep." She waited for him to tell her that Scraps wasn't allowed.

He shook his head. "This way."

Relieved she wouldn't lose her furry friend, Vic followed. "Does the second in command always give newcomers a tour?"

"I asked to do this. I wanted to make sure you found your way to the right place." As in Nyx, not Dei. "I got held up in a meeting." He shivered.

"Didn't have much choice."

He knew she wanted to be here, but he didn't know what she'd seen last night. Vic wanted to trust her gut and tell him, but she would wait until later. Kai hadn't taken away her scythe, and unless she was a fool, she didn't find him untrustworthy. If he had been the type to hurt others, her scythe would've been long gone.

He opened his mouth at her statement, then closed it again. They walked through the courtyard. A large U-shaped stone building surrounded her. Multiple windows over-looked the courtyard. It smelled better here, away from Scrum Creek. There was no escaping the damp smell of Verrin, but the air still felt clearer. An obsidian fountain met them in the center. It formed the shape of a woman holding a scythe. The water trickled down her body, creating a clear sheen over the stone. It created the illusion that the statue shifted, aware of her surroundings.

"You'll be branded first. I heard you won't be living in the dorms?"

"What?" Vic halted. "No, I'm living in the dorms." Her voice rose. "Who said I wasn't?"

Kai's brow crinkled. "I was just told. But don't worry, I can make sure it's fixed after the ceremony."

Did her father think she needed to live at home again? Wasn't it enough that he had control over Vic seeing her sister? "Please, I don't want to live outside. It would be better that I stay with my comrades, don't you think?"

He smiled, and it calmed her down. "Yes, I think so. Are you ready for this?"

"To get branded?" Vic rubbed her bare neck, briefly touching the gicorb. "As ready as I'll ever be. With all the magic we have, I'm surprised they still brand us."

"It's supposed to be painful to remind you that entering

an Order is no light matter. And besides the radiant, you can't use magic to change humans."

"And to remind you that it isn't easy to leave either." Her earlier doubt about choosing Nyx prodded her mind. There would be no turning back once she got branded.

Kai led the way forward, and she studied his back. Did he know? Should she tell him?

"That too." He looked at her as they walked into the building. "Also, you did well in the arena. I was surprised you gave away the stone."

"I was too."

He knocked on a dark wooden door. "It wasn't part of your plan to show sacrifice and teamwork?"

"After nearly getting killed by a mog, I had no room in my brain to consider what the commanders wanted."

She'd promised Yaris she would give him the stone if they worked together. Vic didn't want to be someone who went back on their word. She swallowed. Wasn't that what she was trying to make her sister do? No, her sister never had a choice. There was nothing she could do at the moment. It was time to focus on joining the Order. Her neck itched as if it knew it was about to be burned.

The door swung open, and the room spanned before them. Magic flames flickered in lamps, and the walls, covered in dark stone, swallowed the light. People dressed in black filled the open space. All the reapers had come to watch.

Vic's hands grew cold.

Kai held out his hand and whispered, "I better take your bag with your friend."

She handed him all her belongings and walked to Xiona

in the center of the room. She stood next to a fire, the branding iron next to her.

"Kneel." As always, Xiona showed little emotion and didn't waste words.

Vic clutched her folded scythe and knelt in front of the leader of Nyx. Another person approached and swept Vic's hair aside, exposing the right side of her neck. Then she tilted Vic's head to the side, elongating her neck.

Xiona's face remained emotionless. "Do you need to be held down, reaper?"

"No." Vic instantly regretted her answer. A red-hot iron was about to be pressed into her neck while the whole Order watched. If she flinched, it would mar the mark.

"In entering the Nyx Order, you are tasked with keeping this city safe from the blight. The reaper's vow isn't one to take lightly. Do you swear to uphold all that the Nyx Order stands for, protect the city?"

"I do." Vic thought her voice would shake, but the words came out clear and steady. She clenched her hands into fists, her nails biting into her palms. The words had been the easy part.

The smell of fire overwhelmed her nose.

Vic stared at the iron as it glowed red with heat, the flames dancing around it. Then in one swift movement, Xiona lifted it from the fire and pressed it to Vic's exposed neck.

Vic clamped her teeth down on her bottom lip, and her body screamed at her to move away from the heat. The acrid smell of her burning flesh filled the room, and she swallowed the urge to vomit. She forced down the screams that wanted to break free.

It only lasted a moment, but after Xiona had removed the branding iron, she could still feel her flesh burning. Something ice-cold touched her neck, and instant relief filled her. Her hand touched a bandaged that already covered her neck.

She blinked, and Xiona actually had a smile. "Impressive."

With that, she left the room.

Vic tried to keep her eyes from watering. A young woman smiled down at her. "Heck, Glass, you have some ovaries on you. I think Kai fainted when he got branded."

"Bomrosy, don't you have some gadgets to get back to?" Kai appeared from behind them as the room cleared.

Bomrosy smiled at him and flipped her long dark braid over her shoulder. Her lips stretched into a wide grin, her white teeth contrasting with her deep umber skin. The smile was so natural and easy on her face. Vic's uneasiness from being at Nyx melted away. "Weren't you supposed to be chasing down a swamp monster? Oh, wait." She tilted her head toward Vic. "A freshie took it out for you."

Bomrosy punched Kai playfully. She wore black like all the reapers but didn't have a scythe on her back, which might not matter since it was bedtime for most reapers, and they didn't need to carry around their relics with them. Vic liked to keep her scythe close since she was paranoid that someone might steal it.

It took a moment for the words to register with her. She glared at Kai; he'd said he wouldn't tell anyone about her illegal freelancing.

He raised his hands. "Before you get all mad, I wasn't the only one there, and after the trial, they put two and two together."

"But I'm not—"

"In trouble? No. I don't think anyone wants a reaper of your caliber to get her first-generation scythe taken."

Bomrosy's lips faltered, but she went back to smiling. Her golden eyes warm. "If you're ready, I can show you around. Otherwise, he'll have us standing here all day." She mock-glared at Kai.

Kai handed back Vic's bag, and their fingers lightly brushed, making her arm tingle. "If you need anything, let me know." Kai walked out with the last of the reapers, and Vic found herself missing him.

"Well, blight take me, I think he likes you." Bomrosy nudged her.

"Huh?" Vic blushed. She barely knew the guy, and there was also that small problem of Nyx reapers removing people's orbs, which he might be involved in. "He found me. I think he feels responsible for me."

"Hmm." Bomrosy patted Scraps. "There's nothing wrong with just looking."

She didn't have time to worry about men, so there was danger in "just looking."

Vic gulped and followed her out. "How long have you been a reaper?"

"I'm not." The words were clipped. "I'm the one who fixes your scythe when it gets damaged." Her tone softened. "If the stone breaks, there isn't anything I can do, but other than that, I can fix it. However, it is rare to see a first-generation relic." Her vision grew distant as she glanced at Vic's scythe.

Something must have happened in the past, but Vic didn't want to ask since she'd just met her. "What's the worst case you fixed?"

Bomrosy's voice grew quiet. "Someone came back with only the stone connected to a gicgauge. I still haven't fixed it

yet, but I've seen enough of the inside of a scythe to understand how the stone and tool are connected. I could only
learn how to meld a stone and gicgauge together ... but I
might end up breaking the stone if I tried."

The stone collected the blight, and the gicgauge stopped
the stone from overloading. It was a pain that they could
only gather so much blight before they had to empty the
gicgauge, but it kept their relic safe.

They went down some stone steps that led into a large
room filled with tools and benches. Random bits of wood
and metal lay around the room. The pleasant smell of
lemons filled the air, along with the sweet musk of straw.

"This is my workshop." She bounced over to a foreign-
looking object. "See this?" She flicked a switch, and a glass
bulb turned on. It didn't look like the lamps or magic flames
that Vic was used to.

"What's this?" Vic held her fingers back from touching it.

"Light ... without magic." Bomrosy flicked the switch up
and down, making the light turn off and on.

Vic wanted to touch it. "Wow, the radiant would love
you."

Bomrosy laughed. "I bet. Their leader approached me to
help them, but they aren't my style." She spaced out again.
"B-but it would take a lot of magic-made materials to get to
this point." She gently turned the light off.

Vic had a feeling they stood on the edge of a few uncomfortable subjects for her. So far, she knew not to mention
radiant or irreparable scythes. She liked Bomrosy, but she
understood what it was like to keep secrets from people
you'd just met. Most people didn't have their lives splashed
over the gossip columns.

Other things were strewn about the workshop, and Vic

wondered what else she'd created that didn't need magic. Without magic, the blight would disappear, or so the radiant claimed. Vic guessed it only made sense that without magic, there wouldn't be corrupted magic. The city was held up by magic. If they lost it, they would sink into the swamp—literally. A fun thought.

"I had to pay an imb to work with me, and we went through so many different models. It takes a while to get the glass into the right shape and thinness of a bulb, but when I get frustrated, I move on to something else. I think they put me down here to make sure my ideas don't get out." Her hands fluttered when she talked about a challenge.

Vic felt a sense of warmth around her. "I think this is amazing."

Bomrosy shifted some bits of metal around the wooden table. "It keeps me busy. Xiona must see some value in it." She left out the door, and they went back upstairs. "Up ahead is where you can get meals, if you don't want to make your own food."

Vic quickly glanced inside the massive hall. Large windows let the sun in, and the walls had deep-colored tapestries. The giant hall felt homey. Mahogany tables stretched the length of the room. The imbs must have spent hours in here connecting the wood together with magic.

She followed Bomrosy past the main entrance. Vic saw a large blackboard, and someone was using a wand to arrange letters. When they got closer, she recognized some names.

Bomrosy pointed to the sign. "This is where you'll get your assignment for the night. Most often, you're in the same group every night. You'll get two nights off a week. Since you're still healing, I'm sure they won't make you go out tonight."

Vic studied the names and spotted Kai's. "When will I know what group I'm in?"

"Xiona might still be deciding where to place you, or the different commanders will fight over you."

"Fight over me?"

"It's always good to have an extra person on the team. You might not have noticed them in the stands, but they all saw you fight with your relic. Just don't get on Landon's team." Bomrosy wrinkled her nose. "He's talented but a bit of an ass."

Vic laughed at her expression and took note of all the unfamiliar names on the board. "I thought I didn't have a choice."

"You don't, but it can't hurt to wish for a good fate."

It might be silly, but she wished to be on a certain commander's team.

They walked to the left wing of the structure. "These are where the dorms start. The commanders' and officers' dorms are on the first floor. They're too lazy to go up steps." Bomrosy trailed her fingers along the stone wall.

They walked up three flights of stairs to a long, narrow hallway.

"And here we are. Will you need a sandbox for your cat? If he's trained, you can leave him to wander around the dorm. No one will touch your things."

When they got to the dorm room, Vic noticed a cat-sized hole in the bottom of the door.

Bomrosy laughed. "Never mind. I think Kai already thought of something."

Vic smiled at his thoughtfulness.

They went into her room. A single bed with fresh white sheets sat in the corner. Through the window, Vic could see the center of the city. In the distance, she heard sounds of the awake city: random shouts and cars going over the stone streets. Off to the side, she opened a door to see that she had her own bathroom with a wide sink. She saw the desk in the corner and the thick stuffed chair. No leaks or cracks in the ceiling and not her family home. Most founders would have hated the small room, but Vic loved it.

"You can fill the room with what you want, but the basic things are provided. It's small but clean," Bomrosy hedged.

Vic placed her bag down and let Scraps explore. She hugged herself. "It's perfect." Worries crowded her head about the Order, but the room felt like hers. "And it doesn't smell like mold."

"That sounds like a story I'll want to hear. I'll let you get settled in, then."

"Thank you." She was happy to have a few moments in her new home.

Bomrosy left, and Vic ran her fingers along the stone window frame. It felt nice and cool to the touch. Her neck had finally cooled down and didn't burn anymore, but when she twisted her neck too sharply, it twinged painfully. Vic took out her comforter and smoothed it over the made bed. In the closet, she found a row of black clothing and spare boots.

"It's like they knew I was choosing them before I did."

Only a fool would have turned down the top Order, but most hadn't seen what she had last night. Everything was in her size, and she hung up her meager belongings next to them. Reaper clothing needed to get replaced often, so it was nice to have all the spares.

She ran her hands through Scraps's warm fur. He'd already claimed the sunny spot on her bed. She headed downstairs to the dining hall. There were a few reapers eating, but Vic figured this might be a late snack.

Heaps of food sat in serving dishes warmed by magic flames. She grabbed a paper napkin and selected bread stuffed with various vegetables and fish. Though she was hungry, she didn't want to eat too much. She took her meal back to her room, sat in the chair, and savored the food while feeding bits of cheese to her cat, who'd decided food trumped the sunny spot. Cheese was rare in Verrin. Only a few plots of land were dedicated to animals in the walled city. Most of the space was used to grow food. The sunlight moved across the room until it rested on her in the chair.

Vic placed her head on the chair, making sure her bandaged branded skin didn't touch the back. She stroked Scraps's fur. It didn't take long for her to fall asleep in her new room.

ﾟ✿ﾟ

"MOVE A BIT FOR ME."

The voice startled Vic awake. Light glowed softly in her room, and a young woman sat on the bed. Her hair, a golden red much lighter than Vic's, stayed pinned behind her head. Her face scrunched in concentration as she used her wand on the black sand in her hand. Her pale skin complemented her delicate features. Many said they looked the same, but Vic couldn't see it. Vic was sharper and hardened, whereas Emilia was delicate and soft. Sea-green eyes glanced up, and her face broke into a wide smile.

"You're awake!"

Vic jumped up and threw her arms around her. "Em, what are you doing here?"

The smell of sand filled her nose. Vic had missed it.

Emilia, her younger sister, squeezed her back and stated, "You're far too thin."

Vic leaned back and grasped her sister's shoulders. She couldn't help bouncing on her toes. It felt like ages since she'd seen her sister. "Are you trying to play big sister?"

Emilia hugged her one more time and stepped away. "You need more looking after than I do. I came to bring you to dinner tonight. I think I'm also supposed to make sure you're dressed or clean or something of that nature." Her eyes twinkled.

"Oh, father dearest is worried that I won't show?"

Emilia gripped Vic's hands. "Please come! GicCorp's son will be there, and I'm so nervous."

Vic put her hands to her face and groaned. "Tristan? What in blight is Father thinking having him over when I'm there?"

He knew how she felt about Haven. Nothing like rubbing it in her face that her sister would be taken away. She'd ended that, and now the radiant William had gotten stuck with her. Who would her father set her up with next month?

Emilia returned to the sand she'd left on the nightstand. "I don't know, but your new prospect will also be there. There will be plenty of awkwardness to go around." She molded the sand, her brow furrowed in concentration. "I'm sure you can throw a few tantrums."

"No joke. What are you making now?" After Em had stayed for her duty as a vital, it had been hard for Vic not to feel rejected by her sister. It had taken them a bit to get back to their easy banter. There was still time. Vic held back the words. Nyx Order wasn't the place to talk her sister into leaving. She looked over Em's shoulder.

She placed a tail on the figure. "Your cat. I didn't know you had a cat."

The black sand turned lighter in Emilia's hands as she maneuvered her wand. Vic stood back to watch. She took a deep, satisfying breath, enjoying the normalness of seeing her sister work. She'd spent many nights sitting in her sister's room, watching her create.

The glow of magic filled the sand and formed it to what Emilia wanted. Now resting on her nightstand was a glass version of Scraps.

Emilia stretched her neck and nudged Vic with her shoulder. "Do you like it?"

"Of course." Vic picked up the figurine. It was cold and smooth. She placed it back on the stand. Vic used to have many of her sister's glass figures. Her father had mashed them all into one giant glass ball, which he'd then thrown at the door. Vic remembered her sister's tears as Vic had crunched through the glass and left the house. He hadn't needed to go that far; he'd punished Em as much as Vic that night. That final burst of anger had killed any hope for their relationship. "Thank you. Em, I'm sor—"

"Don't." Emilia's expression softened, and she looped her arm through Vic's. "I wish you could stay away. I'm the one who's keeping you from being free. But soon, you won't have to worry..."

Because you'll be gone. Those final words didn't need to be spoken.

Vic gave her another fierce hug as her throat tightened. "Never think I wanted to leave you. I just couldn't stay there anymore and support ..." She wanted to beg her sister to leave, but she'd tried many times and didn't want to ruin the moment.

They stepped back, their vision watery with tears.

Emilia's laughter shook. "On that note, what do you have to wear to dinner?"

Vic crossed her arms and scowled. "Black shirt, black pants."

Why did she need to put on a show for him?

"Blight, Vic, at least tell me they're clean?"

This dinner would be a disaster.

❧ 8 ☙

WILLIAM

Illiam frowned at his breakfast. The night before had left him with too many questions. After Vic had dropped the line about the reapers, she'd run off and left him to wonder what this could mean for Verrin if they had rogue reapers. Magic would be the city's downfall if they didn't stop it. The radiant had higher morals than reapers from what he could see.

"Did your breakfast do something wrong? I'm a bit sad. I thought that look was reserved for me." Samuel scraped the last of his breakfast off his plate, then snatched a piece of fruit from William's plate.

He didn't try to stop him. "I'm not hungry."

William shoved his plate back, and it slid on the table.

"Ah, more for me." Samuel helped himself and studied his brother. "Did things not go well with your bride-to-be?"

William frowned. "This whole thing is a mess."

"Yes, and messes are bad. Very impure." Samuel snorted and chewed with his mouth open.

William rubbed his forehead. "I'm not in the mood today, Samuel. Can you knock it off for today?"

Maybe he should tell his brother that his beloved magic users were out there making mogs. William swatted his brother's hand away and forced down a spoonful of his food.

"If you mean being my lovable self, I don't know if I can help you, Brother. What's on the agenda today?" Samuel tilted on the edge of the chair, something their mother often yelled at them not to do.

William leaned back in his chair, copying his brother for once. His parents had already left for the day, and if the chairs broke, he'd be the one to fix them anyway. "I have to make my brother see the light."

Samuel did not understand what waited for him. This morning, William had argued with his father that this lesson would be too harsh, but it had been no use. It would only get worse from here on out if Samuel didn't fall in line. He gripped his spoon tighter. Why did he have to do it? Samuel was his brother, not his son.

"Sounds like a productive day. What sob story is on the list?" Samuel's chair nearly reached the tipping point.

His parents had thought that by exposing his brother to stories of loss because of magic, he would see what they were trying to accomplish with the radiant life. It had the opposite effect, but their father thought the tactic today might work. William thought it was overly harsh. His brother sometimes convinced people not to get purified. However, today might be different.

He avoided his brother's gaze. "A person you talked out of purification turned into a mog. Their family wants to get purified, and they also want to speak to you." William couldn't help his tone of voice. The burn of anger filled him, and his brother needed to know what he had cost others.

The smile fell from Samuel's face. "Will, I..."

William clenched his jaw. "You may choose not to follow the radiant path, but you should let others decide for themselves. You'll come with me today. You'll face this family. These are the consequences of your actions."

He pushed back from the table and threw out his food, wasting it. Their mother would complain about it later, but William didn't care.

Samuel bent his head and nodded. His whispered words traveled to the kitchen. "There has to be a better way than this. You can't tell me what you turn people into is the answer."

William ignored him and went into their room to get dressed. The white uniform helped him be the person his father wanted him to be. He could see the good they were doing, but the fact that he was leaving his brother behind hurt him. The white clothes felt like a shield against his old self and a weapon for who he could become.

He straightened his cuffs, giving in to his nerves, and brushed off a piece of red hair. William frowned again. He had to go to dinner and see her again. Part of him wanted to hate her and what she stood for, but seeing her yesterday with his brother had sort of made him jealous. William wished she'd smiled because of something he'd said or that they'd had an easy conversation.

The fight he'd witnessed flashed vividly through his mind. She'd moved like a chaotic flame in the night. Always pushing forward, her hair flowing behind her. Her pale skin had glowed in the moonlight. Then, at the end, her deep green eyes had widened in shock at something neither of them understood. Maybe tonight he could get some answers.

A subdued Samuel waited for him, and they went out into the streets of Verrin, silent for once. William noticed Samuel staring at the surrounding skyline.

"You did what you thought was right." He should let Samuel wallow in guilt, but he honestly didn't enjoy seeing his brother this way. No one annoyed him like his brother did, but he loved him.

Samuel stuck his hands in his pockets. "I think we're both wrong. The blight isn't something that can be solved either way. There's something the whole city is missing."

William glanced up at the swirling blight. "If magic wasn't in this world, you would see a clear sky."

Samuel's gaze softened, and his brother entered a trance-like state. Samuel's voice came out in a harmonic whisper as he said, "Hey, Brother, what color is the sky?"

William frowned in thought. "I'm not sure." The blight changed the color of the sky from day to day, swirling in lazy motions. Today, it was a bright shade of green, like the color of her eyes. William shook his head.

"A nice green, huh?" Samuel smiled crookedly.

"No comment." His brother knew him too well.

Samuel's mood lifted, but the stone home came into view with people gathered in the doorway. Wailing came from behind the walls. The people moved aside when William approached. They didn't make eye contact, as if afraid William would purify them on sight. His voice could go raw from him telling them he would never change them without their consent, but they'd never believe him. He'd learned that his explanations were a waste of time. A radiant would always be isolated outside their own. Over the years, his brother had eased his loneliness. Both of them had watched their friends choose to become full radiant when they'd reached the age of consent at twenty. They were better off, but it still left a sense of emptiness.

They entered the house. The bright light on the inside contradicted the somber mood. Those who weren't family stepped outside. The woman in the center knelt in front of a picture of her daughter. The daughter had come to William last week, and Samuel had persuaded her to find work so she could get charged. Evidently, she hadn't succeeded.

The mother didn't turn to face them until the father tapped her on the shoulder. She peered at William and Samuel with tear streaks on her face. She got to her feet, her hands fisted at her sides. A calloused finger rose and pointed at Samuel.

"You. What do you have to say to me? My daughter doesn't have a body to bury. She's a pile of mushy skin and bone." Sparks sprang from her eyes, and another family member held her back by her shoulders.

Samuel bowed his head. "I'm sorry."

"Sorry? You're sorry? Yet you stand here in your own body, not mush. If you think your advice is so good, why don't you give up your charges for those you don't let become a radiant?" The mother shook as she accused Samuel.

"I-I should have." Samuel lowered his gaze again, his posture folding in.

The mother pulled out of the family member's grip and jabbed her finger at Samuel's chest. With each word, she stabbed her finger at him. "You should be the mush my daughter is. She couldn't find work. She lied to us so we wouldn't give up our charges. You killed her."

The girl's family stood behind the mother in a silent wall, staring at the two brothers. William wanted to reach out. But wasn't this what his brother deserved?

"Ma'am, he thought—"

She glared at William. "I don't care what he thought. He's here. She isn't. You should have purified her like she wanted."

William nodded. There was nothing he could say or do. The woman grieved, and they could do nothing to bring her daughter back. "If you and your family want to be purified, I'm here to help you, but we only purify those who are certain they want a life without magic."

They could change their minds up to the last second.

"I wanted a life with my daughter." Her face fell, and her shoulders drooped. They would never understand this mother's pain.

Samuel fell to his knees. "I won't do this again. Her death is on my shoulders. I'm sorry."

The mother's tears rolled down her face. She stepped back, and her family stood in a line. Six of them in total. "I will die before my other children. They're all of age, and they will make their own choice." Her expression flinty, she directed her last comment at Samuel. "See that you never speak to those who have no choice again. You don't understand our life."

Samuel's face was blank, his tongue mute.

Then the mother took a knife out of her pocket. William shifted forward, but she brought the knife to her neck and winced as she cut. The glass orb fell to the wooden floor with a click. She placed the knife in her husband's hand, and he did the same. One by one, they all cut out the glass orb that allowed them to charge. Once an orb was removed, there was no going back. They would either become a mog or a radiant.

She stepped up to William, her eyes filled with tears and blood trickling down her neck. "I wish to become a radiant and live without magic."

William placed his hands on her head and let her magic flow out of her, then he replaced the magic with the white glow from his relic. Her eyes glowed peacefully, and she stood back and blinked. One at a time, the family came forward. Samuel stayed on the ground, his head bowed.

Once William finished, he gazed at the mournful sight of the family that had lost one of their own. Their expressions didn't speak to the loss anymore. William wanted to kneel beside his brother, but that wasn't what a leader would do.

"Go to the radiant territory. You'll be given your tasks as part of the community," William whispered in the still room.

As a group, they exited the home, leaving splatters of blood and their glass orbs behind.

"They left her picture." Samuel faced William, his voice strained. "Why would they leave it?" Tears streaked his face.

"They're pure now." Those who'd moved on had little need for items of this world.

Samuel stood. "That means they don't feel anymore? They don't care about their daughter? Do people realize this when they get purified?"

"They don't not care. They move beyond."

Samuel grabbed the picture and ran out of the home.

William ran after him. "Don't do this, Sam!"

He caught up with the family strolling in the street and stopped in front of the mother. "You left this behind. Don't you want this?"

The mother glanced at the picture. "I'm going to the radiant territory. We are at peace now."

Samuel shoved the picture in her face. "This is your daughter! Don't you want to take this with you?" His frantic voice rose in volume, and people down the street glanced at the group.

The mother smiled. "There's no need. They provide everything."

Before Samuel could grab the mother, William gripped his arms and held him back. He struggled but eventually fell to the ground, holding the picture of their daughter. The family moved on, not caring about the interruption.

"Why can't you take her with you? Why?"

"They're on a higher level now." Had his brother not learned anything of what the radiant represented?

Samuel curled up and clenched the picture. He threw off his brother's hands. "Don't. Just don't. I can't bear your rhetoric right now."

The other mourners stood outside and stole glances at the brothers. It was his job to keep Samuel from making a scene. "We need to leave."

Samuel let out a short laugh. "Yeah, can't have people see this, right?"

William placed a hand on his shoulder and squeezed. "Why don't we get out of here?"

Eyes that were so much like his looked up. "Fine."

Samuel stood, still holding the picture.

When they reached their home, Samuel walked past the house.

"Sam? Where are you going?"

"Out of here." He set his shoulders and didn't turn back.

William ran his hand through his hair, and his shoulders

sagged. There was no helping his brother. This had only made it worse. He stood outside, hoping his brother would come back, but he never returned.

His mother found him outside the house. "Son, why are you standing out here? Isn't it time to get ready for your dinner?"

"I got back from helping the family that lost their daughter."

His mother clicked her tongue. "Such a tragedy, and our Samuel to blame. I hope this helps him see sense." She lifted her hand and pressed it to William's cheek. "If you two would work together to lead the radiant, I would feel so much better about it."

"I don't see that happening." William followed his mother inside.

She frowned. "Where's your brother?"

"He ran off."

She put her hands on her hips. "You're supposed to watch him."

William plopped down in the kitchen chair. "Should I tie him up?"

She huffed and bustled around the kitchen, clanking pots and pans. "No, but he looks up to you."

"I don't think so anymore." The Samuel who'd followed him everywhere didn't exist. The minute William had taken on his role, Samuel had rebelled.

"What do you think of Glass's daughter? A pretty thing, right? I hear she might be a bit of a challenge, but this is a good opportunity for the radiant." His mother, the expert at changing the topic.

A bit of a challenge? She was fire incarnate, and William

knew that if he got too close, he would get burned. "What's father hoping to gain? The founders won't give up magic."

He pulled at his sleeves, the room closing in around him. He wanted to walk off like his brother had.

"Don't worry, and be a good son."

Wasn't that the answer to everything? Be a good son. Follow and don't ask questions. It was the radiant way. "But if I'm to lead, shouldn't I know what's going on?"

She plunked down wooden plates on the table. "What's going on? I told your father you might not be ready to face those who use magic. With this engagement, she might lead you astray."

"Mother, that's not what I meant. I think I could help more if I knew the end goal." He straightened his cuffs. His foot bounced, and the clammy air got harder to breathe. This home was too small and too dark. Not enough room for him to get air.

She came over and patted him on the cheek. "Do as you're told, and then you don't need to worry about the end goal. Clean up and get ready. You don't want to be late."

Even though he wanted to get out of the house, he didn't want a night with Vic's family. But William nodded and got ready for the dinner. After all, he was a good son.

9

VIC

In the setting sun, the ornate glass walls gleamed with different vibrant colors. It cost a lot to have well-made windows, and the Glass founders had decided to scream their fortunes to the masses. Her ancestors had built these walls with magic. Glass was fragile, but with the help of magic, the walls remained stronger than most stone. But the Glass founders didn't need the protection. Their family's power already gave it to them. They paid dearly for their status and power by giving up one of their own every vital ceremony. The glowing glass doors swung open, but Vic didn't walk through.

"Come on." Emilia pulled on her hand. "It will only be worse if you're late."

Vic ground her teeth and stepped past the gate. The courtyard greeted her with the same glass statues her sister had made. Her favorite was in the middle—an iridescent mermaid that reached for the sky. Her sister had captured the feeling of longing in the mermaid's outstretched hand. The mermaid reached for something she could never have.

Most of the walls were opaque white glass. The ridiculous house was too white. With his white clothing, William would blend in so well they might lose him. The main floor was solid marble, which remained cold year-round. The house always contained sunlight but never warmth.

They entered the foyer.

"I suppose we have to have drinks before dinner?" Vic said. It was too much to hope that they would get the dinner over with. It had to be a show. After all, they were *founders*. They needed to dress fancy and posture, even at a meal.

"Are you sure you don't want to change?" Emilia's forehead creased. "You know we dress up for dinner."

"My shirt is clean." Vic wore her usual outfit of black pants and a black shirt. The scuffed boots finished the look. "I wore my hair down, and I even combed it."

Emilia sighed. "A dress could go a long way in making this less painful." She tried to pull Vic to the wide staircase.

Vic remained planted. "What's going on? Does he punish you if I don't behave?"

Her father had never hit them, but his words hurt enough.

Her sister flinched. "I'm nervous. Tristan will be here."

Vic took a reluctant step. "I'm not wearing color."

Emilia's face broke into a grin. "Okay, hurry!"

They ran up the stairs to Emilia's room. In her sister's room, the walls burst with different colors. It almost hurt to look at, but this was the one place that didn't feel icy. Emilia opened the bright blue closet doors and pushed all her clothes aside. She pulled out a long black dress. "See! I wore this to a funeral."

"How fitting," Vic replied dryly as she took the black

dress from her sister. The material was shiny and smooth against her fingertips.

She pulled off her clothes and slipped on the black dress. It reached the floor, hiding her boots, and hung off her frame. Emilia had always been thinner than Vic, but because of her starvation diet, it fit perfectly.

Emilia stepped behind her and twisted up her hair. The back of the dress dipped low, and with her neck bare, the brand was noticeable against her pale skin. She'd taken off her bandage before coming, and the wound had healed enough. Her bare back felt cold and exposed.

"There. You're ready." Emilia held up a pair of heels. "Unless ..."

"No." Vic left the room. "If I need to run, heels will slow me down."

And this dinner would end in her running out. That was the norm these days.

Emilia smiled. They went to the sitting room and waited for the night from hell to start.

The click of heels on marble told Vic her mother had arrived. Vic leaned back on the sofa. Her mother was beautiful, with every hair, facial expression, and accessory in its proper place. A slip of a woman, she moved with a grace that neither of her daughters could capture. Emilia was better at it than Vic. Her mother's long blond curls sat perfectly on her head, showing off her delicate pale neck. The lavender dress swirled around her as she glided into the room. Her usual smile remained plastered on her face. Only her blue eyes didn't sell the image. Her smile never reached her eyes anymore. Her mother had belonged to one of the many healer houses before she'd married her father. Nothing her mother could do could heal this broken family, so she'd given up. Vic loved her mother, but she also held a great deal of anger toward her.

"My darling daughter, Victoria. I've missed you." She came forward and kissed Vic on the forehead. "I'm so happy you're home."

"I don't live here, Mother." They would have to drag her out of the Order living area, which Vic wouldn't rule out.

Her mother sat on the edge of the light blue sofa between her two daughters. "Oh? Well, I must have misunderstood your father. After the trials, he arranged for you to live here. There must be some mistake."

When Kai had suggested she might not be staying in the dorms his morning, she'd known her father had had something to do with it. "Mother, I need to stay with the reapers. It's easier for my work."

Please try to convince him, she pleaded silently, hoping she would understand.

Her mother checked out more and more the closer to the vital ceremony day they got. Vic couldn't blame her, but moping around wouldn't change anything. Her rage didn't change anything either. They would both lose someone they loved. It didn't matter how they felt about it.

Her mother brushed off imaginary dust from the sofa cushion. "That does make sense—at least until you're married." Her mother smoothed one of Vic's stray hairs into place.

Vic opened her mouth, but Emilia interrupted her. "It must be hard adjusting to a new location. It would be much better if Vic stayed part of the team."

"Of course, darling. I will mention that to your father." Their mother walked to the window. "He must be running late."

Fine with me, Vic thought. Maybe if she said what she wanted in her mind instead of out loud, she could make it through tonight. Doubtful.

The door chimed, and the maid went to answer it. Voices murmured, and then she entered the sitting area with William behind her.

"How wonderful!" Their mother grasped his hands and startled him by kissing his cheek. "You must be William, Victoria's fiancé. I'm Patricia, her mother."

"Nice to meet you." He bowed slightly. "I don't believe we're that far into our relationship yet."

Their mother laughed; it chimed like bells. "Don't be silly. I'm sure it will all work out."

William tried to reply, but Vic shook her head. He clamped his mouth shut and nodded. At least he could read her silent cues. There was hope for them yet. They might not be the best players in the game, but Vic would try for a while.

Vic went to the drink cart. "Would you like a drink, William dearest?"

"It's best if I don't." Clean-pressed as ever, William let her mother guide him to sit across from Emilia. He looked out of place on the expensive furniture.

Vic selected one of the glittering glasses and poured herself a generous helping of whiskey. She took a deep drink and let it burn down her throat. "Are you sure?"

Just thinking about behaving made her thirsty.

"Water." His jaw twitched, and he tried to relax on the plush sofa, but his posture remained rigid.

Vic flashed her teeth and poured herself another glass. "How very pure of you, dearest."

Her mother giggled. "You two are getting along so well." She clasped her hands in front of her, practically glowing.

Vic took another drink and pushed the water into William's hands, spilling it a little. "We get along great. Whoever thought of a radiant and reaper together?" She tapped her head. "Brilliant. Just brilliant. The fact that he hates magic and I use it—you'd never think we'd be such a good match." She sat next to him, the liquid in her glass tipping precariously as she put her arm through his. A clean linen scent filled her nose as she leaned into him. He smelled kind of nice. She cleared her throat. "I mean, look at us. Black and white. Nothing goes together better, right, Mother?"

Her mother's smile flickered. Vic couldn't help but try to crack through the facade. Everyone fell in line but Vic, and so she ended up throwing bitter barbs at them.

"Control yourself, Victoria." Conrad Glass walked into the room.

The mood thickened. Behind him stood Tristan, the GicCorp heir, his sleek brown hair combed to the side. They both wore fitted suits. Tristan's gray suit accented his light skin tone. His gaze went to Emilia, and he walked past their father to take Emilia's hand.

"Lovely to see you." His full lips pressed against her sister's hand longer than necessary.

Every founder of age wanted to marry Tristan, not only because his family ran the city, but also because he was extremely handsome. Vic could painfully admit that she'd had a crush on him back when they'd had classes together. Even though he probably never lifted a finger, his muscles remained enticing under his fitted suits. Tall and with a broad frame, he always was polite and calm, but his presence commanded attention. Back when they were young, Tristan had drawn everyone to him. Vic didn't know how much of that politeness was fake, but founders could put on a show, and Tristan was the headliner. Vic couldn't put a finger on it, but he gave her a weird feeling, although everything these days bothered her. From Tristan, to Haven, to Nyx, her gut told her something was wrong, and she didn't know how to explain it to anyone without making a fool out of herself.

Emilia blushed. "I'm so glad you could join us."

Vic removed her arm from William, who glared at her. He must not have appreciated her earlier comments.

Her father's cold gaze took in the couples. "Victoria, take note on how to act. Let's not make a scene." He strode across the room and tugged her glass out of her hand.

She dug her fingernails into her palms. "Sorry, Father. I wanted to acknowledge the genius behind this engagement."

"Now that you have, you may be quiet." The line of her father's jaw grew white as he clenched his teeth.

"Oh, may I?" She slouched back and crossed her legs. An enormous feat in the fitted dress.

Emilia got off the sofa, her eyes wide, and Vic snickered. This gathering wouldn't make it to the dinner table.

"Glad to see you haven't changed, Victoria." Tristan placed Emilia's hand on his forearm. "What are you up to these days?"

Vic pointed to William as they both got up. "I'm marrying a radiant."

Tristan eyed William in his white clothing, not betraying his thoughts. "I see."

William sipped his water and placed it on the end table,

his face impassive. Vic wondered what he thought of all this, but he was apparently staying out of it. *Smart man.*

Her mother clapped her hands. "Dinner is now ready. Why don't we move to the dining hall?" She smiled at her husband and put her hand on his arm.

William offered Vic his arm, and seeing no reason to be rude, she let him escort her out of the sitting room. She'd never understood why women needed a guide to a different room. Were men afraid they would get lost between the sitting room and the dining room?

Vic blinked. She regretted drinking; it made her feel numb. That was nice, but with her father studying her with his sharp glare, she feared she might slip. After all, she should be quiet. How nice.

They all sat down, her mother and father across from each other and Vic next to her assigned man. The maid placed food on her plate. After going hungry for so long in the last few months, Vic thought she would want to eat whenever given the opportunity. Now that she sat back in her place, she wanted to vomit at the rich display of food. The founders could afford not to finish their meals.

"William, what do you do?" their mother asked.

William's fingers rested on the silverware, and he turned his head. "I take part in the purification ceremonies and help those who don't wish to change into a corrupted soul or mog."

"How nice. Is your business going well, Tristan?"

Vic shoved a piece of food around on her plate. "Guess she's done talking to you."

William picked up a knife. "Most who use magic would rather not talk about losing it." He cut into the chicken. "I don't blame them."

He bit down on the food, and Vic thought she saw his mouth turn up. As a radiant, he might not get meat other than fish very often. The true show of riches would have been beef.

Vic put her elbows on the table and leaned toward him. "I guess this must be weird for you. Don't you live without magic? What do you think of this glass house?"

William eyed the large floor-to-ceiling windows at the end of the dining room. The night sky glimmered beyond. "It's a nice home."

A thud on the table silenced them. Vic saw her father's fist on the table. "Victoria. Enough."

"I'm just making conversation with my betrothed. Am I not allowed to get to know him? Or should we marry right here and now? I guess I know his name and occupation. That's enough, right?" She pushed her plate away, knocking over her wineglass. The drink stained the tablecloth, bleeding out in a wide patch.

Her father pushed back from the table. "Excuse us, please."

William glance between them, and Tristan remained still.

Her father left the room, leaving her behind. Every bone in her body told her not to go, but it would be worse if she didn't. She followed him down the brightly lit hall to his office.

He opened the door and paused at the large black window. They did a trick with the glass so no one could see in, but they could see out. Perfect for keeping things hidden in this room. He poured himself a drink from the glass bar next to the window.

He took a slow drink from the glass. Vic didn't know if

she should sit or stand. She decided that remaining by the door was safest. Her heart ached as she watched her father. After turning down Tristan, she'd dreaded her visits with her father. She closed her eyes and saw the ghost of a young girl who would run into her father's arms. He'd hold her up in the air while she'd giggle and laugh. Reality had found her, and she couldn't stay young forever.

"Do you like your little life?" His tone dripped with disdain. He faced her. "Do you like being a reaper?"

"I do."

He set his glass down on the bar with a clink. "When you didn't meld with one of our family's wands, it disappointed me. I made a misjudgment in giving you the scythe. As my eldest, who isn't an imb, the only thing you are good for is marrying off." He folded his hands. "However, I let you play with your relic. It has given you ideas you shouldn't have."

But you weren't disappointed. Your face was happy when you handed me the scythe. You were proud.

Vic didn't know what to do. What had happened to him? What had happened to turn his expression so blank? Why wasn't he fighting for Em? Why would he let them take her away so soon? He was her father. Shouldn't Haven bother him too?

"If you want me to marry the radiant, I'll marry him. But I will not live here. Just leave me out of whatever you're doing."

It didn't matter. He wouldn't leave her alone until he got what he wanted.

He gently pushed the glass toward the edge of the bar until it fell, shattering on the ground. He stared down at the broken pieces. "Victoria, you've had an easier life than most. It's time to face your responsibilities. You'll not write yourself out of this family." With measured steps, he crushed the broken glass under his heel. "I am the head of this house, and I know what's best for you. As founders, it's our honor to protect Verrin. My sister did her duty, and now your sister will too. They aren't going to their deaths. They'll only be separated from us."

Vic clutched the sides of her gown. "I know what they say will happen, and it doesn't mean I have to be happy about not seeing her again! What more do you want? You win. I already said I'll marry him, and Em will go away. Are you still mad about Tristan?"

She refused to be part of what GicCorp did. They took people away to Haven to purify the magic, but they'd never explained how. Didn't anyone else care about the hole in the story, or were they too scared to lose their places as founders?

Her father picked up a shard of glass from the ground. It cut his fingers, but he didn't flinch. "Dear daughter, you do not understand what you are messing with. Fine, live with the reapers. Just fall in line when you need to."

Fall in line with what? Vic held the question back. "Yes, Father." She felt trapped. The city had become too small. She thought her sister bowed too much to their father, but she did the same, only with a louder mouth. Her loud mouth accomplished nothing. Her loud mouth didn't change the fact they needed purified magic to live in this city. It didn't change the fact that every founder needed to sacrifice a child.

"Let's go back and behave in front of the heir of GicCorp, shall we? He's doing us a kindness. Other families do not get this attention. Every founder family loses a loved one. Mourn in your way, but do it quietly." Her father leveled his gaze on her and crunched through the glass. "Next time, wear appropriate shoes."

"I don't give a damn about my shoes," she shot back.

His eyes darkened, but he didn't reply.

They went back to the table in silence. Emilia's gaze followed her, but Vic didn't look her way. When she sat, she mechanically ate the cold, tasteless food on her plate.

"Is everything fine?" William whispered.

Vic copied her mother's plastered-on smile. "Perfect."

Her father and Tristan talked, with her mother simpering at everyone. The food became a lump in her stomach. She peered at her sister. Emilia smiled at Tristan whenever he looked her way, but when out of his line of sight, she stared off into the distance.

Vic couldn't help it. She opened her mouth. "Tristan, do you know that my sister's an artist?"

He wiped his mouth with the cloth napkin and placed it beside his plate. "I'm lucky enough to have a work by her." He took her hand and squeezed. "Her talents will be appreciated."

"Is glass-making handy when purifying magic, then?" His home, built of stone, was a dark place unlike theirs. "Emilia, do you want this?" Had anyone ever asked the vitals what they wanted? Or did they assume they wanted to be shut away in GicCorp for the rest of their days?

"Victoria—"

Vic stood, placed her hands on the table, and looked at her sister. "If you don't, you can come with me. I have a place at Nyx, and I can support you."

Her mother signaled frantically for the maids to leave the dining room. "This isn't the time for such things."

Their mother actually looked shocked. The whole city would rise against them if they didn't provide a vital.

Her father pushed back his chair, and it crashed to the floor with his abrupt movement. "This dinner is over. William, would you take her home?"

William put down his silverware and got up from the table, but Vic didn't move.

"Em, do you want this?" She desperately searched her sister's face. Any hint that she wanted Vic's help and she would get her out of this house.

Emilia folded her hands under the table and looked away. "Victoria, please leave. It's an honor to serve my city. I'll save many lives." Her gaze moved up. "Including yours. Don't dishonor me anymore. I gave you my answer months ago. Do you think I'm so weak that I can't make up my own mind?"

Vic would have rather been slapped. "I won't be coming back." Her gown swished behind her as she stomped out of the dining room and into the foyer. She shoved the front door open, and it banged against the wall before slamming shut behind her.

Once outside the gate, Vic screamed into the night. It ripped from her throat and cut off with a frustrated sob. A confused couple rushed by her and the man shielded his date from the madwoman.

William appeared behind her, a white form in the dark night. "This is the worse time to say this, but that was not the best time to ask that of your sister. Are they allowed such a choice?"

Vic laughed and tugged down her hair, letting the waves fall down her bare back. "I know that, but I won't see her again."

"How do you know that?"

A tear forced its way down Vic's cheek and turned cold in the night air. "I don't know." She hugged her middle. "Do you ever get the feeling we're bugs caught in a web?"

"All the time," he replied. Vic couldn't tell what he was feeling.

Vic scuffed her boots on the stone. "You don't need to walk me home."

"You're at the Nyx Order now?"

"Yeah."

As she walked, the breeze calmed her hot skin. William remained next to her as they followed the path along the canal. He was a staunch magic hater, but his presence comforted her.

"According to my parents, our marriage is already on the books. Do you get any say?" Vic asked.

"I can't say you're my first choice." He sighed. "If it will help the radiant, I will marry you."

"Geez, thanks." The blight swirled a soft lavender that reminded Vic of her mother's dress. It looked peaceful. "Even if you don't know why?"

"I guess I have to trust my father. Do you trust yours?"

"I used to." Vic bit her cheeks and tugged on her hair. "Why does it feel like my sister's a sacrifice?" She blinked up at William. "Why does it feel like by running away, I'm sacrificing her?"

"Aren't we all sacrifices? Yes, the vitals go into GicCorp. They use all their magic. Rumors say their magic use is so intense they collapse from it every day. They never return. I don't think she will suffer." He turned down the road that led to Nyx. "Will she be happy?" His lips softened. "Is anyone?"

"I guess not." People rushed back to their homes since it

was too late to be out, and Vic strolled with her future husband, whom she barely knew. She'd reached her goal of joining an Order, yet she remained stuck. Those months of starvation had proved to be a childish rebellion. As a reaper, she was useless to save her sister. In Haven, they only wanted imbs.

The gates of Nyx were only a few feet in front of them, and Vic turned to William. "Should we hug or something?"

"No, thank you."

Vic chuckled. "Way to hurt a girl's pride."

He quirked his eyebrows. "Do you need a hug?"

"Goodnight, William."

"Goodnight, Victoria."

Back in her dorm, Vic tore off her dress, leaving it on the floor, and put on her familiar clothing. Scraps rubbed up against her legs. She picked him up and buried her face in his fur. "I messed up."

Vic placed Scraps on the bed and crawled under the covers. She rested and tried to sleep, but the faces of her family flashed in front of her. Then the image of Tristan stayed in her mind. She couldn't be the only one who wondered what happened to the vitals. How could she even find out?

V ic put on her harness, folded her scythe, and hooked it on her back. With a deft twist, she tied her hair back. Dusk approached, and she'd spent the whole day trying to rest but had given up. Even though she was injured, she hoped to find her name on the board downstairs. Her trial wounds had scabbed over and her neck barely hurt. Spending another night thinking about her sister would drive her mad.

After petting Scraps, she left her room without looking at the glass figurine on her nightstand. Following the smell of food, she bounded down the stairs. Vic stopped in front of the boards and searched for her name. It was only her and Kai. She frowned.

"Newbies get one-on-one training." The warm voice came from behind her, making her jump. "And we don't go after mogs. Although you might not have a problem with them, Sparks."

"When will I join a group?"

Kai grinned and leaned in with catlike grace. "You're in my group."

"Oh." Vic didn't know where to put her hands. Something about hunting alone with Kai excited her. Bomrosy had been right: good thoughts had done the trick.

Other reapers milled around the area to see where they were hunting. They remained in the middle like two statues. The smell of cedar filled her nose.

"Don't you want to be under my command?" His low voice soothed her.

"I mean, you already put me in handcuffs. Do you often go out and catch your own members? I have to say, your strategy is strange." She backed away from him and almost ran into another reaper. Why did it feel so awkward around him now?

His face softened. "Just the ones who are worth it. But let's stay dry tonight."

"Got it. No frozen bits tonight." Vic wondered if maybe she'd have a chance to talk about the reapers she'd seen attacking the young man. A nervous energy filled her at the prospect. What would happen to her if he knew about it? She'd been thinking about how she would tell him all day. What would happen to her if she was wrong about Kai?

"I need to charge before we head out. You might as well fill up too."

Vic nodded, and they headed out of the Order and into the streets. A charging station was up ahead. Kai grabbed the handle and placed it to his gicorb. He put his gicgauge on the holder and selected an amount that he wanted to charge. The required blight drained out of his relic for payment. It only took a few moments before it clicked. A final hum sounded, and with that, it was Vic's turn.

She didn't have as much blight to trade for a charge. She'd traded it already for credits to buy food. Kai placed his scythe in the slot.

"You don't need to pay for me." It was nice of him, but she could manage.

He'd selected the charge option already. "Let's call this your welcome gift."

Vic didn't turn it down. Her orb itched, and it was getting low. She didn't want to follow her father, but she'd rather not turn into a mog to get away from him.

"I'll take you on our routes. There'll be others on the route, and they'll take on the mogs if there are any. Most of the time, we run into mogs outside the city gate." Kai wrinkled his nose. "We'll also have rotations for sewer duty. Sometimes, we find people about to change into mogs down there, but it smells horrible."

"I don't doubt it." How glamorous her life was now. Vic shivered. She'd never been outside of Verrin. "What's out there?"

"Miles of nothing but swamp. Those rumors are true. We built up walkways with magic. The real danger is falling into the swamp. Some areas will swallow you whole. We don't go out any farther. There's no point. If there are any other humans out there, they'll turn into mogs if they come our way."

She gulped and followed him down the canal toward the outskirts of the city. It made sense that those who needed blight removed were those who might be out of work. There weren't enough reapers to collect all the blight, but most often, their families didn't recognize the corruption until it was too late and the person had wandered off in search of red-meat options.

Kai ran, and Vic followed. A grin grew on her face. She'd never gotten the chance to hunt with others. There was a thrill in keeping up with someone like Kai. His muscles flexed under his shirt as he ran, his movements smooth. He made it look easy. Vic wanted to spar with him now that her ankle wasn't injured. It would be all flesh on flesh and the force of his attack.

"Enjoying the view?"

Vic paused, lost in thought, then smiled. "Yeah, I saw a cute cat over there."

He snorted and turned down an alleyway. It was darker with only one lone lamp in the middle of the block. "First run. We branch out down these alleys in groups of two. Since it's only us, we'll take the final path. The others behind us will patrol the other alleys."

They found nothing, and in silence, they went to the next road. They stayed next to the canal. Vic memorized all the alleys. She had a feeling she'd need to remember the route for tomorrow night.

They drew closer to the large stone wall. The city had four main gates, and city officers guarded them, more as a warning system if there was another breach. The founders had finally realized that they could get hurt if they didn't maintain the walls. Apparently, many lives had been lost the day mogs had breached Verrin, but no one talked about it.

As they approached, Kai flashed his neck, showing them his brand.

The guards pulled out their wands as they stood behind their stone enclosure and placed them on the iron gate. The bars molded aside, and they ran through to the outside world.

The sky and smells were the same out here. The air was

thicker with moisture. They jogged along the stone path. Their boots echoed in the endless darkness. There were lampposts on the walkway, but beyond that, it was only blackness and the swirl of blight.

The feeling of being watched made her skin prickle as she ran with Kai.

"You already know mogs can take many shapes, and the ones out here are bigger and need more than one reaper to drain it. A group ran ahead, and one is behind. If we see a mog, we run."

"Understood." He must not have thought she'd run. It was pure chance that she'd beaten a mog by herself, and her bruised body remembered all too well how that had felt. If he hadn't bandaged her ankle, she might not have made it through the trial.

Without warning, Kai shot up in the air. Vic halted. Then in the lamplight, she saw a thick, rubbery tentacle around his ankle. Its whip-like arms rose out of the swamp. There were no fingers, and Vic couldn't see a head. It hoisted Kai up, and with horror, she realized the mouth was in the center of all the flailing tentacles. Razor-sharp teeth came into view. Swamp water drained out as it pushed itself up.

Kai thrashed in its grip. "Sparks, run!"

Tentacles shot out at her, and she jumped over them, but there were too many. Kai grabbed a long knife from his harness and tried to sever the tentacle. He struggled as the mog lowered him toward its mouth. Vic pulled out her scythe, unfolded it with a loud click, then slashed at the tentacle arms. The blight warmed her relic as it drained.

"Sparks, listen to me!" Kai slashed at the arms, only a foot away from being dropped into the mouth.

Vic's gicgauge filled as she slashed, but she couldn't drain this one. The mogs out here had had too much time to build up blight. Using the scythe's inner blade, she hooked it around the tentacle and yanked it toward herself, and the tentacle fell off with a thunk. She couldn't reach Kai from the stone path. She needed to step into the swamp to cut the arm off.

Tentacles swung at her, trying to grip her, and she kicked them away.

Kai stabbed the arm with his knife and nearly got through, but his head hung next to the razor-sharp teeth. Without looking up, he shouted, "If you even think of getting in the swamp—"

Vic jumped into the water and sank down to her waist. The tentacle arms immediately surrounded her. She lowered her grip on the scythe and hacked at the rubbery arms. The sharp blade cut through them, but there were more under the water, and they gripped her around the waist. The mog squeezed, and she gasped for air.

A loud splashed sounded to her right as Kai hit the water. His blade flashed. He dove under the water and rose next to her. With one arm under her armpits, he tugged her up, allowing her to cut through the surrounding tentacles. The pieces fell from her.

Kai flung her toward the stone path. Her fingers slipped on the stone, and she fell back into the water. The muck sucked her down, but Vic slammed her scythe on the stone, and from the water, she used all her strength to pull her top half onto the path. Her lower half suctioned down, and she held her legs together and pushed against the side of the stone path. She flopped onto the stone and rolled onto her side to scan the water. Kai's head was above the surface. She extended her scythe to him, and he gripped the wood. His hands couldn't gain traction, but she pulled him close enough to reach him. The mog's remaining tentacles wrapped around Kai. He used one hand to cut them off while Vic yanked him onto the stone walkway.

Her muscles strained against the tug-of-war with the mog. Then with shouts, reapers surrounded her. Blades out, they cut the mog. One of them came to help pull Kai up. In moments, the mog melted into flesh, drained of the blight, leaving a greasy smear on the water.

Vic flopped onto her back and took a deep breath. Then a shadow passed over her.

"Get up." His voice was dark.

Vic swallow and pushed herself up.

Kai nodded to the reapers who had saved them, and then he ran down the path. Vic blinked at his back.

"You better follow, newbie." A reaper with bright green hair grinned. "Good luck."

She forced her battered body to run after him. Her lungs begged for her to stop as they raced. The steady jog from before now gone, they sprinted back toward the city gates. Her clothing clung to her, and the muddy swamp water chafed her skin.

Vic focused on pumping her legs to stop herself from falling apart.

"Kai, wait," she gasped.

"Keep going."

She could do this. They full-out sprinted through their route, checking for blight. Then they were back where they'd started at the gates of Nyx.

Kai turned to her, his eyes stormy and his jaw tight. "We do four rounds. During the first, we jog, since that's when the corrupted come out, and they're hungry. Then we do two rounds walking. The last one before dawn, we run."

No wonder he'd had no trouble keeping up with her in the water that night.

"I'm sorry." She shivered in the breeze, her clothing damp.

"Follow me."

He ran again, and Vic bit back a groan. Her pants clung to her and drooped, the material stretched. She recognized the street they went down and the house Kai had brought her to on the night they met. He slammed open the door and stood facing her, his arms crossed while he tried to take in a full breath of air.

Vic had thought she was in shape, but apparently not.

"So you can run. I wondered after I told you and you ignored me." His wet clothing molded to his shape, and his arms flexed. Dirty water dripped onto the clean floor.

"I wasn't going to leave you there!"

What was the point of working together as a team?

He stepped forward and leaned over her. "Did I or did I not tell you to run?"

"You did." She backed away.

"Do you think you know better than your commander?" He invaded her space.

Vic squared her shoulders. "Was I supposed to leave you to die?"

"What makes you think I was going to die?"

Vic flung her arms out. "The teeth a foot away from your head."

Kai strode forward, forcing Vic to stumble back. Her back met the closed door, and Kai placed a hand next to her head. The smell of cedar hit her nose, even with them covered in swamp water. "I was getting out of it. Then instead of getting to the stone path, I had to rescue you. You put us both in danger because you thought you knew better than me. I've been fighting mogs for a long time. I've been training newbies for a long time. I know how to cut and run when it's only two reapers." He spat out the last words. "I can't trust you with my team if you don't listen to me."

"I'm sorry." He was right. She hadn't trusted him to get out of the situation, and she'd made the situation worse. "I won't do it again."

He stepped back and shook his head. "I'm requesting a transfer. I'm sorry, Sparks. I don't think you'll listen to me."

An ache filled her like a knife digging into her gut. "That's it? I'm out, just like that? I messed up. I won't do it again."

"Should we test that in another life and death situation?"

Vic jutted out her jaw. "No. I'll listen to you in any battle situation."

He raised a brow. "Even if it puts someone in perceived danger?"

"You won't put anyone in danger. Kai, I'm used to being on my own. I didn't want you to get hurt. I thought I was helping." Her chest tightened.

He grinned and laughter filled his eyes. "Well, it didn't take long for you to submit, Sparks. I for sure thought I'd have to teach you another lesson."

Vic's face grew red. "What do you mean? You couldn't have planned all this?"

His chest shook. "The type of mog, no. But I do this every quarter with the newbie. They always think they can save me." He grimaced. "Although, I admit the tentacles were a

surprise. That was a nasty mog." Kai looked at her sheepishly. "The other reapers were close the whole time."

"They all saw me—"

"Disobey an order? Yes. They have orders to stand back
unless they think we might die." Kai reached over, pulled a
juice out of his fridge, and offered one to her.

Vic took a swallow, the cool liquid soothing her throat.
"Is this some sort of hazing?"

Kai finished his juice in one long gulp and tossed the
empty bottle in the trash. "I mean, we both got dunked in
swamp water, but like I said, there isn't a newbie who listens.
It may be a weird welcome, but it serves two purposes."

Vic leaned back against the wall. "To put us in our place
and make sure we follow orders?"

He might be insane.

Kai wiped his mouth. "Exactly. But we're kind enough to
let you shower before we run the route three more times."

Vic groan. "Run?"

He grinned. "Gotta catch up now. The faster we shower,
the slower we run."

Vic darted into the bathroom. Nothing had changed
since last time. With a smile, she pushed his comb askew
again. She got in the shower and let the hot water wash away
the swamp. There were dry clothes already waiting for her in
the bathroom, and she tied up her wet hair and got dressed.

Kai quickly showered after her, and before she knew it,
they were running on the path again.

Though he'd had dry clothing for her, her boots still
squelched with water. "Couldn't you have gotten my other
boots too?"

Kai laughed. "Part of the lesson, Sparks. After you run a
night in wet boots, you'll remember to listen."

"Power trip." She could already feel a blister forming.

She tiredly followed him; her pride wouldn't let her fall behind. She tried to distract herself by thinking of something else besides the lack of air or her burning muscles. Focusing on the muscles in Kai's back didn't help. They made it to the original gate. This time, as they ran the stone path, there was only the sound of their thudding boots.

The second route finished, Kai stopped to let her get a drink of water. She took in more air, and Kai rubbed his brand as he waited.

Vic hesitated. The brand flashed in her mind from the rogue reaper. "When someone leaves the Order of Nyx, what happens to the brand?" She knew she was trying to delay the truth but she hoped still that she was wrong.

"Why?" He rolled his shoulders and stretched out his arms.

"Just wondering if each Order does something different." Maybe she'd missed something in the dark.

"Xiona blacks it out." Kai raised his hands in the shape of a square. "A big black square of shame."

They weren't kicked out, then, Vic thought.

Kai tilted his head. "Why? Did you see something?"

She'd spent the whole night thinking about how to tell him before more people got hurt. She studied his face as she said, "There are rumors of people with brands taking out orbs. You hear a lot of things where I used to live."

Kai's stance widened. "What rumors? I haven't heard of this."

"You're here, and I lived there."

His surprise looked real. She should go with her gut and trust him.

"Uh-huh. Why don't you spit it out? Vagueness doesn't suit you."

Vic rubbed her arms. "The other day, I caught some reapers attacking a young man. They were trying to take out his orb. I stopped them, but he told me this has been going on for a while. When they report it, the officers do nothing."

"You saw their brand?" Kai's whole body tensed.

Vic nodded.

He stepped back, understanding why she'd been hesitant. "They were scythes?"

She nodded again. If he didn't know, then Xiona might not know either. Would a group do this to boost their collection numbers?

"Blight take us." He slammed his hand against the stone wall. "Where?"

"Next to Scrums Creek. I'm sure we could ask people down there and see if there are other reports."

Kai stepped back. "We may not like what we find."

Vic placed a hand on his arm. "I have a feeling this might hurt you more than me. You've fought with them and know them." She would have no trouble putting those rogues away. The people in the poor parts of the city had enough to worry about. The reapers should be protecting everyone equally.

"I'm sure there's an explanation."

Vic smiled encouragingly, but the troubled look stayed on his face.

He ran his hand through his hair. "Sparks, we better finish up the route. Sorry, we'll need to go faster."

"Can't we skip it and go find the reapers?" Her tired body screamed at her.

Kai glanced at the Order's windows. "No deviation. I'm not sure what's going on."

Translation: another commander might be doing this, and they couldn't make their suspicion obvious.

Vic cracked her neck and ran after Kai's departing form. His back remained tense, and she worried for him.

Vic lay on the ground. The cold stone did nothing for her trembling body. Kai splashed water on her face, and she glared at him.

"Get up, Sparks. I want to check the location." He remained tense and ready to move.

Vic took a lazy swipe at him, but he dodged it easily. "Go on without me. I'm going to die here."

He laughed. "You think tonight was bad, wait until tomorrow."

"Ugh, you're psychotic." Vic pushed herself up and wiped the sweat from her neck and face with her shirt. It didn't do much since her shirt was damp. She caught Kai's gaze flicking to her exposed flesh. Vic flapped her shirt. "Like what you see?"

He lifted the corner of his shirt and copied Vic by wiping his face. His exposed abs gleamed with sweat, and the hard planes stood out in the lamplight. "You never seem to have a problem looking. Fair is fair."

"Good point."

They paused, and the air between them thickened.

Vic cleared her throat. "Ah, suppose we should head out?"

No doubt that Kai's attractiveness affected her. Could a commander have a relationship with their subordinate? She should not be thinking about dating right now.

She walked next to Kai back to her old apartment. "What do you think about the orb thefts?"

Kai stared straight ahead. "I'm not sure. I think there's an explanation. Maybe it was someone just getting the blight taken out of them. They might have cut his neck to take out the blight." His brow furrowed. "We discourage reapers from aiming for vital places like the neck. We tend to want the person to live after we get the blight out." He grinned crookedly but worry filled his expression.

Vic sorted through that night. She could tell that Kai was trying to give the reapers the benefit of the doubt, but the man had said that the reapers were taking the orbs. "I wonder if the officers will have the reports?"

Kai kicked a rock, and it splashed into the canal. "Why don't we stop there on the way and ask?"

Vic followed along, and they walked, keeping pace with each other. She thought Kai might be more troubled than he was letting on. Maybe it was the fact he was a commander and hadn't known this was going on. She admitted that what she'd seen sounded crazy. But for him to be taking her claim seriously showed that he listened to his subordinates. That was someone she would gladly follow. He hadn't turned her in when she'd illegally hunted in Nyx territory, showing that he cared more about people than the law. She tried to put together the pieces of the man beside her.

They passed another water-taxi stop, and the empty boats bobbed in the dark water.

"Do you have any other family?" Vic asked.

Kai blinked at the random question. "Yes. My mother, and I have a younger sister."

"Are they reapers too?"

Kai shook his head. "I hold our last relic."

"I'm sorry."

He took in a deep breath. "Don't be. It's just how it ended up. I plan to keep my scythe."

Kai had to provide for his family. Some imbs could get weaker wands, but it was hard for them to earn enough credits to survive. The magic drained too fast. The bright stones built into them focused the magic use and protected the wielder from magic burnout. GicCorp tried to recreate the stones, but each resulted in weaker versions that broke with time. Some founder families had more relics than they needed but would never give them up. Every forty to fifty years, when the vital passed away, they would get a relic back. That was the only notice of Emilia's death they would get.

"Mine is the last scythe in my family. Although my father is disappointed that I'm not an imb, it hadn't bothered him before. When he gave me the scythe, he acted happy that the Glass family had a reaper."

"Your father is an intense man." Kai squeezed her hand lightly.

"*Intense* is one word for it. I suppose he would rather have me be the vital. My sister's more inclined toward art, but she could still run things and keep the factory imbued to produce glass."

"My father and mother lost their wands. This is all we

have left. My sister won't have a wand passed down to her."
His face fell. "She's an imb, so if something happens to me,
that's it. They can sell the relic, but once those credits are
gone, they'll become corrupted."

Vic didn't know what to say. He attacked mogs with no
hesitation, but their job wasn't easy. They could die any
night of the week. Kai wasn't one to leave a man behind, and
he would sacrifice himself to save his team.

They arrived at the station closest to where Vic had seen
the attack. The stations stood out in the gray city with red
horizontal stripes across the top of the stone. An emblem of
a red wand on a blue background hung over the metal door.
She followed him inside. The station buzzed with activity.
Unlike the bright outside, the inside was painted in duller
browns. After being outside in the night, the warm air was
welcome, though it smelled of stale food, unwashed bodies,
and a hint of vomit. Some officers were on alert for trouble,
gearing up shields before they ran out another side door.
Officers carried imbued stones that would warn them of
danger. Vic didn't know how they worked, but near some
charging stations, there would be an alarm people could pull
if they needed help. In the center of Verrin, some lucky officers got their own water taxis or horses.

Other officers argued with people in cuffs. A familiar
brown head caught Vic's eye.

"Samuel?"

Light blue eyes blinked at the sound of his name. He sat
on a metal chair that looked bolted to the ground. "Fire
Girl?" His hands lifted in unison to wave, his wrists cuffed.

"Fire Girl?" Kai took in the new person across the station.

"Hey, that one is new to me too." She went over to
Samuel, leaving Kai behind to talk to the officers. He swayed

a bit, practically tipping off his chair, and reeked of alcohol. Red circled his irises. "What's going on?" She slipped on her eyepiece and saw a slight glow before tucking it away in her harness again. "Are you not charging?" she whispered.

He stood and hugged her by lifting his arms over her head and pulling her in. "Good to see you," he slurred. "I need to talk to you, Fire Girl."

"Why don't I help you out first?" Vic ducked out of his hug and reached for her scythe.

"No, Fire Girl. I don't want you to do that." He staggered and sat down. He clasped her hands and peered at her. "I need you to take care of William. Can you promise me? You'll help him?"

Vic leaned down. "Why are you saying this?" She put a cool hand on his forehead. His skin was on fire, not her. That was strange since most corrupted felt cold.

Samuel closed his eyes, his voice laced with pain as he said, "I killed her. I thought I was helping, but I killed her. Then they didn't remember." He opened his eyes and squeezed her hand tighter. "They didn't remember their own daughter. I destroyed the whole family with my selfish advice."

"Hey now, I think you're being too hard on yourself." Vic had no clue what he was talking about. She'd only met him once, but she didn't think he would hurt others. He probably shouldn't be talking about killing near the officers. Those in the station continued to ignore them.

"Look after William? Please?" He sounded close to tears.

Vic pulled one of her hands away to steady him on his chair so he wouldn't fall on the floor. She doubted William needed anyone to look after him. Samuel sounded panicked and needed her to calm him. "I will, but you'll be there too. Okay?"

Samuel let go of her hands. "Yeah."

"Is someone coming for you?" Vic asked.

"My brother always does." His whispered words were hard to hear in the chaos of the station.

Vic gripped his shoulder. "Why don't we go out together next time, okay? I bet I can outdrink you."

"Yeah, next time." His shoulders hunched over, and he faced the stone floor.

"Sparks?"

Vic jumped slightly at Kai's voice behind her. "Sorry, did you find out anything?"

"No, I didn't. What did you find?" He stood over Samuel, who remained slouched in his chair.

"This is Samuel. He's William's brother."

Kai tilted his head. "And who's William?"

"My brother."

Kai looked at Samuel from the corner of his eye. "That clears up so much."

Samuel waved his cuffed hands at Vic. "They're getting married."

"I see." Kai's face became unreadable.

Vic wanted to sink into the ground. "Um, let's get out of here before the sun rises." She headed toward the door, but Kai stood staring at Samuel, unwilling to move.

"How long have you known her?" Kai asked.

Samuel twisted his wrists in the metal cuffs. "Met her the same day as my brother."

"The one who's marrying her?" This was quickly becoming some sort of investigation.

"Yep." Samuel quirked his eyebrow at Kai. "Do you like her or something?"

Kai's jaw twitched.

Vic grabbed his arm and pulled him away. "See you later, Samuel."

They left the station. The cool night air felt good on her flushed face.

"I didn't know you were engaged." Kai sounded strange.

"Ah, about that ... it's an arranged marriage. I honestly don't think anything will come of it. My family is going through a bit of a transition. I mean, I'm the eldest, and I was supposed to marry someone else, but then I ran off and thought I was free. Then Father came up to me at the trials, telling me I had to marry William." She couldn't stop the words pouring out of her mouth. Why did she owe Kai an explanation?

Kai stepped closer to her as she rambled.

"Honestly, I really don't think we'll end up getting married. He's a radiant, after all, and well, you can see how well that would go."

Kai placed his hand on her shoulder. "I see." He leaned down. "Do you like William?"

"What? I don't know him. I just met him!" Her blood burned as he towered over her.

His lips were mere inches from hers. "You just met me too."

She leaned her head back. "What does that have to do with anything?"

She wasn't sure she was making any sense. His closeness made her shiver.

The corners of his mouth turned up. "I'm not sure." He stepped back. Vic's face grew warm.

He let out a low chuckle. "I suppose we need to find the rogues."

"Yeah." She sounded breathless. What was wrong with her? Kai was smart and attractive, but he was also her new commander.

Get your feelings under control, Glass. She wanted to slap her cheeks but held her hands to her side.

Kai walked to the dock in the canal, and she missed the energy and warmth he radiated.

"The officers said they got complaints, but each one had various explanations." Kai's lips were set in a grim line. "They were flimsy at best, but the officers took the word of the reapers. They wouldn't tell me the names but said they'd forward the information to my commander if I thought it was important."

"Did you?"

"No, not yet."

He suspected Xiona. He faced the alley and glared at the people still out after dark. It wasn't forbidden, just dangerous. People either didn't care or they needed the work.

"How many?" Vic asked.

"There were over fifty reports." He ran his hand through his hair. "Sometimes, when we draw the blight out of a corrupted soul, the orb can break, but that's rare."

A familiar chill filled her. "And they can't be replaced."

"And fifty? I'm in my thirties, and I've only heard of one."

As they got farther from the station, they stuck to the darkness of the alley. "Let's head up to the rooftops to see farther. There's no definite pattern to the attacks, but since the officers didn't look into it, they weren't keeping track."

"This is Nyx territory," Vic said, stating the obvious in the hopes that Kai would correct her.

He nodded. "That worries me. I know the group that patrols this area, and I can't—" He clenched his jaw. "I can't believe they would do something like this." Kai directed her toward a trash bin in the alley. "We can follow their route from the rooftops. They're staying in the city tonight."

Vic boosted herself carefully onto the bin and avoided touching something brown and slimy on the rim. The bin teetered under her feet while Kai tried to steady it. Vic gripped the low terracotta roof tiles and pulled herself up. She planted her feet and gripped the side to help pull up Kai.

The houses and apartments were packed together, with only a few feet of space between, so going from rooftop to rooftop was easy. The breeze blew stronger up here, and they stayed on the move. Kai would grab her hand sometimes when she landed on the next roof beside him. She enjoyed his touch, which surprised her. She'd expected to just marry another founder. Then after she'd refused Tristan and left her home, she hadn't had time for men. *Way to be distracted like a silly kid.* Her legs complained from all the jumping. *You just met him. Slow down.*

Kai steadied her when she stumbled on a rough landing. "Able to keep up, Sparks?"

"Oh, I have plenty of stamina."

He coughed and turned away. Vic smiled at his back; she'd actually shocked him. They stopped and crouched at the edge of a roof.

Kai squatted and hunched over, his focus on the path over the ridge of the roof. It snaked out from a tunneled bridge. "This is the best place to follow them. The rooftops are higher and we can still see the road. We may have to wait a bit, depending on how their routes went tonight."

The quietness of the street grew in Vic's ears. She waited
for the sound of footsteps. If they were on their third round,
they wouldn't be running. Vic lay on her side against the
terracotta roof but kept her head above the ridge so she
could see the bridge. She wanted to sleep. The sound of
approaching footsteps reached them as it echoed over the
covered bridge.

Four figures dressed in black with scythes attached to
their backs came into view. They spread out from each other.
Once they'd passed, Vic and Kai followed silently on the
rooftops.

The group scanned all the alleys with their eyepieces on,
sometimes scanning the water. Vic had learned the hard way
that mogs could be in the canal.

Nothing seemed off. Vic and Kai followed the group,
staying well behind them.

Then a young man came down the road, carrying a pack
of food on his back. He walked slowly under the weight,
most likely coming back late after a long day at the factory.
The reaper closest raised their hand and flicked their fingers
out.

"Nice night tonight," the reaper greeted the person.

The man nodded and said something Vic couldn't hear.
Then in a flash, the reaper brought out a blade. The man's
mouth opened in a wide O, but he didn't move. Then he
released the shoulder straps from the pack, and his hand
shot to his neck.

Kai jumped down from the roof and ran toward the
group, his footsteps silent despite his rush.

"Blight take me," Vic muttered. *Why didn't he wait
for me?*

She swung down and landed with a thud on the stone

ground. Her sore legs wanted to buckle under her. She steadied herself and chased after Kai.

By the time she reached him, he'd caught up with the reaper who'd cut the person's neck.

"What do you think you're doing attacking an imb?" Kai's muscles bunched in his arm as he grasped the person tighter.

The other three stalked forward. Vic touched the victim's arm. His neck was bleeding. "Is your orb still there?"

He bobbed his head and clutched the pack's straps. He ran away from the group of reapers.

"Probably best not to be out after dark!" Vic called after him. She wished they lived in a world where those with less powerful relics didn't have to bend to the will of the founders.

Vic took out her scythe but didn't unfold it. "Kai?"

The other three reapers closed in on them.

"What are you doing?" Kai repeated to the reapers.

Vic didn't know the reaper Kai held, but he wasn't much older than her.

"Sir, I think you better leave." A young woman with a smattering of freckles on her face raised her hands slowly.

Kai's eyebrows shot up, and he lifted the young man's body.

Vic grimaced. "That was the wrong thing to say." She stepped out in front of Kai and faced the other three reapers.

Kai rumbled behind her, "Do you think you have any authority here?"

The young man gasped. "No, sir. Sorry. Just ... it might ... be ... better ... if you ... let this go."

A brief shuffle, then Vic heard a body hit the water. Kai stood next to her. He crossed his arms and didn't draw his own scythe, though three reapers pointed their weapons at Vic.

"Do you really want to fight a commander tonight?" Kai's voice lowered and crawled through the silent street.

He was on her side, but Vic's spine froze. The others stopped advancing and put their scythes back in their harnesses.

Kai nodded sharply. "Get your friend. We're going back to Nyx."

Freckles spoke up, "Sir, we respect you, but please, let this go."

Vic could feel the rage radiating off Kai. His eyes flashed, and they all flinched. "Get him and let's go." His voice left no room for argument.

All the reapers' gazes shifted between one another. They walked past to grab their fallen comrade's arms and pulled him out of the canal. Water dripped down his body, and he bowed his head to Kai, shivering on the stone street. "Commander, I—"

Kai turned away and walked down the street. They all followed him like cowed children.

Vic stayed behind them in case they were stupid enough to run. They acted like they wanted to protect Kai. Her gut clenched.

This is bigger than we know. Vic gripped her scythe, letting the warmth comfort her. They'd found out something they shouldn't have. What would happen now that Kai knew?

They continued down the stone road, her sense of dread growing stronger the closer they got to Nyx.

Emilia furrowed her brow as she shaped the glass. If Vic were here, she would point out the fact that she would get a permanent wrinkle. This piece didn't want to cooperate. She had to finish it today. There was only today.

Emilia bit her lip until it pinched painfully, but finally, under her wand, the last strand fell into place on the statue's face. The eyes were the hardest, and she wanted to get this one right.

Arms crossed, she stepped back to admire her largest work yet. A smile spread as she gazed at the sculpture. One lone tear traced down her cheek, and she swiftly wiped it away.

Sisters. A simple title, but that's what the piece showed. The form closest to her showed Vic in all her glory, her red hair flying around her face. The light reflected through the glass, making it shine from within. Her eyes, always looking forward, had the same fire in them, and her lips were parted in a joyful laugh. Emilia hadn't heard this carefree laugh in a long time, but the memory had stayed with her. In her artwork, she could give Vic the freedom she'd always wanted.

The statue of Vic captured her motion and her passion. However, while the statue looked forward, she also reached back. The long, clear arm stretched toward her sister. Emilia had never made herself before, but unlike Vic, the statue of Emilia showed a calmness. Her eyes gazed at her sister, not in the direction they traveled, and she had a soft, sad smile on her lips. She reached for her sister, but with an artistic eye, you could see she'd already let go of Vic's hand, letting her sister go. She understood what Vic wanted, but she couldn't give it to her. Even if it meant she would never see her sister again, she would devote her life to keeping her safe. Her sister saw her as delicate, but Emilia would prove to her that she was strong.

An ache formed in Emilia's chest. She slapped her cheeks.

"I need to get ready," she told herself and glanced around her room. There wasn't much to prepare. The glass windows made her room, filled with molded glass shapes of all colors, light and airy. Vic had sometimes teased that her room reminded her of an exploded rainbow. Thoughts of her sister hurt. She should have spent her last weeks with her, but Vic had made choices for both of them. Now there was no time left.

Emilia had always been the quiet one, but her art showed more emotion than she ever let out. *I can't let them out.*

If Vic saw her hesitate, she would drag her somewhere and tie her up. Emilia sighed at her sister's overprotective nature.

One wall held containers of different colored sand. She traced her fingers through the grains. The feel of sand always comforted her. Emilia stepped back. It would be better to leave it all behind. She didn't know what she'd need, but her relic warmed her hand. That was probably all they wanted from her anyway.

A soft knock sounded at the door.

"Come in." She folded her hands over her stomach.

Her father entered. His eyes took in the glass sculpture, and he froze. Emilia saw the flicker of defeat in his eyes. Vic saw only an emotionless man because she couldn't see what lay behind their father's once happy eyes. Emilia had learned to see past the surface. This gave her art life. He'd had to give up his sister, her aunt, and now his daughter to protect the city. It wasn't as easy for him as Vic believed.

He stood at the door, his posture as stiff as ever, every proper emotion in place. The corner of Emilia's mouth turned up. Vic had never learned to play their game, the one where you nodded and played along with others more powerful than you. The game let you know when you had to be a dutiful daughter. The game also told you when you'd lost and needed to give in. All the founders played. They all had to lose at least once. To save the city, it was necessary.

"Are you ready? There's time to say goodbye before Tristan arrives." Her father blinked, and his wall of emotion crumbled.

Emilia smiled and placed her hands on his arm. "Yes, Father. I decided not to take anything with me. I'm sure the Nordics will have everything I need for my meditation."

His cold hand grasped hers. They stood like that, daughter gazing up at her father.

"Emilia." Desperation rushed through his face, and his arm shook under her hand. "You can r—"

"Do you like my last work?" Emilia swallowed the large lump in her throat. Tristan wasn't here yet, but she didn't want her eyes to be red. She couldn't be tempted. If she left, the founders could take all the family's relics. Then her family would become mogs. She could cut ties with them and only lose her relic. The founders gave up one of their children for the safety of the city, but Emilia was doing it for her family. That was the only reason she didn't break down.

His eyes glanced away from hers, and a wistfulness came over his face. Her father relaxed, and her heart warmed at seeing her father again.

"You captured your sister." He walked to the sculpture and raised his hand to Vic's cheek. He lowered his hand and turned to the statue of Emilia. "She won't understand."

Emilia's shoes clicked on the floor as she joined her father. "I know." Emilia glanced at the door. "Where's Mother?"

He shook his head. "I'm sorry, she can't."

Emilia tried not to let the hurt show on her face. "I understand."

Her father sobbed in frustration. He stared at the ground, his shoulder's rising and falling. Then one by one, his fingers on his left hand clenched into a fist. He wrapped his other hand around his left forearm. With a jerk, he straightened himself. The wall stood strong once more.

The musical notes of the doorbell rang through the house. They both stilled.

Emilia recovered first. "He's here."

Her father offered his arm. They walked together to her bedroom door. As they passed through the threshold, Emilia tugged on her father's arm and stopped. She took one last look at her room and the glittering sculpture at its center. The handle felt cold in her hand as she gently shut the door on another person's life.

They continued forward in silence. In the sitting room, Tristan already stood next to the drink cart.

"Do you have time for a drink?" her father asked.

Tristan shook his head. "I need to get back to my family. I came to get Emilia. The others are arriving today." He smiled, showing his teeth.

Emilia admitted Tristan stood out amongst all the others. His brown hair fell softly across his forehead, and when he smiled, a dimple appeared in his right cheek. His shoulders were wide enough to give him a lovely stature. He would make an amazing model for her art. She gently bit her tongue. She didn't want to immortalize him in her art. He was beautiful, but something behind those eyes didn't sit right. They were older than normal.

She'd never mentioned this to her parents. When her father had told her that she was to be a vital, she hadn't understood what that meant. In school, they'd made it out like a grand adventure. Emilia took a breath of the sweet air in her home. She wasn't Vic. She understood the meaning behind the actions of those in her life. Even though she didn't understand Tristan yet, she had a strange feeling she didn't want to. His old eyes frightened her.

Her hand didn't leave her father's arm. In a moment of weakness, she gripped her fingers into his flesh. He didn't react, but she knew he felt it. *Protect me too, Father.*

She let go, the moment gone. She smiled at Tristan. "Shall we, then?"

Tristan nodded. "My mother's so excited to help

everyone prepare for their meditations before the ceremony." He scanned the room. "Are your things packed?"

"There's nothing I need from here."

If he found that odd, he said nothing. He offered her his arm, and she slipped her hand on top of it.

Tristan nodded to her father. "We will see you at the vital ceremony." He patted Emilia's hand. "There is nothing to worry about. I know this must be hard on you, but I assure you that Emilia will be well taken care of in our home."

Something flickered in her father's eyes. "I have no doubt."

Good job, Father.

Tristan escorted her to the front door, her father following.

Emilia stopped.

"Is something wrong?" Tristan asked.

Her lips parted. "I'm sorry, but I would like to give my father another hug."

Tristan smiled understandingly.

She stepped unsteadily toward her father, then wrapped her arms around him. *Just a moment. I just need this one moment, please.* Her father tightened his arms around her.

"Protect her," Emilia whispered.

He gripped her tighter, but they both knew they needed to release each other. With another slight exhale, she dropped her hold. Her father's arms fell to his sides. She turned away and put her hand back on Tristan's arm.

They walked past the doorway to Tristan's waiting car. The imb driver waited outside and opened the door for them. She slid inside, and Tristan followed her.

With a hum, the vehicle started, and they drove away from her home. Emilia stared out the window. The city of

Verrin was all stone and water. Part of the center of the city was kept polished and bright. She thought it lacked in color.

"Forgive me. I don't think I understand why I can't see my family."

Tristan shifted next to her and tapped his long fingers on the armrest. "They explain this in our history. The magic you will use connects you to the device in the corporation. If you leave, you will lose that connection and your life. We keep trying different things, but it doesn't work to purify the blight. What we use is an ancient relic made before our time."

Emilia nodded, pretending like she understood. "Couldn't families visit?"

She shouldn't press, but there was something he wasn't telling her. Now that she was stuck, maybe he would tell her. Apparently, if imbs came in contact, they would also attach to the relic. It was never clear.

"Are you doubting your purpose?"

She had pushed too much. "No, I guess things weren't really explained." She smiled brightly. "I have no doubts."

They made Haven vague on purpose, and that very vagueness didn't work for Vic, though it comforted most families left behind. Vitals were heroes going in to fight something, but no one knew how.

He nodded and didn't respond. He never did. His old eyes saw too much.

The ache in her chest grew the farther they drove, filling her ribs and making it hard to breathe. She rubbed her fingers together, wishing she had a pouched of sand with her.

The dark stone walls of GicCorp rose in front of them. They passed through the first gate. Many workers milled about the main area, where they brought in the corrupted magic and turned it into the purified magic for the population of Verrin to charge their orbs. Different stone buildings all connected to the charge lines out in the city. She remembered this much from a school trip.

They drove farther into the Nordic estate. In the first area, they hosted social gatherings among the founders.

They pulled up to the main entrance and stopped. Tristan held out his hand, and she took it, letting him help her out of the vehicle. Her heels clicked on the stone.

The main entrance loomed over them. The white, smooth pillars were familiar. They walked through the main entrance, and the large stained-glass dome made their skin different colors.

Tristan noticed where her eyes rested. "Maybe you can make another window for the home."

"Perhaps." She wasn't here to make glass. They both knew it. She'd rather he didn't bother faking it.

He led her down several identical hallways and opened a door into a white, airy room. From the floors to the curtains, everything gleamed white.

"This is where you can stay until the vital ceremony. Afterward, you will be taken to Haven with everyone else." He paused as she walked farther into the room. "There's clothing for you. Did you need anything else?"

A new life? She placed her hand on a plain white end table. "Everything is wonderful. What will my duties be while I'm here?"

"My mother will be by to greet you and tell you what they need. You'll spend your last days in meditation, preparing to leave this world behind." He stepped forward and reached out to brush back a strand of her hair. "You're exquisite."

She forced herself to remain still. She felt no excitement at his touch. She lowered her eyes in fake bashfulness. "Thank you." What did he want? He saw something she didn't. What did he mean?

"I'll leave you to get settled." He shut the door, and his footsteps disappeared down the hall.

Emilia went to her closest and ran her hand over the clothing. Jewel tones and expensive fabrics. She stepped back and took in her white room. Would her new family appreciate a rainbow explosion? She regretted leaving her sands behind. Wouldn't it have been kinder to let her spend her last hours with her family than here, sitting with her thoughts?

She slipped off her heels and let the cool stone floor soothe her feet as she padded to the window. Sitting down in the alcove, she grabbed her wand and felt the comfortable heat of magic flowing through it. She'd figured she'd used up all her magic finishing the statue.

A tiny amount of magic trickled down her wand, and she swirled a pattern in the clear window of her new room.

She wondered how Vic's first day as a reaper had gone. Maybe her mother would finally smile for real again. Would her father survive the choice he'd made? Emilia laughed. Did they have a choice? They all could have died together. She knew that her father regretted that she needed to leave.

"I'm the dutiful daughter." *I'm also a fool for not asking more questions.*

She molded the glass until her magic ran out. The wand's warmth turned cold. She stared out at the city of

Verrin. The glass that used to be her friend now separated her from everything she loved.

"But if you're happy, I can survive this." She rested her forehead against the cool glass and waited for her new duty in her too-white room.

V ic helped Kai escort the four reapers to the holding cells in the basement of Nyx.

"Commander, you need to understand that it's in your best interest to let us go. We won't even mention this." Freckles tried to plead with him one last time with her hands on the bars of the cell.

Vic wondered if they were acting too rashly by turning in the reapers.

They left the basement and walked toward Xiona's office.

"What do you think they're doing?" Vic asked.

"Warning me that someone powerful gave them the order." He quieted as other reapers returned from their routes and filled the halls. "What I don't know is if it's Xiona or someone higher up."

In Nyx, there wasn't anyone higher than Xiona. Could it be someone outside the Order? "If we tell Xiona and she's in on this, we could end up like them?" Vic pointed back to where they'd left the other reapers.

"Maybe."

"Comforting." Nothing like an exciting first day at work. Despite everything, she might end up where she'd started: starving in a smelly room.

At the end of the first floor, they went to Xiona's room and knocked on the wooden door. They both listened, but there was no answer. Kai pulled her to him. "It might be better if you weren't there when I talk to her."

"Oh?" In all fairness, she was the one who'd dragged him into this. If it all went south, she should be there. She couldn't stay quiet now that she'd confirmed with Kai that reapers were killing people.

His grip tightened. "If it's something we're not supposed to know, I'll be more protected than you. You're an unknown, and she might not risk you knowing."

"She'll kill me?"

He released her arms. "No, she wouldn't kill you. Just maybe kick you out." Weary, he leaned back against the stone hallway.

Vic smiled wryly. "And my brand's just healing too." She touched his bare arm. "I think I need to be there and tell her what I saw the other night." It felt wrong to leave Kai on his own. After all, he'd just given her a lesson on teamwork. She might be ignoring the part about listening to orders again, though.

Kai pushed away from the wall, and they left the door to Xiona's office behind. "It isn't necessary. I'll tell her all she needs to know."

"Will you, now? I guess I'll meet with her on my own." She didn't need his protection.

"You're going to be stubborn." Worry crossed his face. "Is there any way I can convince you that this is a bad idea?"

Vic stayed out of politics, and she'd actually run away

from them when she'd thought she'd have to marry Tristan. "It'll be fine."

If she could only believe those words, that would be great.

"Let's grab something to eat while we wait for Xiona to get in from her patrol." Other officers padded to their rooms and nodded to Kai.

"Now that's a great idea." Vic wanted to sleep too. It was getting harder to stay upright.

They walked to the dining hall. Most reapers ate breakfast in the late afternoon, but the hall also had food available after patrol.

Vic, for once, didn't feel very hungry, so she piled fruit onto a plate and sat next to Kai.

He eyed the amount of food on her plate. "That's all you're eating, Sparks?"

"I thought I was hungrier than I was." He didn't have much either.

With his fork, he stole a strawberry from her plate and popped it in his mouth. "Delicious."

"Excuse me?" She grabbed his roll, took a bite out of it, and put it back on his plate.

He stared at the mutilated roll. "That's just cruel."

She nudged him. "You started it."

He settled on the wooden bench and pushed his food around on the plate. "My sister always stole my strawberries."

Vic crunched down on a grape and juices filled her mouth. "So it's my job to supply you with them?"

He smiled whenever he mentioned his sister. Vic liked that talking about his family made him relax.

"Didn't you know that's the newbie's job? To feed her commander?" His eyelids lowered, and his gaze heated her.

"Is it?" She moved closer, their thighs touching under the table. "You fed me first."

"I was afraid you'd starve to death before the trials happened." He took her hand and slowly rubbed his thumb over her palm.

Food forgotten, she pushed the silverware to the side. "I thought you would pile food at my door."

He leaned down, his face inches from hers. "Would you have taken it?"

"Probably not." Her heart thudded.

"Are you two eating each other for breakfast?" They jerked apart. Bomrosy stood over them. She quirked her eyebrow. "Xiona's back. Someone told me you were at her office earlier and may need to see her, but I could leave you to throw Kai on the table and have your way with him."

Vic jumped up and brushed her hands over her body. "I'm going to wash my dishes."

Bomrosy laughed as she rushed to the side of the hall to wash her dishes. They only employed cooks. The reapers were responsible for cleaning what they used.

Kai wasn't far behind. His arm brushed against hers as he washed his dishes. She nudged him.

He leaned down and whispered, "Since there's no patrol for us later, why don't we do something?"

"After confronting Xiona, sounds like a plan."

They smiled. Her nerves eased, but small jolts filled her. She didn't know if it was Kai or the fact she was about to talk to Xiona. Since seeing Samuel this morning, Kai had stood closer to her and touched her more than normal. Vic liked it.

Also, the jolts might have been from the possibility that they'd rot in a cell. That brought out end-of-the-world vibes.

They waved at Bomrosy as they left, and she winked at them.

"I think I might kill her," Kai muttered.

Vic laughed. She wanted to take his hand but restrained herself. He was now close enough that their arms touched. His touch comforted her. They walked down to the end of the hall. Large double doors with two scythes carved into them waited.

They burst open, and Xiona stood before them. A bit of dirt stained her black clothing, and her hair was a little mussed. Her brown eyes had dark circles under them. Up close, she stood shorter than Vic. At the branding ceremony and at the trials, she'd felt taller.

Xiona held open the door. "Are you coming in or not?"

Kai went through the doors, and Vic followed him. A large desk took up the center of the room. Another door in the back likely led to her living area. Windows on the wall behind the desk had a view of the front courtyard, and the blinds were open, letting in the morning light. Neat stacks of paperwork sat to the side of the desk, and Xiona's scythe remained within reach from her desk chair. The whole place didn't have much in the way of personal items or furniture, but it was immaculate.

Xiona waved briskly at two chairs, and she lowered herself into her chair behind the desk. "This couldn't wait until after my shower?"

"I thought you would want to know what we found out." Kai talked in a steady tone, his posture giving nothing away.

"Does this have to do with the four reapers you put in the

cells tonight?" Xiona folded her hands on the desk. Her face remained calm.

"When we were on patrol tonight, Vic informed me that she'd seen reapers trying to cut out the orb of a citizen. I wanted to confirm this, so we looked into the area where she saw it."

Xiona leaned away from her desk. "What about your training?"

"We finished it first."

Did she really care about training over this? Vic felt knots form in her stomach.

"Continue." Xiona tapped her finger.

Kai remained on the edge of his seat. "We then saw this patrol attack someone and try to cut out their orb."

Xiona pushed forward and carefully placed her elbows on her desk. "Why would they be doing this?"

"I'm not sure what the motivation behind this is." Kai's shoulders tensed.

Xiona placed her palms flat on the desk in measured movements, not taking her eyes off Kai. "Do you think they're following orders?"

"Yes."

One by one, her fingers slowly tapped on her desk. "And you think the orders came from me?"

"Yes."

Vic jerked. He'd mentioned that in passing, not that he believed it.

The two of them stared each other down, the tension in the room growing thick.

Vic bit the inside of her cheek.

"Kai, do you know why?" Xiona's face remained blank, and all her fidgeting stopped.

"The reapers are doing too good of a job."

Wait, what did he mean? Vic wanted to talk, but one glance from Kai and she stayed silent. Were reapers clearing out the blight too fast?

Xiona tilted her head back, and she let out a loud laugh that didn't fit the mood of the room. "Yes. In a way."

Vic's skin grew cold as Xiona stared at her, finally acknowledging that another person was in the room. "I suppose I have you to thank for this. I didn't know if Kai would be open to this plan, but now I get to find out."

Vic swallowed, wishing she hadn't come in the room with Kai. "Happy to help."

Xiona snorted. "Well, Kai, are you with me?"

"I am."

Her heart fell through her center, and she was surprised it wasn't beating on the floor.

"What?" she yelped. He was with her?

His gaze pierced her. "I am with her on this plan. There isn't enough corruption to be purified. This way, it stays controlled." As he spoke, she saw his face flinch.

Vic jumped up. "You have to be kidding me? You're in favor of corrupting souls?" Forget her heart falling out; it had gotten ripped out. She'd thought she could trust him.

Xiona held up her hand. "This way we can keep them controlled. We know who will get corrupted, and we can drain them."

"You're killing people. Without the orb, you can't save them." This didn't sound right. Wouldn't it be easier to prevent them from charging? They were letting them turn into corrupted souls. "If they're only corrupted souls, that isn't much blight, unless you let them become mogs. Mogs can go after others, so you aren't killing one person, but their family members too."

"A small sacrifice," Xiona replied while still sitting calmly at her desk as if they were talking about the weather.

"I bet the ones you choose would care. Or are you only choosing those without high-end relics? After all, how important are they? We have to make sure the founders get charged, but forget the rest." Boiling rage rose inside Vic. When she'd found out she was a reaper, she'd thought she'd be protecting people from getting the blight. It turned out they were giving out the blight. "How many reapers know what's going on?"

Xiona took a piece of paper out of the stack and examined the writing on it, going about her day. "I don't need to explain myself to you. I saw a problem, and I solved it. Nyx now has the resources to feed and clothe the reapers."

That could mean anything. Vic didn't know if other Orders were doing the same thing. In the past year, she'd noticed there wasn't enough charge to go around. Even last month, she'd needed to trade in more blight or credits to get charged. She could have become corrupted if she hadn't gotten into Nyx.

"Even so, you don't get to play god," Vic spat, her mind a swirling storm. Her sister was leaving to protect this madness?

Xiona placed her paper to the side and folded her hands. "Says who? Who will stop me? You?"

Vic squared her shoulders. "I can do my best." The words had flown out of her mouth. Anger took over her body. She didn't have backup. Her commander had told her he agreed with this plan. It was her against Nyx, and she didn't know how many reapers were involved.

"Very well." Xiona nodded, and before Vic could react, Kai had grabbed her scythe out of her harness.

She twirled to block him, but he already had her relic. Vic darted forward, but Xiona appeared behind her and gripped her arms, pinning them to her back. A click sounded, and something cold rested on her wrist.

"With this, you can't leave the grounds of Nyx without your commander. You're a recruit, and I would hate to lose you." Xiona smirked. "I think you need time to see how life really operates on the outside, founder brat. In this walled city, we have little choice."

With a push, Xiona let her go, and Vic stumbled forward. Kai lifted his hands to help her, but she shoved him away and righted herself. She glared at him when hurt flashed across his features. What right did he have to be hurt? He'd taken her relic from her. A new pain filled her, and it numbed her. She'd trusted him, but he'd proved he was no different from the founders, stomping on the weak to raise himself up.

Xiona snorted. "I think the love birds need to have a talk. Take her to her room. You get to deal with her until she can see things clearly." She blinked slowly. "The fact you're the daughter of a founder may be the only thing keeping you alive. How's that for privilege?"

Vic tried to kick her, but Kai pulled her from the room. When he shut the doors behind them, she jerked out of his grip. She tried to walk away, but sharp pain burst up her wrist.

"You can't leave the grounds, but she failed to mention you also can't get more than a few feet from me." He held up a ring on his finger. "I can't remove it. Only she can."

Vic clenched her hands into fists. "This is a sick joke."

What kind of masochist invented such a thing?

"Sparks ..." He stepped closer.

She held up her hands. "Don't call me that. Stay the maximum distance away."

The tingling ran up her arms, and she rubbed the pain that lingered.

He walked. She had no choice but to follow. They went down to Bomrosy's workshop.

Bomrosy was bent over something on the table. When she straightened, it made a loud clicking sound, and Bomrosy yelped in glee. Then, in mid-celebration, she saw them waiting.

"Finally got it to work. I hope you two don't think this is a make-out room." Vic avoided Kai's gaze and folded her arms. Her smile faded. "Don't tell me you already hate each other?"

Vic turned her head away from Bomrosy.

Bomrosy smacked Kai's arm. "What in the blight did you do?"

"Keep this in your lockbox." He must have handed her the scythe.

"Why do I need to keep this?"

Vic stared at the wall. If she saw her scythe disappear, she might not be able to hold back her tears.

"Follow orders." Kai's words shot out like a whip.

"Fine, then."

Vic heard the shuffle of footsteps, then a series of clicks, and a slam told her Bomrosy had locked away her scythe.

"Let's go."

Vic turned to follow him and glanced to see Bomrosy standing in the middle of the room, looking confused. She mouthed something to Vic, but Vic turned her face away to follow Kai.

His shoulders were stiff, and he paused in the hallway. "I'm not sure where to go." His voice was soft.

Vic studied the stone floor. She had no power. A slow burn in her body made it hard to focus. She tried to shove any attraction she had for him into the dark corner of her mind. It was only a physical attraction. She only respected his abilities and didn't know him much as a person. *Keep telling yourself that.*

He let out a frustrated sigh and stepped forward. She didn't walk beside him. She could tell that made him feel awkward.

Her tired body walked of its own accord. She wanted to sleep but didn't want to be in the same room as him. She visualized punching him in the face, then replaced his face with Xiona's.

When they continued out of the Order, she paused, and he took her down a different path, not toward his place but farther up the city.

"What now? Can't I just sleep?" Fatigue filled her. She'd pushed herself beyond her limits tonight. Every step on the stone path hurt, and the blight-covered sun made her squint.

"I need you to understand."

Vic snorted and followed him. The stone road widened as the canal shrank. Only narrow water taxis could go here. Most of the homes had some greenery; they were in the farming area, so it made sense. Every tree or plant in Verrin produced something that could people could eat.

Kai took her to a stone house where a graceful woman stood in front, hanging a clean white sheet on a line. Some didn't like to use the imbued appliances to save credits. She shook out another item of clothing and hung it up with deft fingers. Her movements reminded her of Kai's but less brutal.

Kai stopped at the gate. "Mom?"

The woman turned. Her face lit up, and she dropped the shirt she'd been about to hang. "Kai? What are you doing here?" She ran up and wrapped him in a hug, her hands clasped tightly. She backed away and glanced at Vic. "Who did you bring with you?"

"One of my new members."

His mother nodded. "She looks strong." To Vic's surprise, she hugged her as well. Her warm body enveloped her, and Vic melted into this stranger's arms. She missed her sister. With everything piling up, she felt too exhausted to think.

"Do you mind if we rest?" Kai asked.

His mother patted her back before letting Vic go. "Your sister's still asleep."

"I only need my room."

Kai led her into the house. They went up a narrow flight of stairs, and at the top, the ceiling slanted in, but the whole space was one room. It was a simple room with a bed and a desk facing the window. A worn sofa sat to the side with a colorful knitted blanket tossed over the arm. Kai motioned for her to take the bed.

Vic almost refused but didn't know what point she'd be making. He shut the dark curtain as she fell into bed. She heard him rustling on the sofa.

She turned her back to him, and in the darkness, tiredness overcame her. Images of her sister, Kai taking her scythe, and her father's restrictions danced in her mind's eye. Her fingernails bit into her palms, and silent tears fell. It was too much. She'd finally gotten into an Order, but it had become more of a mess than her home.

"Why did you bring me here?" she asked.

After a long pause, he said, "Get some rest. I want you to understand something. I don't think you'll forgive me, but I want you to understand. And we're both too tired to talk now."

She didn't reply. In a way, she already understood, but it made her feel powerless and alone. She took short breaths to calm herself. In the coming days, she wouldn't get the luxury of crying.

A thin line of light escaped through the curtain in Kai's room. Watching the line make slow progress across the wall calmed her. From the other side of the room came Kai's steady breathing. She didn't know how long she'd slept, but it hurt to move, and she was happy to stare at the light for a while. Her thoughts had quieted. Right now, she had to deal with Kai. What she needed to do about Nyx didn't matter at the moment.

The steady breathing behind her stopped, and she heard him shift. "Are you awake?" he asked, breaking the silence in the room.

"Yeah."

Vic pushed herself up and stared at the wall. Kai let out another sigh. She tied up her hair and waited for him to explain.

"I can smell food downstairs."

Vic cleared her throat. She traced circles on the stitching in the blanket. "Do you really want to have this talk in front of your family?"

"Will you not look at me?"

Vic glared. "What?"

"Do you think I should go against Xiona to her face? I have no clue how deep this goes. We don't all have founder blood to keep us safe." His posture stayed relaxed, and his expression pleaded with her to understand.

"I'm a Glass, so I can do what I want?" When the words left her mouth, she knew it: a founder got more chances than everyone else. She could afford to be rash. Xiona had even said as much.

"Basically, yes." He crossed his arms. "I told you I'm the only one in my family with a relic. What do you think will happen if I lose it?"

Her anger with him melted away, and her frustration with herself grew. He was trapped like her. "You'll let her keep doing this?"

She understood what he stood to lose, but she still pushed him.

"Are you not understanding my situation? What do you think would happen if I told her I didn't agree and wanted to stop her? Use your head, Sparks." He slammed his hands on his legs.

He would lose his relic. Xiona had the power. Then his family wouldn't get enough credits to get charged. "I understand, but what they're doing is wrong."

Kai laughed. "Do you think I don't know that? But I need to see how far this goes. I'm one man. It may not make me a hero, but I will put my family first and play along until I can't anymore. You would too." He rubbed his forehead, and his shoulders bent with the weight of his responsibilities. His family could remain safe for a while longer.

Vic thought of her sister. She sighed. It still hurt, but she had to admit she was angrier at the fact that they were trapped in this situation with Xiona. She'd let her anger get the best of her in Xiona's office. She should have thought about Kai's situation too.

"I get it. What are we going to do?"

They needed to navigate this situation delicately. Vic liked to face things head-on, and most of the time, she tended to overreact. But Kai was right. She could, and being a founder could get her out of many situations. It wasn't fair to expect Kai to mouth off like she did.

"You have to play nice so we can convince her to get rid of the band on your wrist." This would be more challenging for Vic than facing a mog.

"Play nice," Vic said dryly. "Somehow, I don't think she'll buy it."

Kai crossed over to her. He reached out slowly, but Vic didn't step away, letting him rest his hands on her arms. "I will get your relic back. I'm sorry, but I didn't want you in there."

She raised an eyebrow. "Would you have told me everything if I hadn't been there?"

"I doubt you would have let me not tell you." He went to the desk in the room and sat on it. "I won't let this go. Xiona, along with who knows how many reapers, will be watching me. Getting my relic taken away will help no one."

"Yeah, yeah, I get it. I was stupid." She'd lost her relic. And for what?

Her heart still ached. Her stomach rumbled at the smell of cooking. He smiled at her. Her feelings felt mixed. She understood, but part of her wanted him to take her side. Em had always told her she shot off too quickly and wanted people to take her side all the time. Vic's family was as safe as they could be, and she needed to understand that Kai's family wasn't. Xiona and Kai were right: she had privilege. It came with its own chains, but it also provided a shield. Her actions affected others, and she needed to be careful.

A quiet moment passed between them. Without saying anything more, they left his room and followed the smell of food to the kitchen.

A miniature version of Kai sat at the wooden table and snatched a piece of fruit from the plate. Her thick russet curls were tied in two adorable poofs atop her head. A yellow shift dress complemented her skin, which was slightly darker than Kai's. He did spend most of his time outside at night. Mischievous brown eyes glanced at the duo, and a smile that might have melted Vic's father's heart graced the young girl's face.

Kai's mother lightly smacked the girl's hand. "Leave some for your brother and his guest."

"His kissing friend?"

Vic choked at the remark, and they both looked at the doorway.

"This is my sister, Remi. You already met my mother." Kai leaned forward and messed up Remi's hair. She batted his hands away but kept smiling at her brother.

His mother set more dishes on the table and hugged her son again. "You can call me Una," she told Vic.

Vic nodded and fiddled with her fingers. Kai placed a hand on her back and guided her to the chair next to Remi.

The young girl snuck glances at her. Vic could see some of Kai's personality in his younger sister. They had the same eyes, but she had less worry in them. "Are you kissing friends? My friend at school told me that if you kiss a boy, you'll get a baby."

Vic nearly spat out the food in her mouth.

Kai shot his sister a look. "I think you and your friend need sex education classes."

"What's that?" She shoved another one of Kai's strawberries in her mouth.

Vic smiled at the exasperated look on his face.

"Don't worry about that yet," Una told her daughter and put more eggs on Vic's plate. "You're far too thin. Don't they feed you at Nyx?"

"I haven't been there long," Vic mumbled. Having a mother take care of her brought up memories of her childhood.

"Kai needs to bring you around more often. We barely get to see him." Una stroked her son's hair.

He smiled and grabbed her hand. "I'll try."

Una released his hand and patted his neck before taking a pan off the stove.

Vic watched the family. She could see how Kai carefully watched them, like he was afraid they might disappear into the next strong wind. Vic wanted freedom from her family, but seeing them together, she missed what she had. She hadn't taken the time to understand the change in her father. Em had told her that their father acted defeated. Vic had scoffed at her. To her, he'd shown his true colors of wanting control over everything.

They finished up, and Kai hugged his mother and ruffled his sister's hair again. Remi ducked, but her face glowed.

"We need to get back," Kai stated.

His mother nodded and waved at them as they left out the door.

Vic stayed next to him on their walk back to Nyx.

"Kai, I know you have a lot to lose, but this affects them

too. I think we need to reach out to the other Orders and find out if they're cutting out orbs too."

"I know." His pace slowed. "Do you suppose we should burst in and ask? We might be watched by Xiona's reapers."

Vic thought. "We can follow their patrols, see if we notice anything."

Kai rubbed his forehead. "Nice plan in theory, but how?"

"Bomrosy." Vic grinned. "I wonder if she has anything to help us out." Vic held up her band.

"She might be on Xiona's side," Kai stated.

"True, but I don't think so."

"Based on?"

"A feeling."

"Great."

The afternoon sun rose high in the sky under the pinkish-orange swirls of the blight. They made it back to Nyx and Bomrosy's workroom. This time, Bomrosy banged on something so hard it broke. With a curse, she went to retrieve the fallen item.

"Back, are we?" She raised a tool at them and waved it at their faces. "Ready to tell me what in the blight is going on?"

"You know you aren't in charge here." Kai gave her a condescending look.

Bomrosy wielded her tool like a weapon, and Vic was sure she wanted to stab Kai.

Vic stood between them. "Okay, why don't we just sit?"

Bomrosy plopped down on a bench and glared at them.

"What we're about to tell you could put you in danger," Vic hedged. Maybe they shouldn't tell her.

"How can I help? Is it about the destroyed orbs?" Bomrosy asked.

"You know?"

Bomrosy spun her tool in her hand. "Just because I don't use magic, people think I don't matter. They also talk too much."

Kai straightened. "How many Nyx reapers are involved?"

Bomrosy set aside the tool and put her hands on her knees. "I can't tell you an exact number, but I know which group is for sure helping. I was sure you were in on it, Kai." Her shoulders slumped. "I figured you needed to keep your family safe. I've been tracking them on my own. It's been hard since it would look weird if I left at night." Shadows filled her face, and Vic could tell it was more than the rogue reapers bothering her. She'd only met Bomrosy and didn't want to push her to share something private.

"Do you have the names written somewhere?" Kai asked.

Bomrosy rustled in a toolbox near her and handed Kai a slip of paper. "Xiona kept it to her inner circle from what I can tell. But there are some reapers I'm unsure about."

Vic sighed in relief. "See, I knew we could trust her."

Bomrosy lightly hit Kai. "You thought I'd be okay with this?"

Kai read the paper and handed it back to her. "You thought I would be!"

"No, like I said, your mother and sister are relicless. I didn't think you would want to, but you aren't in a great situation."

"We also hoped you could help us." He held up the ring, and her eyes widened. "Is there a way we can get this off or disarm it? We'd like to patrol other reapers and see if other Orders are cutting out orbs as well. We can cover more ground apart. Also, we can leave one person here as a decoy."

Bomrosy stood and went over to what looked like a pile

of junk. "I was messing around with one a few months ago for fun."

"Weren't you supposed to be repairing it?" Kai asked flatly.

She put her hands on her hips. "Are you here to lecture me or thank me for my genius since now I can help you?"

Kai raised his hands and lowered them. "I bow at your genius."

"That's better." Bomrosy produced a wristband and a ring similar to what Vic wore. "I can't turn it off, but I found a cool way to block the magic signal for two hours at most. After that ... well ..." She shook her arm in a pantomime of a shock.

"Comforting." Vic took the band and saw the small button. "I guess if I pass out from shock, you can come find my butt and carry me back."

Kai took the ring and pocketed it. "As long as someone sees one of us going into my room, we should be fine."

Vic glanced at them and put away the band. It felt like the three of them were facing something bigger than they knew. Her sister was about to go away to keep the city safe. It was Vic's job to protect this city, even if it had betrayed her.

⚜

VIC'S SCYTHE ON HER BACK SETTLED HER NERVES. BOMROSY had retrieved her relic before she'd slipped out of the window at Nyx. Due to the lack of express water taxis, it had taken her an hour to get to the far side of the city where Dei patrolled on the other side of the farmland. She wouldn't have as long to follow them tonight.

Every other night, after their normal patrol, she and

Kai switched off to watch other Orders and groups from Nyx. If they had time, they stopped and asked locals if they'd been attacked. The Boreus territory so far was clear. Dei didn't patrol in a populated area, which gave them a reason to believe that Dei wouldn't have a chance for much orb cutting. It gave Vic hope that only Nyx was wrapped up in the plot to create more blight. If the other Orders found out they were cheating the blight collection numbers, they would be enraged. GicCorp provided extra money to match the blight collection. Dei held the third spot and didn't get as much money as Nyx. Xiona likely wanted the top numbers for blight collection either for pride or because she really thought this was best for her reapers because it provided them with more money. Vic couldn't imagine how Xiona could kill people to improve Verrin's economy.

A group of four reapers appeared through a wheat field, and Vic stayed back. There wasn't much cover out in the farmlands, and she'd already staked out the orchards.

Every time she'd seen Xiona this week, she'd had to control her facial expressions. Making matters worse, she had to stay with Kai. Their relationship felt off, and though there was an attraction, neither of them wanted to make a move while in forced bondage. Also, she was engaged to someone she hadn't seen in days.

Vic crouched as she ran after the reapers.

Focus. Worry about your love life when people aren't getting turned into mogs.

She paused when the group branched out. Each reaper ran in a different direction. This never happened. Reapers always stayed in pairs. She poked her head up higher to see where they were going.

"See something interesting, Nyx spy?" someone asked behind her.

Vic jumped and turned around. "Ah. No. Just checking out the farmland."

The woman folded her muscular arms and glared at her. A long scar ran along her scalp, visible through her short black hair. "Every night this week, reapers have reported that someone's been watching them. You aren't as sneaky as you think. We're trained to notice our surroundings." Her copper eyes narrowed as if she thought Nyx's training wasn't as good as Dei's. The moonlight highlighted the bronze glow of her skin, and her lips pressed into a thin line. Her prominent nose complemented her features as she glared down at Vic. This woman could have given Vic's past teachers a run for their money as far glares went. She would not want to cross this woman, but she would want her on her side in a fight.

Vic took a step back, stumbling around for a lie. "We aren't watching you. We made a deal to get some extra fruit with the Orchard founder. We have to pick it up before the market opens." This was the best excuse she could come up with. She and Kai should have figured out a better cover story.

"Fruit? Want to rethink that lie?" Vic stood taller, but she felt shorter in her presence. The woman's muscles were impressive, her figure beautifully curved under the standard reaper black.

Vic grinned. "I'll head out and not bother you again." She sidestepped away, only to feel a vise-like grip on her arm. The other three reapers rose out of the field in the dark.

"I think it's best if you share your fruit story with our leader, don't you? She may want in on this early morning fruit deal."

"Heh." Thinking she might make things worse if she struggled, she followed the woman through the field.

"Becks," someone called to the woman holding her. "Do you want me to run ahead?"

Becks didn't loosen her grip. "Tell Nel we caught one. The other one must not be here."

They waited for me. Vic groaned inwardly. With Vic in front of them, they forged through the fields. Vic doubted it would go over well if she asked Becks to let her go, so she let the woman hang on to her.

They approached a stone wall. The Dei Order was more simplistically built than the other Orders in the city. Beyond the wall, stone huts were grouped together, with a one-story main building at the center. Surprisingly clean and tightly packed stone filled the courtyard.

Becks led her through the courtyard, and instead of the sound of the canal, the soft whispers of clucking chickens sounded from their roosts. Out here, the air smelled more of growing things than mildew. People looked down on Dei's blight collection numbers, but Vic thought this Order might have the better location, even though it was far from the center of town.

Thick wooden doors protected the main building. The lamplight was bright inside. Rough-hewn tables and long benches dominated the space. The Dei Order leader stood over a large table at the front of the room. Her rumpled clothing didn't look much different from what she'd worn at the trials, and the black color made her white skin stand out. She had a long face graced with an angular nose, and as they approached, her gray eyes took them in. Nel dismissed the other reapers with a nod. She sat down in the chair and put her dirty boots up on the table. Bits of mud flaked off on the

table, and Becks flinched. Vic didn't blame her. If Nel did
sewer runs, who knew what was on the bottom of those
boots.

Becks huffed. "Do you have to put your boots up there?
This is where we eat."

Nel tapped her boot on the table, letting more mud fall.
"You can leave. I need to speak with the number-one pick."

Becks muttered something Vic didn't catch and left her
in the hall with the leader of the Dei Order.

Nel stared at Vic, unmoving. "I hear you're into early
morning fruit deals?" she asked blandly.

"Fruit's good for you." Was it better for her to stick to the
lie? Heck, she could come out and tell her what Nyx was
doing. And if Nel threw her in a cell, then she'd know for
sure that Dei was in league with Nyx in stealing orbs.

"Hmm." Nel pulled out a knife from her boot and traced
the blade with her finger. "I think it would be best if you told
me the real reason a Nyx reaper is spying on us."

Vic followed the movement of the throwing blade. "I
mean you no harm. I was off duty and taking a walk." A
sheen of sweat covered her skin. She glanced down at her
wrist. Her buffer would soon wear off. She might be
twitching on the ground in a matter of minutes. Traveling
out to Dei never gave them much time to do recon, and this
side trip wouldn't help.

"A walk." Without sitting up, Nel flicked her hand, and
the knife sailed across the room.

Vic's hair on the right side of her head fluttered. She saw
a few hairs fall to the ground.

"We aren't doing anything wrong." These last few nights,
Vic and Kai hadn't seen reapers attack innocent civilians on

their routes. But Dei could have sent reapers into the city to hurt people.

Nel pulled out another knife and twirled it between her fingers. "Fresh little reapers like you shouldn't get involved in espionage so quickly after trials—unless you're disposable."

Vic agreed with her, but she'd chosen Nyx, so she would try to help the Order. "What if I brought my commander here?"

"No. Talk now." She stabbed the knife into the table. The thunk echoed in the empty room.

Vic's heart pounded in the silence. "Nyx is turning citizens into mogs by taking out their orbs. They're creating a supply of corruption since we're running low."

Nel slid her boots off the table. "Really?" Her laughter filled the room. "Xiona's playing more games." Nel leaned back again. "Damn fool should have joined me here. She will lose her head."

"You aren't doing this?" Vic's method of blurting out the truth worked at least three out of four times. She tried to be more cautious for Kai. The bracelet would go off soon.

Nel pressed a finger against the blade embedded in the table. "No, I'm trying to protect people. If there isn't enough purified magic to charge, that's GicCorp's problem. We find plenty of mogs out here in the middle of nowhere. The supply is fine." She watched the blade wobble as she removed her finger. "You have to realize they might not be using it for what you think they are."

"What?"

Nel spoke slower, saying, "Our numbers did not go down. Nyx numbers did not go up or down. Boreus numbers did not go up or down." She raised her hands. "So where is all the extra cleansed blight going? I don't think we had that many new babies who needed to be charged."

"Why does Xiona think we need more blight?"

Nel grinned. "Why indeed." She slipped the knife away. "I'm guessing you want something?"

"Your help in stopping Xiona." Might as well get it out there.

"Oh, is that it?" Nel yanked the blade from the table. "No."

Vic stepped closer. "Innocent people are getting turned into mogs, and no one's doing anything about it." She didn't know why this had become her problem as a new reaper. Shouldn't the commanders care more than her?

Nel took her time standing, and she walked over to where Vic stood. She still held the throwing blade in her hand. "You want a reaper war? How many lives will be lost then?"

"I'm not asking for a war, just to stop her."

Nel stopped in front of Vic and flicked her forehead. "I can't run in there and tell her what to do. Only GicCorp has any authority. If I try anything, it will be an act of war."

Vic rubbed her forehead and glared at the Dei leader. "The whole Order can't be doing this."

She put the blade back in her boot. "It isn't my problem."

"Didn't you say it's your job to protect others?"

Nel let out a long breath of air. "I'll help if you get GicCorp involved."

Vic almost fell back into one of the tables. "You want me to tell GicCorp?"

"Look, little green bean. Nyx gets the most money because their numbers, although unchanged in the monthly report, are always the highest. I wondered how they got so much blight when they only cover a bit of land outside the wall." She smirked. "Now I know. If you tell GicCorp, then Dei will have the best numbers after we beat out Boreus."

Vic rolled her eyes. "Wow, how noble."

"Numbers mean food in the belly. Can't eat justice." Nel turned and went back to her table. "Let me know how it goes."

"Sure, thanks for your help. I guess I'm free to leave?" Nothing like giving Vic more to do. She didn't blame Nel. Kai knew that the officers or founders would eventually need to get involved. The biggest fear for Vic was, what if the founders didn't care?

"Sure. Next time bring fruit."

Vic shook her head and left the building. The other reapers watched her as she went outside the Dei walls. Once beyond the gate, she took off at a run. She didn't know how many hours had passed. She needed an express water taxi immediately.

She pumped her legs and ran through the fields. When she hit the trees, two figures appeared in the dark. It was too late to stop, and she ended up bowling them over.

"William?"

Then the band activated, sending shocks down her body. The burning sensation made her stomach twist, and she vomited bile on William's white shoes. The pain bloomed from her wrist.

He grasped her arms gently. "Victoria, what's wrong?"

"Take me to Nyx. Back wall."

"What?"

The shocks coursed through her, and she fell back against him and saw his worried blue eyes as she passed out.

❧ 15 ❧

WILLIAM

A loud thud woke William. He sat up in his small bed and saw his father glaring at him.

"Where's your brother?"

William glanced at the empty bed. "I don't know." He had a feeling his father was about to tell him.

"I received a communication from the station across town in the Boreus district. Your drunken brother is there. Go get him before others see."

His father left and slammed the door. William rubbed his face and groaned. Samuel usually only went out once a week, but this whole week, he'd snuck out night after night. William was tempted to tie his brother to his bed. A flash of anger filled him. This shouldn't be his concern.

He ran a hand through his hair and got dressed in his older clothing. On his way out, his mother handed him a cheese sandwich and patted him on the cheek.

In the early morning, the swirling blight was a deep green color intermixed with a dark blue. For something so evil, it looked beautiful. William stomped his way down the path, letting the morning walk wake him. Maybe he would be calmer by the time he arrived. This whole week, what had his brother been thinking? Something hadn't been right since they'd visited that family, but it wasn't like his brother had ever been right.

William walked the narrow alleys and nodded to other radiant he passed. Smiles in place, they began their early morning duties. This whole time, he had heard nothing about his upcoming wedding. His mother had mentioned that they were going to the younger sister's vital ceremony in a few days.

He went over a stone-covered bridge. Victoria had been taking up too much of his mind lately. The sun rose in the sky as he arrived at the station. The officers nodded to him and went back to get his brother. They knew him.

William crossed his arms and prepared a look of disapproval. Not that it mattered. His brother would keep doing what he wanted and not care that William wasted hours walking to stations to get him every day.

They pulled his brother out and removed the cuffs. His brother stumbled toward William, his face down. His hair had thick mats, and he smelled more than usual. William grabbed his arm and took him out of the station.

"See you tomorrow!" an officer joked.

He let go of Samuel, and his brother wobbled on his feet. "What has gotten into you? Do you have to go out every night and get drunk?"

Samuel muttered, "They forgot her."

William sighed in frustration. "I know. I know. It isn't your fault. You need to get over it. You know it looks bad on me when you do this?"

Samuel stared at the ground.

"Can you at least look at me when I'm lecturing you?"

Samuel laughed and raised his face. His eyes ... they had red rims around the iris. His lips were cracked, and faint red lines crossed his face. William's throat tightened.

"You need to charge. Come with me." William pulled him to the nearest charging station.

Samuel yanked out of his grip. "Don't pull me."

"Fine. Then walk over there and charge yourself. You're at a dangerous level."

Samuel leveled his gaze at William. "I gave away my credits."

William tried to grip his brother again. "Fine. Use mine."

"No."

William paused in the middle of the pathway. "What do you mean, no?"

Samuel staggered but crossed his arms. "I won't charge."

"You can't be serious. Why in blight's name wouldn't you charge?" What was this new game he played? Didn't he realize it was dangerous? William took a deep breath to avoid screaming at his brother in the street full of people.

Samuel swallowed. "I don't deserve to. I'm done. This is my penitence."

William shoved open the folding green door to the station. Samuel tried to yank away, but William overtook him and put the charger up to his neck. There was no click. He looked closer and saw a long cut on Samuel's neck.

"You've got to be kidding. You cut it out?" William dropped the charger, and it clunked against the side of the station. A numbness filled William, and his world became a living dream. His brother surely hadn't done this. William brushed his brother's hair out of the way, hoping he'd misheard or seen something else. The long red cut was still there, mocking all of William's efforts. He couldn't believe it. His brother had ended his life. A sense of abandonment filled him.

Samuel pushed William's hand away, stepped out of the station, and took off. "Leave me be, Brother."

"If I have to take you to a reaper every day, so be it!" He slammed the door shut behind him and followed his brother. "How far do you expect to get?"

William caught up to him and wrapped his arms around Samuel's, forcing him to march forward all the way home. Samuel didn't try to break away, but William held firm.

Everyone glanced at the spectacle. At home, William shoved Samuel inside.

His mother and father stood.

"He cut out his orb."

His mother gasped, and his father glared at his younger son.

"Get him cleaned up," their father snapped. Other than those words, they showed little concern that they were about to lose a son.

Samuel went to the bathroom, and William heard the splash of water. His father stared at the candle flame in the middle of the table. Light came in through the window, so the flame would soon be put out.

They said nothing. William waited for them to show any sadness. His mother shook her head like this was another inconvenience from Samuel. His father stared for a moment. William understood what his gaze meant: his brother was his responsibility. They'd already written Samuel off, probably months or years ago. The weight pushed him down. They all knew there was no coming back from losing an orb. William sank to the floor, head in his hands. It was over.

༄༅༅༃

WILLIAM WATCHED HIS BROTHER WAKE UP FROM A SHORT NAP. Samuel's now dry hair was mussed from him sleeping on it wet. He blinked at William in the corner.

He tossed his pillow at William. "Could you be creepier?"

"Probably." William threw the pillow back, and it landed with a thud next to Samuel on the bed. "Get ready. I want to take you somewhere today."

Samuel rubbed his red-rimmed eyes. "Are we going on a date?"

William stepped out of the room. "You could say that." The informal white clothing felt awkward. The radiant clothing was mostly handwoven, though they did buy some materials. It was his father's goal to be completely independent of magic-made items.

He grabbed the pack he'd prepared in advance, and Samuel appeared. William handed him a sandwich, and Samuel ate it as they walked out of the house. He pushed the empty feeling to the back of his mind. Today, he only wanted to be with his brother.

The blight swirled in vibrant purples and reds.

"What's the plan for our date?"

Neither of them wanted to talk about what would happen to Samuel. The warm day helped put William at ease; he hoped Samuel's corruption would hold off while the sun stayed high in the sky.

William rolled his shoulders under the weight of his pack. "We haven't spent much time together with my radiant training. I thought we could have a normal day." He glanced at his brother and tried not to notice the red around his light blue irises. When he reached to straighten his cuffs, he remembered he wore a shirt today and not his radiant uniform.

Next to him, Samuel folded his hands behind his back and peered at the sky. He did that more and more these days. "I don't suppose we're getting drinks?"

William bit his tongue. "We can later if you want."

Samuel nearly ran into a lamppost. "Okay, who are you?"

"I'm still your brother." William gripped the straps of the pack. "I don't get to be myself anymore and thought it might be nice to get to for this last day." He stopped talking when he felt his throat getting tight.

"Last day?"

William didn't want to hide from his brother. After all, he might turn into a mog, even today.

"You know. You already know," William whispered. Samuel had harassed him day in and day out that he'd changed. "I have certain responsibilities. This is what I have to do. I hope you understand. But I think we never got a day ... a day to say goodbye to who I was. I want ... I want it to just be you and me."

"I understand." He'd already made his choice, and now William had to live with it.

"Let's go," William whispered. He forced on a smile. He looked into the eyes that were his mirror. "Why don't we not worry about that today?"

Samuel lightly punched his arm. "Okay, then."

There was a timer, but today, they would ignore its ticking.

William led them away from the center of town. In the eastern district, they reached the farmland that spread out for miles. This section took a break from the stone and canals. The water branched out to irrigate the land, and streams edged the orchards. Any unused water looped back around into the canals. William headed to the orchard, and Samuel followed.

"Remember?" William asked.

Samuel pulled at a leaf from one of the trees. "We used to come here all the time as children." He quickened his pace and settled down next to the stream. "I used to beat you all the time in our boat races."

When you didn't have magic, you had to find other ways to play. "Beat me? I think your memory is getting worse."

"I clearly remember winning all the time. You would throw a fit and drown my boats. Such a sore loser." Samuel tried to splash William with the cool water.

William ducked away and pulled out paper from his pack. "Prove it."

Samuel raised his brows and smiled. He grabbed a stack of paper and folded a boat. William folded along with him, the smooth paper creasing under his fingers. It took a few tries, but the memory of how to make a paper boat came back. His finished product didn't look water-worthy, but it would be a good tester. As they worked under the shade of a tree, the breeze cooled them down from the hot day. William didn't enjoy being dirty, but as he sat on the grass, he didn't mind if his pants got stained today. The air was fresher here than in Verrin, and the trickle of the tranquil stream relaxed William for the first time in months.

Samuel held out his boat, and it didn't look much better. He laughed at their creations.

"Want to test these?" William asked.

They knelt next to the stream and hovered their boats over the water.

"Three ... two—"

Samuel dropped his boat.

"I realize why you won so much." William snorted as they watched their boats bob down the water.

"But you do remember me winning." Samuel whooped as his boat went over the drop first.

"You honestly don't think that counts, do you?"

"A win's a win."

William mockingly glared at his brother, who finally grinned sheepishly.

"Fine. I won't cheat."

They each grabbed another piece of paper and folded them. This time, their boats had cleaner lines. When they dropped them in the water, William "accidentally" splashed water onto Samuel's boat, sinking it.

"Ha! See, this is how you win." Samuel again splashed at William.

The cool water hit his bare arms, and William smiled at his brother. "I don't know what you're talking about."

Samuel scoffed. "You always had this way of speaking so people would believe you."

"It's a talent." He dried his arms and hands on his clothing.

"Mother and Father never realized you misbehaved as much as I did." Samuel took another paper.

"Oh, I got just as many spankings as you."

"Until I hid the paddle." Samuel winked.

William chuckled. "I knew it was you."

The warmth of the afternoon sun shone down on them. William took out a few drinks from his pack and passed them to Samuel. The cool beer tasted amazing as they raced boat after boat.

William's smile stayed on his face throughout the whole

day. The sound of their laugher echoed in the orchard. It was almost nightfall by the time they ran out of paper.

Samuel fell next to William, his cheeks flushed. He stared up at the sky. The swirls darkened as the sun got ready to set. "Are you happy?"

William took a long drink. "You're very concerned with that." Did Samuel think that if he turned into a mog, William would be happy he was gone? The ache he'd tried to ignore all day came back and burned in his chest.

Samuel twisted a blade of grass between his fingers. "Don't you think we all deserve to be happy? This world is broken, and there's something missing, don't you think?"

"You mean magic versus no magic?"

Samuel tore the blade of grass in two. "There's something off with magic and the radiant life, not to mention the vitals."

William focused on the swirls in the sky. "This is what we have, though." A feeling he couldn't control rose in him. He didn't have the power to figure something else out. The radiant path might seem extreme, but turning into a monster was the worst outcome. He studied his brother, with his slight smile and light blue eyes. His body would mutate until he didn't recognize his family. He might try to eat them.

"If you think about it, the radiant path is a hard one, but you won't admit that we don't turn into monsters."

"You know a reaper won't fix this, Brother." His soft voice mixed with the sound of the stream.

Removing the orb had been suicide. They both knew it. Getting a reaper to drain him could buy them a week at most.

"You also have this unwavering responsibility to me."

Samuel closed his eyes, and tears pooled. "I know this wasn't a goodbye to your childhood. It was for me."

William's fingers dug into the ground. "Samuel, you know I ..."

Samuel sat up. "I know."

William choked, then gripped him in a hug. When he let go, they stared at each other. Everything remained unspoken, but they understood each other, even if these past months, they'd bickered about the radiant life. They still were brothers.

Samuel looked up at the sky. "What color is the sky, Brother?"

"I'll find out someday." Selfishness filled him, and William couldn't let go of his brother. He understood what Vic would go through in losing her sister. He didn't have to lose Samuel. He could keep him. William placed his hands on his brother's head.

While Samuel stared into the colorful swirls of blight at dusk, William pulled out the magic and blight inside him and replaced it with the whiteness of a radiant.

When it was over, William fell to the ground, tears dripping down his cheeks. This was what he'd had to do to save his brother. Part of his soul had been ripped from him. He had to believe this was better than Samuel turning into a mog, but he'd never wanted this for Samuel. A few moments later, he felt a hand on his side.

"Are you okay?" Samuel asked.

William sat up, and the shell of his brother sat there with a smile and clear eyes. "Yes. Let me take you where you can find a place in our society."

"Wonderful." Samuel kept smiling, but it wasn't him.

None of the mischief remained. It was like any other smile now.

William's vision blurred as he packed up the empty bottles and stray papers. Samuel stood calmly, waiting for him. William swallowed hard and continued to work. He picked up a boat they'd never sailed. It was his brother's. In the growing darkness, he held the last paper boat.

His vision foggy, he stared at the blight that had taken his brother from him.

He tucked the boat in his pocket, and instead of taking Samuel back to the city, he sat down and stared at the sky with his brother, the weight still heavy on his shoulders.

What color is the sky, Brother? "I'll find out someday."

❧ 16 ❧
VIC

"What did you do to her?" Kai whispered angrily.

Someone held her in their arms. They smelled like fresh linen hung in the sunshine. She decided not to open her eyes and curled her body into theirs.

"Nothing. She ran into me then went into convulsions. She told me to take her to the back wall."

She recognized that voice. "Sally Sunshine, is that you?"

"She's waking up," William said, stating the obvious.

"Give her to me."

"Who are you?" Her frame was jostled as William stepped back.

"Her commander. And who are you?"

"Her betrothed."

Vic groaned. "Stop it. My head already hurts." She shifted and gasped. "Okay, my whole body hurts."

She blinked her eyes open and saw William's jaw very close to her face. "Can you put me down?" Vic winced. "Slowly."

He hesitantly lowered her to her feet. She gripped his arm to steady herself. Vic looked up and saw Kai glaring at her hand on William's arm.

"For blight's sake." She let go of William and wobbled.

They rushed forward to steady her.

She held up her hands. "I'm fine." The sun rose, and she looked over and saw Samuel. She smiled. "What are you doing back there so quiet?"

He didn't respond and kept facing forward.

"Samuel? Samuel?"

He turned, but his eyes were dull and a faint smile was on his face.

Vic stopped a shout of rage from leaving her throat. Her eyes zeroed in on William. Her voice was low, anger rising in her. "What did you do to him?"

He looked away.

She grabbed his shirt. "What did you do to him!" She shook him, and Kai pulled her back as she tried to kick William. She staggered. "You didn't have to do this!"

"I didn't have a choice. He cut out his orb." His shoulders slumped forward, and this was the most rumpled Vic remembered seeing him.

She jerked out of Kai's grip. "What?"

She'd seen that he needed to charge the other day, but why would he do something suicidal?

William's eyes flashed. "His orb is gone!"

Vic shoved him. "I could've helped!"

William caught her hand so she couldn't shove him again. "How? You know it only works once or twice at best."

"We get him another orb." Vic knew the situation was hopeless, but she couldn't help it. The ghost of Samuel's laughter and true smile lingered in her mind. She barely knew him, but losing his easy-going cheer hurt.

"You know that doesn't work. This was his only option. He chose this." William's eyelids were swollen from shed tears. He acted like he barely existed.

Vic clenched her jaw. "It looks like he chose to be a mog." She waved her hand at Samuel. "Not some brainless light lover."

William stepped closer. "You met him twice. Don't pretend to know what he wanted or who he is. You're just a magic-addicted bitch. Go back to your founder life, where you can have anything you want." He spat the words. This was the first time Vic had seen William lose control.

"Fine, I'm privileged. He loved you. How could you do this to him? Where were you when he cut out his gicorb? Too busy chasing after what Daddy wants for you?" Vic wanted to hurt him. All the pain and frustration she'd gone through this last week had found a target in William.

William straightened his shoulders. "I don't need to hear this." He nodded to them. "Enjoy your day." He walked away with Samuel following.

Vic stared after them, her eyes burning. Samuel had needed help, but she'd been too focused on the orbs. She hadn't seen that he no longer had his.

A hand rested on her shoulder. "I'm sorry."

"Is there a way to undo this?" Vic cupped her cheeks. Her body hurt, and her mind felt ragged.

Kai shook his head. "I know nothing about the relics the radiant possess. Putting magic in people never turns out right. Also, taking out your orb is a death sentence."

In school, they taught that some imbs had experimented with imbuing others with magic. Either the historians had never said what had really happened to those people, or it was too graphic for children. Apparently, whatever had resulted had made it forbidden. The rings and scythes took away power, but the rings could also put something else back in. No one knew what. What purified radiant could tell them?

"He didn't want this." Vic's heart felt heavy. She stumbled again.

Kai helped her walk to the wall. "What happened tonight?"

Vic stared down the path where the brothers had disappeared. "Dei knew we were watching them."

She explained what Nel wanted from them.

"She wants us to get GicCorp involved. That way she'll be the number-one Order."

Kai paced behind the back wall of Nyx. "This whole time, I thought Dei didn't care about numbers."

"It turns out she likes to eat."

"Don't we all?" Kai sighed. "I don't see how we'll get into GicCorp."

Vic waved her hand. "Founder's daughter. Might as well use all my privilege for something." Bitterness sounded in her voice. Separating herself from them was impossible.

Kai pointed at her band. "Also, you missed this, but because of the constant shock ..."

She held up her arm. The buffer had become blackened and cracked.

"We might need a new one," Kai finished.

"Or we can cut off your finger," Vic teased.

"Ha. Let's try asking Bomrosy first."

Vic nudged him. "It's only one finger. What do you need it for?"

He traced her chin. "I can't think of anything." He leaned down, his gaze moving over her face.

The whole week had been awkward. Vic leaned into him. Her sore body felt warm next to his. "Maybe we should give it a fond farewell."

She pressed closer to him. Her heart pounded. She'd shelved any feelings she had for Kai since they had more important things to deal with. Now, she let her walls fall a bit.

"I still think there's an easier option." He pulled her closer and pressed their sides against the cool stone of the back wall.

"Spoilsport."

"We could cut off your hand." He traced his fingers down her arm.

Vic smacked him. "Yeah, I don't need my hand."

He laughed and helped her get over the wall. She landed with a thud and rested her hands on the ground to steady herself. He jumped over after her.

"I think you need to lie down before we get involved with GicCorp."

Vic closed her eyes and stood. "I'm fine. Let's see if Bomrosy has another buffer for us."

Kai shook his head and grabbed her. She shouted in surprise as he went to his open window on the first floor and tossed her in.

"Thanks." She stood and rubbed her bottom.

He winked. "Rest first. Bomrosy will still be there, and Xiona's not going anywhere either."

He helped her onto his bed and took off her boots. Vic snuggled into the mattress and relaxed. Kai lifted the covers and snuck in next to her, the blanket separating them and his face next to hers.

"You're something else, Sparks." He gently tucked a strand of hair behind her ear.

"Is that a compliment?" There were laugh lines at the corners of his eyes.

"I've grown fond of you."

"Fond?"

"Since I nearly froze my bits off."

Vic snorted. "How romantic."

He pulled on a strand of her hair. "I aim to please."

Vic drifted off as he radiated warmth next to her. When she woke up, Kai sat at the desk, gazing out the window into the distance. She stretched with a groan. "See anything interesting?"

"I thought being part of the highest Order would help out my family, but soon, I may be in the lowest Order." He smiled ruefully.

Vic swung her legs over the side of the bed and stood next to him. She grasped his shoulder. "Will your family be okay?"

Kai put his hand on hers. "As long as GicCorp doesn't blame us all for padding the numbers, we should be fine. Maybe they won't withdraw all their support."

"I can't say I know Tristan's father very well, but he seems like a reasonable man."

Ethan Nordic ran the founders. He wouldn't like Nyx's cheating. He ran a tight ship, and she wondered how much chaos it had caused when she'd refused to marry Tristan. She'd let her father deal with the aftermath. Part of her was surprised that her father hadn't dragged her back home.

Vic tied her hair back with a tie she kept in her pocket. "Let's see if we can save your finger."

They walked out of the room, Vic tried to ignore all the stares from the other reapers. She didn't know how many knew Xiona was punishing her. Nothing like not belonging in her new home. With the founders, she'd been used to feeling isolated since she openly stood against Haven. So much for a new start.

They made their way to the workroom with Kai holding on to Vic's scythe. Bomrosy stood over a bulb giving off light while Kai locked Vic's scythe away again.

"It's lasting longer?" Vic reached out to touch it.

Bomrosy smacked her hand away. Her teeth flashed in a smile. "It's hot, so I wouldn't touch it. It's lasted a whole week so far." Her eye glimmered. "I also have something better for you two." She held up a black box the size of her thumb.

"Cute?"

"Yes. Very cute. It also blocks small amounts of magic. I can't get it to work on a larger scale, but it uses the same currents as the non-magic light."

"And this means?" Vic couldn't follow what she meant half the time.

"We can take off the band."

Vic shot her wrist forward, and Bomrosy placed the device on the band. She clicked the lever, and Vic felt a shock. Then the band loosened and fell off her wrist.

"We should probably put it back on," Bomrosy mused.

"Probably, but I need to go out anyway. I can put it back on when I get back." This would ensure she had enough time to see Ethan.

"Where are you going?" She placed the device inside a container and handed it to Vic.

Vic smiled. "To make a deal."

"Fine, keep your secrets. I think you're trying to protect me in some weird way, but I'm already in waist deep."

Vic hugged her lightly, the smell of leather filling her nose. "The less you know the better off you'll be."

She raised her eyebrow. "You know I know the most of everyone?"

"True." Bomrosy wasn't a reaper. If there was a fallout with GicCorp and Xiona didn't insist on keeping her, what would happen to her? "Take care of yourself. I'll see you later."

Vic left the room with Kai, and they went back to his room, Vic hiding her wrist from sight. She got ready to jump out the window.

Kai lightly grabbed her arm, stopping her. "Don't you think I should go with you?"

"The Nordics are secretive. They won't like me coming to see them about this, and I'm technically in the same circles as them." She patted his arm. "Plus, you're the decoy."

Kai gripped her shoulders and brushed his forehead against hers. "I'll make a great decoy. All my years of training and I get to sit on my ass."

Vic bit down her grin. "A fine ass to sit on." She glanced around the back of the Order to make sure no one was out training, then with a quick wave, she jumped down. Her legs wobbled a bit, but she tried not to let it show since Kai watched her. Another look around and she scaled the wall.

She stuck to the alleys as she made her way to the GicCorp headquarters. In the late afternoon, people headed home before night fell. Workers came out of various founder factories. In the north, GicCorp transferred the blight to where it would be purified in Haven. The vitals stayed in their own section of the city, away from the rest of the population. The heroes of Verrin.

Vic made her way past the front gate to the family entrance. A short, stately man greeted her.

"Victoria Glass. I need to see Ethan Nordic about something I've uncovered."

The man lifted his nose and huffed. "He's busy. Perhaps you can arrange a visit through your father."

"This is reaper business, and it has to do with the Order of Nyx. He'll want to hear this personally. If I'm wrong, you can take away my relic." Not that she had it with her, anyway.

"I will inform him you're here, but he's a busy man. He doesn't have time for nonsense."

"Neither do I." Nervous energy filled her, and she bounced slightly on her toes.

The man shut the door in her face, and she heard his footsteps walking away. She realized he might not tell Ethan Nordic she was here. The sun set, and Vic stood outside the door as the last of the workers left. Some gave her strange glances.

The door creaked open. "He will see you."

Vic smiled brightly. "I thought so."

He sniffed and walked away, leaving Vic to chase after him. The entrance to the Nordic home was as stunning as she remembered it. The stained glass in the ceiling darkened with the setting of the sun. Her sister had always liked to look at other work by those in the Glass sector. Now, Vic tended to notice it too.

The man took her to the right and led her down a hallway. He opened the door to a large, impressive office. The whole thing was spread out, with a large black desk in the center. It might have been made from one solid stone. The wooden floors were stained gray, and the shelves behind the desk had objects Vic didn't recognize.

"Sit here and wait." He gestured to a few wooden chairs with black cushions.

Vic didn't feel like sitting, so she paced the room and let her footsteps echo on the wooden floor. She stayed that way for an hour. The sun set, and the blight swirled in an ominous yellow through the windows.

The door opened behind her, and Vic turned to see Xiona. Her face twitched, but she tried to keep her expression normal.

Xiona silently shut the door behind her. "I think we both knew there would be no compromising with you."

"I'm not sure what you mean." Vic tensed and distanced herself.

"You were never going to be okay with corrupting people. I had to give you a chance because of your founder blood." Xiona strode closer to Vic.

Vic's body urged her to run. She stepped back to put some of the furniture between them. If Xiona was here, that could only mean one thing. "The Nordics already know you're padding your numbers."

Xiona twirled a pair of cuffs in her hand. "You could say that."

Vic swallowed, then it hit her. "They told you to do it." Of course they knew.

She stepped forward. "Come now, little newbie. Let's take you to your new home."

Vic took the wooden chair and threw it at Xiona. She dodged out of the way. The chair slammed into the wall and clattered to the ground. Vic rounded the desk, grabbed the strange objects, and threw them at the commander's head. Some of them hit and shattered against her.

Xiona glared and swiped away the fragments. She grabbed her folded scythe from her harness and used it to knock away some of the thrown objects. Xiona crunched over the broken projectiles, jumped onto another chair, and landed on the desk. Vic veered to the side, nearly tripping on the desk chair, but now she had a clear shot at the door and darted to the exit. A flash caught the corner of her eye, and she saw a blade coming around toward her neck.

Vic dove, and the blade swooped over her head.

"Killing me now?" Vic scrambled backward on the floor to get away from the vicious blade.

"No loss for me."

Xiona lunged forward. Vic rolled out of the way and barely avoided the blade as it came down on the wooden floor, chipping the perfect wood.

"Nordic might not like that you messed up his floor." Vic gasped as she jumped to her feet.

Xiona smiled and swung at Vic. "The blood will be harder to clean up."

Vic's jaw tightened, and she sidestepped another swing of the scythe. Xiona had more reach with the weapon. As soon as she swung again, instead of dodging, Vic caught the wooden handle and yanked, bringing Xiona forward. Vic kneed Xiona in the stomach, and then she clutched Xiona's head and slammed her knee into her nose.

With a grunt and a crunch, Xiona toppled. Her relic clattered to the floor. Vic stole the relic and ran out of the room. Her mind raced. Where could she go in this city? The walls felt more like a prison now. She could beg Dei to hide her? She ran down the hall, and then in front of her stood six reapers. She halted and tried to run back, but they surrounded her.

She swung the scythe and hit a few as they came at her, but she was outnumbered. They tackled her and pinned her arms and legs down. They parted as Xiona approached.

Xiona stared down at Vic. She picked up her relic and pressed the blade to Vic's neck. Her skin broke open—just a nick but warm blood dribbled down her neck.

"Let's get this one a new brand." Xiona removed her blade, and the other reapers dragged her out of the Nordic house. With all the hands holding her, it was impossible to budge. Vic tried to twist her arm away while she hung in their grasp. Did all the founders know what was happening to the people of Verrin? What about the vitals?

A sick feeling overcame Vic as she glanced at the passing city in the darkness. There wasn't anything beyond the walls except blight and swamp. There was nowhere to run for those who didn't like what the founders were doing. Helplessness filled her. She had to try. She needed to keep Kai and Bomrosy out of this mess she'd found herself in.

They reached the Nyx Order, and they dragged her to the room where she'd received her brand.

"Start the fire," Xiona ordered.

A few reapers ran forward and brought the flames to life.

"You're all okay with hurting others and letting them get corrupted?" They made her kneel on the stone floor. The heat of the fire caressed her skin.

The reapers ignored her as they worked. Five of them held her down, and one came up to hold her head to the side, exposing her neck.

Vic couldn't see very well, but Xiona put something in the flames.

"It's easy to take you out of the Order, Victoria Glass. Keep in mind how little power you hold. It doesn't matter who your daddy is," Xiona sneered.

Vic twitched as Xiona held up another brand, this one a solid square. The heat from the new brand singed her hair as it drew closer. She pressed the brand to Vic's neck.

This time, she wasn't gentle, and it seared into Vic's flesh. The smell of her own burning skin filled the room. Pain lanced down her side. When Xiona finally withdrew the brand, Vic felt a layer of her skin go with it. She bit down on her tongue and trembled as the mark burned.

Xiona stared down at her and tossed the black branding iron back into the flames. It clunked against the burning wood. "Take her to the lower cells."

Delirious from pain, Vic felt them carry her away. They went down some steps and to a wall in the back of the holding cells. One of them pressed a hidden latch, and the stone wall opened. More stone steps led down farther into the ground.

Human waste hit her nose, and they dumped her in a cell. Blackness overcame her as she stared into a pair of red-rimmed eyes.

Vic winced as she turned her head, the brand still raw. She touched the brand gingerly and hissed. They hadn't bothered to bandage it before throwing her into the cell. Maybe if she died from infection, it would make their lives easier.

She scanned the dim cells, and she was alone in this one. There was a young woman in the cell next to hers. It had to be who she'd seen before passing out. The woman huddled next to the bars and shuddered every so often.

"Hey, are you okay?" Seeing she was locked up in a dungeon, probably not. "Why are you here?" Maybe that was a better question.

The young woman raised her head. Deep red rimmed her irises, and black veins branched out on her face. It wouldn't be long before she changed. At this stage, they'd already lost their human self.

"Hungry."

Vic slid farther back until she felt the stone wall behind her. "Yeah, me too."

The woman continued to stare at Vic.

"I don't plan on being your next meal." Something wet soaked into Vic's shirt from the wall.

The woman blinked hungrily at Vic.

"Nice place you have here." Vic looked everywhere but at the woman. She hadn't known about these cells, but she'd only been at Nyx for a few weeks. She had a feeling most Nyx reapers didn't know this place existed.

The metal bars were melded into the stone by magic. Vic placed her hands on the damp metal to see if any were loose. Kai might know she was here, but he couldn't do anything. His family needed him more. He might have a hard time explaining why Vic hadn't been wearing the band. She didn't know if Xiona would believe him. There was a reason Xiona had never told him about what they were doing to the citizens, and if Vic knew anything, it was that Xiona wasn't a fool.

If Ethan Nordic was part of this, other founders might be involved. Tristan, his son, likely knew as well.

Vic sat in the middle of her cell. She needed to get out of here first. Then maybe she could think of what to do about GicCorp. She placed her chin on her knees. The world had to be bigger than Verrin. Maybe she could get her relic and take her chances out in the swamps. This would mean leaving Em and Kai behind. She hoped there was something better out there.

A pattering of footsteps interrupted her thoughts. Xiona stopped in front of the bars to her cell.

"Like your room?"

"Could smell better." The secret dungeon didn't get any outside air. "When did your job become about profit instead of saving people?"

Xiona ran a finger along the metal bar of the cell. "No one gets charged if there isn't enough blight to purify. Remember that, Glass."

"I'll try. It gets harder when you see innocents who are barely surviving getting sacrificed." She dug her fingernails into her legs and let the pricks of pain give her courage.

Xiona's expression grew cold. "What would you know about their lives? You spent a few months on the streets and now you understand their struggle? Deep down, you knew Daddy would come and save you before you starved."

Vic jumped up and slammed her hand on the bar next to Xiona's face, but she didn't flinch. Pain flared in her hand from the strike. "You don't know me either."

"Rich girl problems. I'll pass. Ready for the show?" She approached the cell of the woman now rocking back and forth.

"What are you going to do with her?" Vic asked, but she already knew.

"Sometimes, it's easier to have the mog change here."

Vic's throat felt dry as she glanced at her neighbor.

Xiona's voice grew quiet. "Pay attention, rich girl. No one cares about the poor."

The woman in the cell moaned, a deep feral sound of pain, then a sound like bones cracking followed.

"It's reforming," Xiona noted in a bored tone.

"She."

"It doesn't matter." Xiona took out her scythe and flicked it open.

The woman's bones crunched, and the skin broke open, reforming. The blood and muscle turned black as her head elongated. The ligaments and muscles squelched around the bones. Her moaning spoke of hunger and pain. In one slobbery gulp, the mog scooped up the glops of skin that had fallen off its body.

Vic had never seen the transformation since most corrupted souls went underground before it happened. Before the mog could adjust, Xiona thrust her scythe in and absorbed the blight. As a new mog, it didn't need more than one reaper. Its skin and bones fell into a heap on the ground, and some of it leaked through the bars into Vic's cell.

"I'm surprised you don't feed it to make it larger."

"Only for the trials."

Vic swallowed. "You don't go out and find them?"

Xiona stepped back from the melted skin. "Is there a special on naivete today? Had you kept your little nose out of everything, you would have been happy here."

"I guess my nose is too large." Vic stepped away from the mass of skin creeping into her cell. "Are you going to do that to me?"

Xiona flicked her scythe shut. "Can't."

"I'm in a cell. How is my family name protecting me?" If her father didn't know she was down here, he couldn't help her. They might have a problem explaining to him how she'd gone missing.

Xiona stared at Vic, her dark eyes searching for something. "Your birth gave you something, but you probably won't like what it is."

"Gave me what?" Vic frowned. All the webs connected in her mind, but there was something left unsaid.

"I think you've learned enough. Your fate will be sealed soon." Xiona sneered. "Maybe you would have been better off poor."

Her footsteps echoed up the stairs, and the stone wall grated shut. The other cells were empty, but her orb was still in her neck. The only way out was through her cell door, and she would have to wait until someone opened it. The smell of the mog filled the dungeon, and there were no windows to let in fresh air. Vic stayed in the corner and knew she would only get one chance to escape.

Hours passed, and she didn't know what time it was anymore. The grate sounded, and she heard more than one set of footsteps.

"This was better than marrying me?"

Tristan stood in the basement next to Xiona. His clean and expensive contrasted with the dirty cells.

"If you knew about these cells, then yes." She shouldn't have been surprised since she'd assumed earlier that he was involved.

Tristan looked her over and avoided the small puddles that gathered on the stone floor. "Get her cleaned up and under control."

"I don't know why you care," Xiona replied

"She wants her there." He smoothed his lapels. "It's the least I can do for Emilia and the vital ceremony."

Xiona shook her head. "You will regret this kindness."

"Perhaps." His bored gaze spoke of power and money that could solve any problem Vic might create.

"What's going on?" Vic asked.

Dread filled her. How would they control her? Put her on a leash for the ceremony? That would raise a few brows among the founders.

"It saddens Emilia that you won't be there. As a gift to her, you'll go." His eyes hardened. "After all, she has a higher calling, and this will be the last time you see her."

Vic's hopes rose. This was it, her way out.

Tristan's calm voice stated her fate: "Maybe we should

purify her. That would solve many problems." The corner of his mouth turned up. This must have been the plan all along.

Her heart sank. She recalled Samuel's glazed eyes. A film of sweat formed on her forehead at the thought of becoming a radiant. "No need. I'll be good."

Xiona scoffed. "I'll get a radiant here. It'll make her more cooperative. Good thinking."

Tristan nodded. "Emilia cares so much about you. I hope this gift will give her peace before she enters her *new life*." His teeth flashed at the mention of the word *life*, his tone flattening.

Vic grabbed the bars. "What do you mean? Why does it sound like Emilia won't be alive?"

"Don't you know you won't see her again after today." He frowned, his previous look fading and the company line remaining intact. "Unless the radiant don't understand what's around them, so maybe dinner will be the last place you see her."

"Why? What are you going to do to her?" She tried to grab him through the bars. The metal scraped against her skin.

"You know the vitals keep us alive and safe. They live a *happy life* in Haven. She will be part of that. Much better than making glass." Shadows crossed his eyes.

Vic shook as she gripped the bars. She wanted to take him by the hair and slam his face into the metal. All she could do was stare at him angrily. Vic wanted to throw herself at the walls or do anything besides just being trapped here, waiting for her life to end.

Tristan spoke, "Do it soon. We'll need to clean her up after. The ceremony is only a few hours away."

They left as if they'd discussed the weather and not the stealing of Vic's magic. This couldn't be it. The way he'd spoken about the vitals had sounded off. They protected Verrin, which had been all well and good until it was her sister leaving. He'd made it sound different from what she'd been taught. A sick feeling filled her. Vic paced the cell and slammed her hands on the stone. Blood came off in a smear, and she resisted the urge to scream.

When the grating of the door sounded again, she positioned herself to attack. They weren't taking her magic without a fight.

"Very dirty down here."

William had never looked so good in his ridiculous white uniform. He stood next to Xiona and six reapers. He was more rumpled than usual, and there was a wildness to his eyes.

William looked hesitant. "She doesn't want to become a radiant."

Xiona brought out a large key ring. "It's better if you just do your thing, okay?"

"Understood."

Xiona opened the door. Before Vic could bolt, the reapers pinned her down and chained her to the wall. Then Xiona shoved William in and locked him inside.

"This should be a private moment, even if she's unwilling," William stated.

"I don't care. You have five minutes."

Vic backed into the wall. The chains provided her little movement. "What are you doing?"

"They wanted my father, but he wasn't around." His back to Xiona, he widened his eyes, his pupils moving. He was telling her something, but he couldn't say it.

"How are you okay with this?" Vic asked.

He got closer but blinked in a weird pattern. "There's too much magic in the world. Accept this fate and live a pure life."

His eyes widened and squinted over and over, but Vic couldn't read what he wanted her to know.

If she could get to her sister's ceremony with her mind intact, she'd drag her out of there. The way Tristan had talked about the vitals made her more nervous about her sister leaving. How could she save her sister if William purified her?

William made his eyes go blank, then normal, then blank again, continuing the pattern. Did he want her to pretend to be a radiant? He quirked his brow as if asking if she understood.

She could try. Vic made her eyes lose focus and tried to smile vacantly while William blocked her from view. She focused on him again, and he briefly nodded.

Xiona clanged something against the metal bars. "Hurry up, radiant!"

"Hold still, magic user." William reached toward her with his relic.

Her throat tightened. She had to trust him. She struggled against the chains until he placed his hand on her. Then, just like she'd seen during his cleansing ceremony, she relaxed and fixed her face to look like a radiant.

"It's done." William gave her one last look before he turned. He acted worried that Vic couldn't pull it off.

Vic pictured her sister's face. *I have to.* Her anger toward him about his brother still thrummed inside her, but his eyes were red, and his gaze flittered around the cell as Xiona entered to release her from the chains. He was hurting too.

"About time."

Vic let her arms relax at her sides, and she waited for William to tell her what to do. Her mind raced, and she focused on keeping her expression easy.

"Let's go, radiant." Xiona turned her back, and Vic's gaze flicked to William.

He nodded again. She must have been doing okay.

Vic schooled her expression and let William guide her. Part of Vic wanted to burst through and run, but if she did, she might never see her sister again.

"I should stay with her since she doesn't yet have an occupation. She may get lost." William took hold of her hand and led her out of the cell.

"Fine. We need to clean her up."

"So you said on the way here." He held her and didn't shake. Vic admired how calm he stayed.

Vic didn't dare glance around, so she couldn't see Xiona's face. William guided her up the stairs, his hand warm in hers. Her mouth already hurt from smiling for so long. Was she really that angry of a person that it hurt to smile? Xiona stepped in her line of sight and led them to a room with a shower. A light green dress hung in the corner.

"Can a radiant bathe themselves?"

William bristled next to her. "Yes." To Vic, he said, "Shower and get dressed. Be quick."

Once the door shut, there was no need to tell her twice. She looked for a window but found none. Part of her wanted to run out of the city, but she couldn't leave her sister behind. They would make it in the swamps. With her fighting skills and Emilia's glass making ... they probably wouldn't stand a chance, but the fate that awaited her was ominous.

Vic let the water clean off her time in the cell. She

washed fast since she didn't know when Xiona would be back. After the shower, she toweled off and slipped on the dress and shoes. It was a simple yet elegant dress fit for a founder. There was a bandage next to the sink for her to cover her neck. Only a few people knew of her rebranding. Her vision blurred as she covered the ugly black square on her neck. These bandages were not imbued. It figured Xiona wouldn't give her relief from the pain.

She sat down and arranged her face into a blank expression. It was so odd, but she had to remind herself to blink.

The door opened, and William took her hand again and led her out. Then her heart fell when she saw Kai next to Xiona.

His words came out harshly as he demanded, "What did you do to her?"

Vic didn't dare look at him directly. He could ruin everything.

"She's safe now. Don't worry," William replied.

Kai took a step closer, but Xiona blocked him. "I thought your loyalties were not in question. Why do you care what happens to her? You can get any woman to sleep with you."

Kai backed off, and William led her away. She wanted to reach out to him, but he would understand. He wanted to protect his mother and sister. Right now, she needed to protect her sister.

She followed them down to the courtyard where a car waited for them. Xiona waved them inside.

"You're to take her to the ceremony and then give her to your family when it's over." Xiona slammed the door shut.

When they pulled out to the road, Vic relaxed but stayed still. The driver would notice something, and he used his magic to run the car. William said nothing either, his gaze on the swirling blight in the sky.

They arrived in a mass of cars and slowly inched up the drive. Guests got out one by one, and when it was their turn, the greeters recognized Vic. They smiled at her, but she stayed expressionless.

Some of them gave her and William a wide berth, as if they thought they might get purified next.

It made it easy for William to navigate through the crowd. They found a place to stand near the wall to wait for the ceremony to begin.

"What's the plan?" William asked without looking at Vic.

She kept up her blank expression. "It'll have to happen after. I need to get her alone."

"I don't see that happening."

Vic squeezed his hand. "Then I'll blow my cover and drag her out."

He sighed and adjusted his cuffs. "You may be better off letting me take you out of here rather than breaking your cover. If GicCorp thinks you're a radiant, you'll be safe in radiant territory."

Safe? She could do that. Be safe and free. She could pretend to be magicless for the rest of her life. Smiling and following orders. Never hearing from her sister again. She tried to puzzle out Tristan's intonation when he'd talked about the vitals. Had she imagined the way his tone had been off when he'd talked to her? Her heart gave a sharp pang. How had things fallen apart so fast? Her father had changed, their house had fallen apart, and the reapers were now the bad guys. Now here she was, trying to rescue her sister while surrounded by founders.

The crowd quieted down, and Tristan walked to the

stone table with his parents. An elegant metal rod with a marble handle waited next to a paint palette. Emilia, a vision in a cream gown, stood between their mother and father. The rest of the vitals formed a semicircle around the Nordic family, with their parents next to them.

Vic looked at the parents' faces. Most had a sense of pride, but there was also sadness in the air. Those left behind were told that they'd live out their lives connected to magic and have their own families. The vitals looked nervous, and a few retained calm smiles. After all, they were heroes.

Ethan Nordic spoke, "With the blight entering our world, many were lost to the corrupted magic. Our founders made a way to purify the magic, but it requires isolation and a connection to this new relic. For those who are connected to it, if they go too far away, they will die."

Ethan continued, "Those with the strongest relics are the only ones who can connect to the magic." He put on a kindly expression. "Given this power, we understand the sacrifice we must make. All of us here have said goodbye to our children, knowing they will save the city while we run it in their trust."

He waved his hand toward the vitals. "It's an honor to know you. Step forward and get the brand. Tonight, we celebrate you." He bowed and faced the crowd. "Let us honor them."

Everyone in the room bowed low to the vitals as they received the new brand. A white circle was placed on their necks with paint. It wasn't a permanent brand, so Vic didn't understand why they called it that. The vitals would have no other occupation in the city, so was this supposed to make up for what they were leaving behind?

Vic noticed she was holding on to William's forearm. Her nails dug into his uniform. He put his hand over hers. Was William actually comforting her?

"Stay in character," he whispered.

Vic curled her toes in her shoes. She loosened her grip and watched her sister smile at various founders while Tristan led her around the room like a prize. Why did he stay so close to her? He looked at her sister's face with an expression Vic didn't understand. There was an odd softness in his gaze. It couldn't be love, but it looked that way from where she stood. Did Tristan actually care for her sister? She bit the inside of her cheek. It couldn't be. His cold posture in the dungeon only hours earlier had shown a man who couldn't love. Could he? It didn't matter. Once her sister went to Haven, Tristan couldn't get to her either. Right? Her head hurt from all the questions, but she didn't have any answers.

She almost flinched as William went into the crowd. Vic made sure her face didn't change, and she let him lead her. Now that they were surrounded, she didn't dare ask what he was doing. Radiant didn't have their own thoughts. When the founders saw Vic, shock filled their faces, and they immediately whispered to the person standing next to them. Their stares drilled into her back. Soon, they would all know that the heir to Glass was a radiant. What would happen when her father found out? Or did her father not care anymore?

William halted, and she nearly tripped. Her father stood in front of them, his face blazing with rage.

❧ 18 ❧
VIC

Vic forced herself to remain a brainless radiant as her father stood shaking, with the whites of his eyes showing and his skin flushed red. He wanted to kill someone, probably William.

"What did you do to my daughter?" His shout silenced the room. If they hadn't been looking before, Vic was sure they were looking at her now.

Her father's lips pressed into a thin line, one hand clenched at his side while the other held his wand, pointed directly at William. Imbs didn't have much as far as combat training with magic, but she'd once witnessed her father shred a wooden post using glass. She shivered, and William backed up.

"Sir, if I may talk with you in private, I can explain." William raised his free hand in a peaceful gesture.

Her father's face darkened, and the silent room deafened her. "Explain now. I don't care what these gossips hear."

Vic noted William's hesitation. He couldn't tell the room that a Nordic had ordered him to purify a founder. If it came out that William had forced a purification, he would be hauled away to the holding cells at the station.

"You have ten seconds to answer me. I know my daughter would never choose to be a mindless fool." He reached into his pocket, where he kept a pouch of sand.

From the crowd, Ethan appeared next to her father and placed a hand on his shoulder. "Old friend, let's figure this out in the next room."

Vic's father flinched and nodded sharply. In the silent room, they followed Ethan out of the supposed celebration and down the hall to his office. Her father pulled away from Ethan the minute the door shut, and he glared back and forth between Ethan and William. Vic stood with her fake smile and glazed eyes. She tried to think dull thoughts to remain calm in her father's presence. A bead of sweat traced down her forehead and into her eye. It burned, but she didn't dare wipe it away. Did the radiant wipe away their sweat? The whole room could probably hear her heart beating. She knew too little about how to act.

"Conrad, I know this is unfortunate, but this is something Vic requested." Ethan sat down calmly in a cushioned wooden chair and gestured for her father to sit. He ignored William and Vic.

Her father remained standing and stepped forward. His voice was raw with anger as he said, "When was this decided?"

Ethan shifted in their direction. Her father noticed the movement, and he stepped back, still gripping his wand.

"I'm not sure when *your daughter* decided this, Glass."

A scary coldness filled Vic. Did he mean that her father was involved in what GicCorp was doing? He opened his mouth, then glanced at William and shut it again.

"I think I would like to talk to you, *my friend,* about what my daughter decided *without telling me.*"

The loaded conversation filled the room with tension. They didn't want to talk in front of William. Nordic clearly held all the power here, but maybe he'd brokered a deal with her father. She could only assume they had some sort of dealing, but whatever the deal was it wasn't good. Could this be the reason for his change in demeanor over the last year?

What are you doing, Father? Vic thought. She wanted to shake answers out of him. Saving her sister from this mess was the one thing she could do. Whatever her father had done affected them all.

"Why don't you and Glass's daughter stay here for a bit so we can get back to the party? She's upsetting people with another foul choice of hers." Ethan rose as smoothly as ever. Her father would lose two daughters today, and it didn't bother Nordic.

Her father stiffened and glanced at Vic before following Ethan out of the room. A wave of pain and sadness hit her. Her father quickly schooled his expression into an emotionless mask and left the room.

"I think we stepped into something," William's voice broke through the room. Its tiredness wove around Vic.

"All our fathers are up to something." Vic dropped her hand from William's arm. "Since they couldn't find your father today, you're involved by default."

William weakly pulled on his cuffs. "It doesn't really matter, does it?"

"What do you mean? Whatever they're doing involves turning people into mogs to provide blight. You don't think they matter?"

"If they would choose the path of the radiant, they

wouldn't need to worry about corruption." His voice no longer held the conviction it used to.

Vic scoffed. "Don't you realize that if you hadn't been called, your dad would have purified me against my will? How many people has he purified without permission?" His father had to be breaking radiant laws by changing people willfully. Forget radiant laws; it was a law in Verrin too.

William used the wooden chair for support. "Sometimes, you don't have a choice."

Vic let out a short laugh. "Like your brother? Did you tire of bailing him out of confinement? Tired of him giving the radiant a bad name?" Vic squared her shoulders and got into William's face. "He wouldn't get in line, right? Took care of a problem and saved him, right?"

His breath hit her face as he exhaled. He backed away. "Don't talk about my brother. You know why I had to do it, and it had nothing to do with those reasons."

"Someone has too. You know what he wanted, and you still changed him." Vic told herself to stop, but the words poured out anyway. "You took away his choice and did what you wanted!"

William reached up as if to shove her away but stopped himself. "I saved you today. Don't forget it. If they find out you're not a radiant, I might as well run off with you."

Vic snorted and kicked the chair. It clattered as it fell over. "Like I'd want to be stuck with you out in the swamps."

"That's your plan? Survive in the swamps?" William laughed. "How will your sister live out there? Can she fight? Oh, and what does she want? Are you thinking about that?"

"Worry about yourself and your dissolving morals!" Vic paced to the door and wondered how long they needed to stay in here and away from the crowd. At this rate, it didn't look like she could get close to her sister. Maybe she should pass her a note? She doubted they would let William get close to her either.

William trembled with anger behind her. "Don't claim to understand my beliefs. You magic users know nothing of what the radiant do."

Vic clicked her tongue and pointed at him. "Purify the unwilling. Got it figured out, thanks."

"You know what? Why don't you stay here and figure this out on your own? You're bound to drag me down. I might as well get a head start." He pushed past her to the door.

"Verrin isn't that big. Where are you going to go?"

"I can survive in the swamps the same as you."

Vic blocked his hand from the doorknob. "Oh, really? Are you going to turn mogs into light lovers? Be careful when you touch them. They bite."

The door flew open, knocking into them, and William swung to face it. There in white stood her sister. Her mouth opened, and she flung herself at Vic. "I knew it. You aren't a radiant."

Vic's arms automatically went around her sister and squeezed. The smell of lilies filled her nose as she held her sister. "Blight, this is luck. How did you get away? Wait, no time. We need to get out of here. Think you can open the glass window without making a sound?" Her stance relaxed. This was the stroke of luck she'd needed. She wouldn't have to separate her sister from Tristan.

"I only have a few moments, so I can't stay," Emilia replied.

"Yeah, I got that. Let's get out of here." Vic grabbed her hand and took her to one of the back windows. William followed behind. Vic ignored him. He could follow them if he wanted, but he wasn't coming with them past the wall.

Emilia pulled her hand away from Vic's. As her fingers slipped away, Vic glanced back.

Her light green eyes softened. "I'm not leaving, Vic."

"You have no clue what the Nordics or our father is involved in. Trust me, we need to leave. There's something going on with Haven." She didn't need to get stuck behind the stone wall and figure it out too late.

Emilia shook her head. "No. I can't."

"Um, you can. Follow me and we can get out of here." Vic reached for her sister once more, but she moved back. "Em, I'm not joking. Before, I might have selfishly wanted you to stay, but there is something wrong with Tristan."

"What makes you think I'm joking? Where in the city do you plan to run? The sewers? You know they'll find you. Yes, Tristan is strange, but he won't be with the vitals."

"I'm leaving Verrin." The moment those words left her mouth, Vic's throat dried up.

Emilia gripped her arm. "You can't. You'll die out there."

"Thanks for the vote of confidence. We're strong. I'm sure we'll be fine." Vic found it hard to believe her own words as she tried to sell Emilia on the idea. Verrin suddenly felt tiny, and Vic struggled to breathe.

Emilia looked at Vic's back. "You don't even have your relic." She took Vic's hands, her fingers cold. "I have to stay. If I don't, they'll come after you. Just live, okay. This is part of what I need to do as a founder. I'm keeping you all safe. I know you wanted me to leave when you left the house, but I stayed so I could save you."

Emilia pulled away, but Vic clutched her hands. "What

do you mean? What do you know? Why isn't anyone telling me anything?"

Emilia gently released her hands. "I know they need us to keep the city safe. Even though it isn't the life I imagined, we are needed."

"Blight take me, can't you and Father see this isn't helping anything? What are you protecting?" Couldn't she see there was something wrong? Vic raged at her lack of solid evidence.

"You."

The word floated in the room.

"I didn't ask you to." The life of a vital was an honor, but Vic felt like her heart was being ripped out.

"I know this may sound selfish, but I'm doing this more for my family than the city. Vic, did you ever stop to think that all this 'something is going on with the vitals' stuff could be in your head? I know you want to keep me here. I know it's hard, but I'm saving you. Can you believe in me for once?"

The door opened, interrupting them. Vic blanked her expression and stared at Emilia. Tristan walked into the room. She could fight Tristan and grab Em.

"You're missing time with your parents. Did you get to say goodbye to your sister?"

Emilia stepped back, and Vic caught a small shake of her head. She was telling her not to do anything stupid.

Frustration built to the point of exploding as Vic watched her sister take Tristan's arm. She didn't know what he was doing? How could they trust the Nordics? What did he know about the vitals that they weren't saying?

"Radiant, you might as well take the former Glass heir away. She isn't needed here, and she's upsetting her family.

Making such a selfish decision has hurt her family even
more." He went back to the door. "She turned her back on
them months ago."

Vic burst forward and punched Tristan in the nose.
Warm blood sprayed over her hand and arm as he fell back.
His dumb eyes spread open in surprise.

"Blight consume you, you monster maker."

Vic raised her foot and slammed it into Tristan's side. He
rolled away from her and stood, blood running down his
chin. He swung at her.

Vic bent out of the way of his punch, and it grazed her
side. She used his forward momentum to thrust her leg into
his. Then she elbowed the back of his head, shoving him to
the ground. He'd be down for a moment. Vic grabbed her
sister's hand.

Emilia jerked away and shook her head. Then she
looked past Vic. "Take her, please."

A hand closed around Vic's wrist and pulled her from
the room. Vic jerked against William, but he ran. Emilia, still
as a statue, remained in the doorway.

"No!"

Emilia smiled, and went back inside the room and to her
calling, her white dress fluttering behind her.

Vic tried to yank free from William. "Let me go, you light
lover."

He was stronger than she'd thought, so she tried to
trip him.

He halted and grabbed her shoulders. "Don't you get it?
You're putting her in danger! Open your eyes and see she
made a choice. She's protecting you. Now I'm protecting you
too. Don't drag us down even further."

Can you believe in me for once? Vic swallowed and nodded.

William took her hand again, and they ran out the back of the Nordic mansion and over the stone courtyard. Vic barely noticed any of the workers moving out of their way. She let William lead her out onto the street. She didn't know what would happen. The Nordics and Nyx wouldn't want the city to know what they were doing to people. However, they couldn't let them go; they would want to bring Vic back in quietly. Next time, they would make sure she was purified and William too, unless his father had some pull.

Their footsteps slapped against the stone roads. They reached the main canal and ducked into an alley. He dropped her hand. Vic missed the warmth. His breath came out in gasps, and his face was flushed from the run. Vic leaned against the wall and took a deep breath. Her thoughts wouldn't focus. All she could think about was her sister going back to Tristan.

"What's the plan?" William asked.

Vic ran her hands through her hair, and the motion helped calm her down. "I-I don't know." The thought of going out to the swamp by herself did frighten her. Endless darkness and mogs once the sun set, all of them trying to eat her alive. If she stayed, Xiona or GicCorp would find her in the walled city. Once her gicgauge was full, she would likely die.

"You can still come with me."

"How long until they find me?"

"Change your name?" William suggested.

She let out a sad laugh. "And my face? Maybe I need to warn the other Orders." Had Dei gotten any updates from Kai? But he wouldn't know about Nordic's involvement.

"Are you going to live outside of Verrin?"

Vic took another breath and thought about her options.

Em wouldn't leave. Kai was stuck at Nyx, his position precarious. "Will you be okay?"

"I'm going home. If they want me to get purified, it doesn't matter." He faced the swirls of blight in the sky.

"You're giving up?" She had mixed feelings about the radiant, but she'd thought he was stronger than that.

William's jaw twitched. "I don't see purification as giving up, reaper. It's an honor to live without magic."

Vic rolled her eyes. "Fine, then. Enjoy your life. Thanks for saving me."

She didn't need his help, anyway. He could go back to his light-loving life with all his brainless friends. She glanced out of the alley and got ready to run. She grabbed the bottom of the dress and tried to arrange it into tied-up shorts. The result was a bunched-up dress that looked like a diaper.

"Next time, get out of your own mess."

She glared back at him. "Don't worry, I will."

Vic took off and left him behind in the alley. She ran through the city. No one paused at the strange woman in a bunched-up dress as she ran past them. She stuck to the alleys as much as she could to avoid people. She ran over the bridges that went over the canals in the city. Citrus hung in the air as she hit the orchards.

As far as she could tell, no one had followed her out to Dei. She stopped at the gate and met her old friend Becks.

"Ah, the little redhead is back. I take it you want to see Nel?"

Vic took a moment to breathe air into her strained lungs. She shivered now that she had stopped running. "Is she here?"

Becks jerked her head, signaling for Vic to follow her to

the main building. Vic tried to piece together her thoughts before seeing Nel. She didn't know what the commander would do with the information about GicCorp's involvement in turning people into mogs. Vic thought she could at least tell her so that someone besides Kai and William knew. Then maybe she would vanish. If she tried to help Kai, it might only hurt his family. She didn't dare go back to her family. A soft pain filled her chest. Her father might need her, but she had a feeling he wanted her to stay away. What did they know about the vitals? They'd chosen not to tell her anything. She should be the one protecting Em. She should have been born an imb; then she would be the vital.

Her thoughts stopped as she entered the building behind Becks. The temperature dropped, and Nel stood in the same place Vic had seen her last.

"Don't move around much?" Vic asked.

Nel barked out a laugh. "You'd be surprised at the paperwork I get stuck with now. I wish for the days when I ran around in the swamp." Nel pushed aside a stack of papers. "I work out here just to see other people during mealtimes." She sat back and put her dirt-covered boots up on the table. She smirked at Becks's frown. "But you aren't here to help me with paperwork. What's the news? I haven't seen anything about a scandal in the news reports."

"That's because GicCorp has been part of it all along."

Nel raised her eyebrows but didn't look surprised. "Ah."

"You knew, yet you sent me to him?" She stepped closer, but Becks stepped in to stop her.

"Had you disappeared, I would've had my answer."

"Oh, how kind of you to sacrifice me." Vic glared at her and wanted to punch her in the face. Her knuckles still smarted from hitting Tristan. Apparently, this was how she solved problems now.

Nel blinked her gray eyes. "Sorry, green bean. I have an Order to protect. You joined the wrong team." Her gaze traveled down to Vic's collarbone. The bandage covered her new brand. "Looks like they kicked you out."

Vic felt isolated in front of this woman. "Yes, I belong nowhere. I told you, now you know. Goodbye, then."

Vic turned to walk out.

"Where're you going, green bean?" Did Nel sound concerned? Vic did like the coarse woman, but it angered her that Nel wouldn't do more.

"Over the wall." Did it matter anymore? No one could do anything, and Vic didn't want to become a radiant.

"In that dress?"

Vic opened the door. "What do you care?"

The door slammed shut before Vic could leave, and Becks stood in front of it.

Vic crossed her arms. "Tell your guard dog to move."

Nel strode forward. "Eh, she isn't very well trained."

Becks glared at Nel. "Watch it or I'll pee on you."

Nel laughed and stood in front of Vic. "No relic and in a dress. I wish you would have chosen my order." Was Nel impressed?

"It's too late now. Let me go." Vic had given her already-known information. She was done with this city.

Nel sighed. "Let me at least get you clothes, and I have something for you from your friend."

From a friend? "Who?"

"Follow me."

Where else did she have to go? She followed the leader into a room at the back of the hall. Piles of clothing and personal items littered the room. "It smells like a mog died in here."

"Hush or I'll keep this for myself." Nel held out the relic. It gleamed in the dim light.

"How?" Nel didn't respond. "Bomrosy?"

Nel handed it to her.

Vic gripped the scythe in her hands. "Oh, Bomrosy, you'll get into trouble." How had she known she'd end up here?

"Most likely. Her best bet will be to tell them that someone stole it. I don't think Xiona will believe it, though, but she enjoys having the tech girl as a pet." She handed Vic a glass figurine of a cat.

Vic willed her eyes to stay dry. She caught the cold figure in her palm.

Nel dug through a pile of clothes and handed Vic a pair of pants and a shirt.

Vic took the clothes with the tips of her fingers. "I don't know if I want these."

"Put the clothes on. You won't die from the smell."

"Are you sure about that?" Vic called out as Nel left and shut the door behind her.

She took a cautious sniff of the offered clothes. They smelled like mildew. She quickly undressed and pulled on the borrowed items. She grabbed a pair of boots sitting in the corner. They pinched the sides of her feet. She slid the glass figurine into her pocket. This was all she had left of her sister. She left the messy room behind her. Nel waited outside for her.

"So, green bean, what are you going to do now?"

"I want to see if there's anything beyond the wall." Not that she had much choice. It sounded better than giving up.

Nel smiled and walked out a side door, waving for Vic to

follow. "Too bad your head got out of your ass too late. It would have been an honor to have you in my Order."

Vic gripped her relic. "There isn't any honor as long as the people of Verrin are dying."

Nel gave Vic an odd look and walked with her outside. "Maybe so."

The moment Emilia turned away from her sister, she wished she could follow her, even out to the swamp. If the Nordics lost Emilia and Vic, they might go after them. She didn't understand, but they wanted one of the Glass sisters. Her hair stuck to the paint on her neck. Tristan stood in the room, covering his bloody nose.

Emilia wanted to smile, but she furrowed her brow and placed her hand on his arm. "What can I do?"

He glanced down at her, and a strange look came over his face. "You would choose me over your sister?"

Did she really have a choice? Verrin would be overrun with mogs without the vitals. Why did he make this personal? Emilia hugged her waist to calm herself. She had only a few moments left of her normal life, then she would find out what it really meant to be one of the chosen. The wait was almost worse.

"I thought you might need help." She didn't know how to answer his question. She would only drag her sister down.

Emilia had never trained in combat. Her sister couldn't have been serious about living in the swamp. Her sister wouldn't really leave her behind in the city, even if she lived in Haven. Emilia wanted to know that her sister was out there, living and finally happy. This was all she wanted. Vic would rather make up conspiracy theories than let her go. Emilia smiled to herself. She would miss her.

Tristan looked himself over in the mirror, wiped the blood from his face, and took out a comb from the inside pocket of his suit coat to fix his hair. The swollen nose was the only sign that something had happened. "Let's get back to the others."

Hope rose in Emilia. This would give Vic a starting chance. She didn't know why Vic had faked being a radiant, but she had a feeling it involved Tristan. "Okay."

She forced herself to place a hand on his arm and plastered a pleasant expression on her face as she went out into the room full of founders.

She caught her father's gaze a few times, and he wore his mask well. She wanted to tell him that Vic was okay, but she stayed next to Tristan. Why did he stay so close to her? This was the easy part. After this, she would move to the back of the manor and never see these faces again. Mr. Stone stood next to the bar and laughed, his face red as always. Vic had never liked these parties, but she'd claimed Stone made them worth it, even though he was a jerk. Maddox Stone, his daughter, frowned at her father. She and Vic used to be close friends. Emilia didn't know if they spoke anymore. The Branch founders bowed their heads as they approached. They never said much and were quite dull. The gossips, those looking for advancement, matches, and deals—Emilia found herself missing this strange life of posturing. The other vitals, also dressed in white, wandered like ghosts. It was like they were dead and trying to accept the fact they wouldn't exist in this life anymore.

The party wore on to the early hours of the morning. Ethan Nordic called it when Stone passed out, and six imbs carried him out to his vehicle.

"Everyone, say your final goodbyes. Remember, they are with us still."

"Shall we?" Tristan asked.

Emilia nodded and followed him. He finally took her to her parents. She hugged her mother, and she shook in Emilia's arms. Emilia didn't know what to say to her mother to make it easier. She let go, then hugged her father.

She took a chance and whispered, "She's not."

She wouldn't know if her father understood, but she'd tried.

She stepped back to Tristan. "Goodbye, Mother. Father. I-I'm honored to be your daughter."

"There is no need for worries. You're still with us." Tristan's hand tightened around hers.

Emilia forced back the tears that wanted to fall. It was best to go with her head held high.

One more exchange of pleasant expressions and Emilia left with Tristan, her heart behind her.

She let him lead her and the others to the back of the manor. The Nordic house was connected to the commune of the vitals. Two giant onyx doors stood at the end of the hall. It seemed as though they were walking into a tunnel of nothingness. Tristan pushed on the doors, and they swung open with ease. A breeze rustled her hair, and the usual musty scent of Verrin filled her nose. Even with magic, they couldn't get rid of the mildew and mold that clung to Verrin.

The doors shut silently behind her and the others. This was it. She'd gone through the ceremony. Now she would see what happened beyond the onyx doors. Some stayed silent, and others sobbed in the darkness, their minds filled with goodbyes. What the relic did with their magic, no one knew. Emilia didn't know if she wanted to find out. They stepped outside to the walled section of the city. Two guards flanked another set of onyx doors. They followed Tristan. Their white clothing glowed like the radiant.

Tristan paused at the doors. "I can only go in so far with you. Once you cross over the second threshold, you will connect with the relic. The others will meet you at the gate and show you to your homes. Thank you for this honor." His old eyes singled out Emilia.

Shivering, she broke eye contact and waited as the doors opened. They went inside, and the doors shut with a deafening thud. They shuffled forward to the next gate, and Tristan paused while the gate opened. He gestured them forward.

The iron gates clanged shut behind them, and they all huddled in a group, staring into the dim light around them.

"What do we do now?" someone asked.

Emilia turned to look behind her, but Tristan wasn't there. She stood in the dark. Then figures came out from the darkness, holding lights.

Emilia didn't recognize anyone. It also didn't help that masks covered the lower half of their faces.

A man appeared at the front of the group. "Ah, another group of fools."

With that, he threw what looked like powder in the air. It floated down over them, and the vitals fell to their knees.

The words sunk in as the group grabbed the front line of vitals as they passed out.

Emilia backed into the iron gate as screams filled the air from those fighting to stay awake.

I'm sorry, Sister.

V ic cracked her neck. How kind of Nel to show her the door to the swamp and let the imbs lift the iron gate to let her pass.

The smell of rot filled her nose, and the water bubbled to the surface. In the distance, something splashed. Daylight still shone down from the blight, so she didn't need to worry about mogs. Yet. She stood on the stone path and gripped her scythe. When she'd made this brilliant plan in two seconds, it had seemed like the better option. Faced with endless swamp, she thought maybe she should go back to pretending to be a radiant.

Vic laughed, and the sound filled the surrounding emptiness. Pointless. If they caught her, they would make sure she became a radiant this time. Out here, she would become a mog. She sat on the stone path to enjoy the bleak scenery of the swamp.

"My sister chose them," Vic told the empty swamp.

The swamp didn't answer. After all, a swamp didn't have answers. Her sister had done what was expected of her to save the city. That was the understanding the founders had with the city. People accepted that the rich sacrificed their children to save them all. Did they know that they were being sacrificed too?

Vic sat helplessly, finally free from her family obligations. Free from any obligations. On her own. Being alone out in a swamp wasn't what she'd had in mind.

"So this is my life now." She meandered down the path. "I can steal a boat and go farther, or I can wander on the path until the Dei reapers come through every night." Maybe she could beg them for food or sneak in and out to empty her gicgauge. If GicCorp closely monitored the charging station or credits, they would know she was around collecting blight.

She flicked open her scythe. "Well, swamp, I might as well go down fighting."

No matter what she did, it led to crap. Maybe some kind reaper would find her scythe and use it well. Or maybe it would sink to the bottom of the swamp. The last scythe of the Glass house.

She pressed her forehead to the warm handle. "Give me one more battle."

Her scythe didn't answer either. All these inanimate objects didn't communicate very well.

Vic faced the swamp, her feet planted on the stone and her knees relaxed. The sun set, leaving violet swirls of blight above her. The tall magic lanterns came to life, signaled by the growing darkness, and cast a dim glow on the path. Part of her mind screamed at her that she was a fool, but Vic found it hard to care about anything at the moment. Rage burned through her. Rage at herself for not being enough for her sister to leave her duty. Rage for not being born an imb so she could take her sister's place. Her body went numb as she thought of everything she'd messed up, including judging William for not wanting Samuel to become a mog.

A loud splash sounded in front of her. A dark shape rose out of the water. The waves hit the stone path as it sloshed toward her.

What did she know? Nothing. She knew how to kill mogs, so that was what she would do.

Its large form drew closer. It had a massive head with multiple gleaming eyes that blinked in unison. Two, four, six arms drew themselves out of the water. At the end of each arm, two-fingered hands with long claws protruded. The mog's thick skin drooped from a life spent under water. As always, the smell of a rotted mog overcame the musty swamp. The stench of dead flesh and bone. Vic placed the blade of the scythe between them.

It paused and smacked its large mouth, filled with small teeth good for shredding. Its eyes focused on Vic, like it wondered why there was only one reaper standing there.

"Well, hot stuff, don't let me hold you back. Let's go," Vic taunted the mog. This would be fun.

It clapped its long arms together, trying to grab her. Vic spun around the arms and cut into the mog. Her scythe burned in her hands as it collected blight. Vic let out a laugh. There was no way that her gicgauge could hold enough blight to end this mog. Did it matter?

The mog pushed itself onto the path and blocked her way. It had long legs, and its upper weight caused it to hunch over. With a burst of strange speed, it flung itself forward, using its arms to propel itself.

Vic balked in surprise. The thing had slogged so slowly

in the water. She turned and ran back down the path, though the iron gate would trap her and the guards might already be on the lookout for the woman with the black square brand.

Its feet slapped the stone behind her, and then it yanked on her hair, flinging her backward. She skidded on her back, her hair tangled in the mog's fingers.

It swung its arms and her body followed, ripping the hair out of her head.

Vic screamed as she fell, her landing softened by the swamp. The cold, dirty water felt good on her sore scalp, but her legs sloshed as she tried to back away from the mog. It wanted to stay on the path where it could attack faster.

Her back was to the swamp where she didn't want it to be in case another mog appeared.

She gripped her scythe. The situation wasn't ideal. She couldn't get back onto the path without the mog grabbing her.

Footsteps thudded in the distance. Vic tried to see the figure.

"Sparks, what in the blight are you doing?"

Kai's voice broke through the swamp like a beam of hope. He dove toward the mog, blade flashing, and the mog turned away from Vic to face the new threat. Vic sloshed out of the swamp, pulled herself onto the path, and rolled on the ground. She thrust her scythe at the mog's long legs.

A large gash showed up on its inky skin, and her scythe filled with blight. The mog drooped as she and Kai slashed into it. Finally, a pile of misshapen bones tumbled to the ground.

Vic took in a deep breath. Her clothes dripped water. Her skin would become permanently pruney at this rate.

"Looking good, Sparks." Kai held her in his arms. She let the smell of cedar fill her. "I thought ... I thought you were a radiant."

Vic buried her face in his neck. "I might as well be."

He pushed her shoulders back. "What's this, some weird sacrifice?" He shook her. "What do you think this will prove?" His fingers tightened against her skin.

Vic hugged herself. "What's the point? There isn't much I can do. I lost my sister. I lost my family. I have nothing."

"We aren't done yet." His grip tightened around her arms.

"Oh, are we going to raid GicCorp?"

Kai dropped his arms. "Why not?"

"What?" Was he crazy? Did he think the two of them could take down the organization that ran everything in Verrin?

"I don't think that's what we should do first. But why not?" His gaze grew distant. "I think we both know there's something wrong with GicCorp, but we need to be smart." He glared at her. "Going out into the swamp isn't smart."

Vic snorted. "I wasn't claiming I was. What's this big plan?"

"What if we started with taking over Nyx?"

◈✦◈

VIC FOUND HERSELF ONCE AGAIN SHOWERING AT KAI'S apartment. This place wouldn't be safe forever, but maybe long enough to make a plan.

She put on Kai's clean set of clothes and left her feet bare while her boots dried.

Kai put a bowl of soup in front of her.

She cupped her hands around the warm bowl.

"Bomrosy and I have been trying to figure out if anyone else is in Xiona's inner circle. We keep landing on the same six. The rest of the Order seems to know nothing." He helped himself to a bowl.

That made Vic feel better about Nyx. If she hadn't caught the rogue reapers that night, Xiona might have had more time to expand her inner circle.

"The fact is, I am second in command. If something happened to Xiona ..."

Vic paused in the middle of eating. "You would be in charge."

"I think we can use the power of the Order to infiltrate GicCorp." He tapped his hand against the table.

Vic took a bite and said with her mouth full, "But GicCorp will still come after me."

"True. That's a problem." He focused on his dinner.

She finished the food and leaned back in the chair. "I guess I get to hide out in the cells."

"How many saw you as a radiant?"

"Only all the founders." Tristan had made sure to put her on display. He probably hadn't cared that Emilia wanted to say goodbye. He'd wanted to humiliate her or maybe her father.

Kai looked thoughtful. "Could we play it off as a joke?"

Vic flinched. "That I played a joke on my family?"

She was already infamous for leaving her family. "That would be expected from a spoiled rich girl?" She'd already left them, so what was her reputation as a founder? Though she was mad with her father, she would never do anything to hurt him this much. The rest of the city didn't know that.

"The only ones who know what really happened are

Xiona's inner circle and the Nordics. If you come out as a joke ... what could they do?" He finished his meal and set the bowl on the table.

Vic pointed to the black square on her neck. "There's also this."

Kai frowned and reached out to touch the raw flesh. "This won't be easy."

"You're making it sound like something is possible." Covering up the large black square on her neck would be impossible. What could they do? Paint her skin and then paint on scythes? With how often she got soaked, the paint would rub away.

"Only something painful." He lightly traced the edges of the black brand.

"Great."

That was how Vic ended up lying across Kai's table with a stick in her mouth and a blade to her skin.

She removed the stick. "Shouldn't we have a professional do this?" Her voice sounded higher than normal.

"Too many people will know. There are already too many we need to keep silent."

"Silent, as in kill them?" Coldness filled her stomach.

He stilled. "Is it worse than killing imbs?"

She'd never killed a human before in her life. The mogs had been human once, but she didn't see them as human. She turned her head away, exposing her neck to him.

"I don't know." Her voice was quiet in the empty room.

Kai rubbed something on her skin to numb it.

"The bandages should help with the scarring, but it won't be perfect. I may have had a healer friend steal these for me." He grimaced. "I didn't tell him why I needed imbued bandages to help skin grow," Kai rambled, probably more nervous than Vic. "It just needs to be perfect enough to rebrand you before any other Nyx reapers see you."

"How many times will my neck be burned?" Vic put the stick back in her mouth.

"Hopefully only once more?" Kai took a deep breath and focused on her neck.

Vic turned away from him and swallowed. The cold blade scraped her skin. She cried out and bit down on the stick. Hot tears flowed down her cheeks while Kai skinned her neck. Her warm blood dripped onto the table as he pressed bandages to her neck. Kai couldn't go too deep, but he needed to get down to the layer of her skin that wouldn't show the brand. He followed behind with imbued bandages. Vic tried to think of something else besides her skin. She didn't dare move, or the sharp blade might hit something important. Rawness coated her throat as she forced her neck to remain still. She wanted to jerk away from the torturous blade.

When he finished, he sat back, his hands coated in her blood. "I never want to do that again."

Vic wanted to pass out on the table. "How in the blight do you think I feel?"

They met each other's eyes and laughed.

"Blight take us, we are screwed." Kai's blood-coated hand trembled.

"Most likely."

Kai reached out to put on a new bandage. The magic wore out faster with the amount of healing it needed to accomplish, but he had plenty of bandages to spare. Vic eyed the supply as he went to the sink and washed her blood off his hands before returning. "It's an honor to go down with you."

"I bet you're wishing you'd left me in the canal?" Vic couldn't leave the table, her body immobile from the strain of trying not to move while Kai had skinned her.

"Never." He pulled her up so she sat on the table. "You are trouble, Sparks, but you opened my eyes." He cupped her face, careful to avoid her fresh wound.

She leaned into the heat from his hands and tilted her face up. Their lips met, partly in desperation over what they were about to do. They pushed their bodies closer as their lips melded together. Heat pooled through her as she stayed in Kai's arms. His lips moved slowly against hers, and she pressed against his hard chest. Her fingers trailed down his neck as he kissed her. Tonight, they couldn't know how it would end, but together, they could steal this moment. She allowed herself to get lost in his touches and not think of everything falling apart around her. He kissed her, and he was solid and warm. Too soon, they stopped and held each other while their breathing filled the silence.

They separated, and he pressed his forehead to hers. "I didn't know that skinning you would be such a turn on."

"Just don't tell anyone."

The corners of his mouth turned up. He lightly brushed her hair away from her forehead. "It'll only be the two of us against Xiona and her group. Even if we think more reapers are involved, the reports were only in the sections that matched those six's routes."

"That was stupid on their part." Vic couldn't understand why they hadn't branched out.

"They're most likely only the tester group." He picked up another bandage and put it over her slowly healing skin. "It might be best to keep your hair down so no one can see it if the bandage falls off."

"She really didn't make an announcement or anything?" Vic furrowed her brow. It was unlikely that Xiona wouldn't say anything.

Kai lightly pressed the bandage over her neck. "I think she's waiting for the news to come out about you being a radiant. If you left to become a radiant, it would make more sense than her kicking you out. After all, you're a founder." He glanced at the clock. "We better get moving if we want to capture them before the patrols get back."

Vic shifted from him and instantly missed the warmth. Bits of pain ran down her neck as the bandage pulled on her skin. She placed her hair around her neck and slid up the hood of her sweater.

As she waited, Kai placed manacles and vials containing liquid into his pack.

Her eyebrows rose. "If you're planning on knocking them out, I don't think we can carry all of them back at once."

Kai closed his bag and stood. "If we can lure them here first, it should help with how far we have to carry them. I don't know how we'll move them into the cells under the Order. If only the usual number of reapers are on patrol, we'll still need to worry about the reapers who aren't with them. Then hopefully Xiona will assume that the four we attack tonight were killed by a mog so no one will go looking for them. Xiona will be harder to catch." Kai ran his hand through his hair. "Nyx reapers would only believe a mass attack of mogs took out Xiona."

"Rumor planting. I guess it might work as long as it can't be traced back to us."

They didn't have much time to execute their plan. It needed to happen before news of Vic's transition to a radiant came out so she could claim it was a prank. She couldn't bring much more shame to the family. If the founders cared so much, then Emilia's sacrifice would make up for the Glass name.

He cracked his neck as they got ready to leave. "The best team taken out will be the hardest to believe. This is a normal occurrence for reapers. Xiona has lasted a long time for a reaper."

The cool air hit her face as they left. The blight was now a bloody crimson in the sky. They needed to get beyond the city walls without the guards seeing them. Kai took them down a dark alley and lifted a metal grate in the ground. The smell of sewage hit Vic's nose.

She stepped back. "You're kidding?"

"Ah, Sparks, you haven't had the pleasure of sewage duty yet. You're in for a treat." Kai winked.

"Blight, stone, and a founder's ass." Her nose stung from the stench.

Vic breathed in the fresh air and gestured for him to go first. He disappeared down the tunnel. She placed her hand on the edges, stepped on the slippery ladder, and pulled the grate over her head before descending. She tried to breathe through her mouth, but she could practically taste the foul air. She pulled her hood tighter over her face, burying her nose in the fabric.

Kai walked next to the sewage river, and she followed him in silence. The tunnel was tall, so they had plenty of space. On the side of the sewage river was a stone path. Imbs came down here to fix any problems during the day. Spider webs clung to the dim lights, and claws skittered on the stone as they ran in the tunnels. They didn't speak so they could listen for any approaching mogs. Vic didn't look forward to their trip home, carrying or dragging the other reapers through the muck.

They made it to the grate without interruption. The path through the swamp appeared past the bars. With minimal clanging, Kai broke the lock open. Now they needed to wait for Xiona's patrol to come through the swamp. They would need to jump into the swamp to get to the path, then run after them and take them by surprise. They removed their boots to avoid being weighed down by them. Vic waited in the tense silence. There was nothing else to say. They would either fail or succeed. The hard part would come after the battle. The unsaid truth was that they would try to subdue them but might be forced to defend themselves.

Vic swallowed at the distant sound of footfalls. Kai turned to her and nodded. He squeezed her hand, then got ready to jump. The first two reapers passed at a fast trot. Kai and Vic waited until Xiona and the other reaper had appeared in their wake. Their eyes met. Vic rolled her shoulders and scooted out of the tunnel to grip the edge with Kai. They hung as low as possible so as not to make a loud splash. They both released the edge and fell into the water, landing with her knees bent. Water and mud clung to her as she pushed forward to the path. Kai reached it first and put his hand out to help her out of the water.

Their feet padded silently as they chased after Xiona. Someone shouted from behind them as they spotted Xiona's back. Xiona turned to face them, and Vic froze. She took a quick look behind her. Behind them stood the other members of the group. They blocked the way, each with a grim expression on their faces.

Footfalls sounded behind her, and Vic pulled out her scythe. Kai mirrored her as they put their backs together.

"Seven on patrol?" Kai asked.

Xiona lightly tapped her scythe on the path. It made a dull thud in the swamp. "I keep my allies close. I hoped I was wrong about you, but I had a feeling you wouldn't like the new Order."

Vic's heart pounded. They could have faced four or three reapers, but not seven. Kai tapped her left thigh. They would go through the three reapers and run. Their rebellion had ended in a moment. Now they would both be on the run.

They took off toward the fewer reapers and stuck together to force their way through on the edge of the path. The middle reaper swung at her head, but she blocked the blow with her folded scythe. Kai chose to crash into the reaper on the right side, shoving them into the swamp. Vic's attacker closed in, but Kai and Vic stayed on the run. Vic blocked the scythe, giving Kai the chance to bludgeon the reaper in the head. The reaper fell, and they ran to where they'd left their shoes with the other reapers sprinting down the path.

The wind tore her hood back as she ran.

"We can lose them in the sewers."

Vic didn't answer, just followed as the sound of Xiona and her reapers closed in behind them. They jumped into the swamp. Vic was jolted back as someone grabbed her sweater. She reached up and clawed at the hand, but it held firm. More hands gripped her. Kai turned to see what the commotion was about. Holding out his weapon, he came back.

"Kai, go!" Vic pulled on the neck of her sweater to get some air.

He ignored her. Vic kicked out and made contact. A deep grunt filled her ears, but they didn't drop her. Vic couldn't see Kai, but the hands gripped her tighter and forced her up. The reapers pinned her legs down and her arms behind her. Someone forced her head up. The reaper Kai had attacked lay on the ground, and next to him, Xiona stood in front of Vic with her opened scythe pointed at Kai.

"You're killing your own?" Xiona asked, her voice flat.

"My own doesn't kill those we're supposed to protect. I thought you knew this. You're the one who trained me. You told me that our honor as reapers depends on defending those who are weaker than us!" Vic could hear the pain in his voice.

She couldn't see Xiona's face, but she saw her back stiffen.

"You don't know the lengths I've gone to to protect everyone." Xiona stepped back and nodded to the two reapers holding Vic. The other reaper stood next to Xiona. "Stand down or we will drown her while you watch. The other option, since you are like a son to me, is that I will let you and her live out your days in the cells."

Vic tried to shout as Kai dashed at Xiona, but the reapers thrust her head under the swamp water. Her mouth filled with the muddy water, choking her. Her lungs burned for air, and she futilely tried to squirm out of their death grips. Her head grew foggy, and her body went limp. It became oddly peaceful as the water took her. She faded, and her last thoughts were of her sister as she blacked out.

I'm sorry, Sister.

William couldn't look at his brother as they faced his father when he arrived home. Samuel's vacant face had become his personal ghost. Vic's accusation filled him. The fact that he'd forced the change ate at him.

"I appreciate that you filled in for me today. I think you're ready to take on more responsibilities." His father patted his shoulder, making William feel more like a good pet than a son.

William stared at his father's hand like it was attached to someone he didn't know anymore. He looked back at his father's proud face. "Do you mean turning people against their will? Using our power as a weapon?"

His father's hands rested calmly at his sides. "Son, I think you understand after helping someone like your brother. He was doomed for destruction. Now, he's on that higher plane we all desire."

William pulled at his cuffs. "He didn't desire it, though. We both know that."

His father let out a condescending sigh. "Sometimes, you have to choose the right path for others."

A strange, sick feeling rose in William. "How many people have you made this choice for?"

His father guided Samuel to the table and eyed William. "I don't like your tone. Don't tell me I misjudged your morals?"

A short laugh fell out of William's mouth. "Morals? The ones that say we never change people against their will? Are those the ones you want? Or these new morals where we judge what's best for humans." He shook as he faced his father. The carefully built world they'd made as radiant was collapsing. They thought they were better than everyone. They were pure and soon to be free of magic completely.

In a fit of rage, his father slammed his hand on the table. The dinnerware rattled, and Samuel sat calmly through it all. "I thought you could see how broken people are because of magic. Don't you understand that we can't fight their brainwashed ways? They think life without magic is a horrible fate. Some will see reason, but we must show others."

"How many, Father?" He took a slow breath. He needed an answer.

"Do you think they would rather become a creature that eats people?"

"How many, Father?"

His father meticulously straightened the crooked dinnerware. "Choose your questions wisely, my son."

William laughed. "Or what? You will purify me too? Might as well. I can't stand to look at my brother and feel the shame at taking his life." It was all a lie. A lie. The walls of their home closed in, and the mildew smell filled the air. It was so hard to breathe in there.

"A higher plane!" his father shouted and threw a plate at William.

He didn't dodge, and it smacked him in the shoulder. He welcomed the pain. The plate shattered on the floor.

"I don't know if I believe that anymore." The words fell from his mouth without emotion. Words that challenged his whole faith.

His father stood in front of him. "That magic user founder got to you, didn't she?" He gripped William's shoulders. "We won't marry you to a founder. You're too easily corrupted, it seems."

William brushed away his father's hands, went to Samuel, and grabbed his hand. "Let's go, Sam."

They walked by their father.

"Where are you going? Without purifying blight, you can't charge. You'll become a mog."

"So be it."

His father held up his hands, and William thought he might be the next one purified. He stared down at the man who had lied to him and made him believe they were doing something helpful. Was his whole life a lie? His father dropped his hands and looked away.

William straightened the white cuffs of his radiant jacket and left with his brother following behind.

❦

NOW THAT WILLIAM AND HIS BROTHER WERE HOMELESS, HE wasn't sure what to do. A numbness overcame him as he wandered down the streets. If a mog attacked them, that would solve all his problems. He glanced at his brother, and his jaw tensed.

"I will find out what color the sky is, even if it kills me. Until then, I will protect you." After that? Maybe he would let fate decide which punishment he deserved for forcing the change on his brother.

"Maybe if Vic is at Dei, they will help us?"

Why not? They didn't have any other allies in the city. Vic hated him, but she cared for Samuel. William didn't have any money to rent a place in the slums.

The bitter citrus smell haunted him as they crossed the orchard into Dei territory. William tried to think of anything besides the moment when he'd purified his brother. The sound of the stream mocked him as they passed.

"What's your business out here, light lover?" A stocky woman appeared from behind the line of trees close to the Dei Order.

Against his better judgment, William lashed back. "I'm allowed to walk out here if I want." He could have slapped himself. So much for trying to get help.

She reached for her scythe. "Yes, but today, it might be better if you walk somewhere farther away."

The warning in her tone left no room for questions. Before she chased him away, he thought he would try to find Vic. "I didn't mean to be so defensive." Even though she was the one who had used a slur. "I'm trying to find Vic. She said she might come here and talk to the head of the Order."

The woman crossed her arms. "Many people are trying to find the founder brat."

Right about now, Vic was probably enemy number one

to GicCorp. William didn't know if he should trust this woman, but he also had a feeling he wouldn't get past the gate if he didn't tell her everything.

"I was with Vic at the vital ceremony. I don't know how much you know, but I helped her get away by pretending to turn her into a radiant. It's very important that I talk to her. If she's there, I think she'll want to talk to me." William shifted and tried to look trustworthy. Magic users already hated him, so he wasn't sure how to appear harmless.

The woman stared at him, and the wind in the grass made more noise than their breathing. "Vic isn't here, but I think Nel may want to talk to you."

William tried to keep his face calm. "Really?" He hadn't thought his honesty would work.

The woman sighed and gestured for him to follow her. William tapped Samuel's shoulder, and they trailed after the woman. Past the wall, the courtyard filled with reapers. It looked like they were planning a massive patrol. Various reapers wrapped their hands, and some swung their scythes in mock battle. Thick tension hung around the reapers. It didn't feel like a normal raid, but what did he know?

Inside the building, there was a cacophony of sounds as people rushed around the room. It all centered around a tall blond woman with flashing gray eyes. They cut through the traffic, and his guide went to the woman he assumed was Nel. She whispered something in Nel's ear, and the woman focused on him.

"Come here, radiant."

He pulled his brother up with him. Only a narrow table remained between them. William glimpsed stacks of papers in front of her. They were filled with drawings of buildings.

"Eyes on me," she said, her voice cutting through his snooping.

"Sorry." He didn't know what was happening, but it felt like they were preparing for battle. William laughed to himself. What a ridiculous thought. "I'm looking for Vic. She said she wanted to come here and warn you, but I don't know if she made it."

Nel pushed some papers under others. "What did you want to tell her?"

What did he want to tell her? As this woman stared down at him, he felt silly for coming to Vic for help. "I need help. But if she isn't here, we'll leave."

Nel leaned to the side and took in Samuel. "Is that your buddy?"

William tensed. "My brother."

Someone came up and shoved another paper in Nel's hands. She scanned it, and her jaw tensed. Her voice boomed across the hall. "We go now!"

William flinched and stepped back. "What's going on?"

Nel smiled. "Vic got taken captive. I'm afraid she can't help you." A reaper tossed a scythe at her, and Nel caught it in a smooth movement. She walked around the table, and the commanders fell in line.

William scurried next to the commander. "What can I do?"

Nel adjusted her gear. "Unless you know how to fight, there's nothing you can do. I assume there won't be anyone wanting to get their soul sucked out." She slapped his arm. "Go back home and get help from your daddy."

William couldn't be sure, but he had a feeling she knew who he was. "That isn't an option."

She raised an eyebrow. "Oh? Well, then good luck." Without a backward glance, she ran out with a flood of black-clad reapers behind her. They hardly made a sound as they emptied out into the courtyard.

William and Samuel stood in the deserted hall. "Guess we should lock up?"

He raised his hand and looked at the relic wrapped around his finger. He was useless. The best he could hope for was maybe getting a third-generation wand.

They walked out of the deserted Order. "What should we do?"

His brother cocked his head.

"I will find my purpose with the others," Samuel said, his voice monotone.

William had never given him a task. Even in that he'd failed. Anger rose in him.

"No, Samuel, what do I do?" he yelled in his brother's calm face.

"Do what you must." His blue eyes blinked slowly.

William burst out in laughter and fell to his knees in the dirt-covered courtyard. He buried his face in his hands and screamed into the silence. The eerie sound echoed in the dark. Screams tore from him as he stayed on his knees, a white ghost with his brother standing next to him. His voice raw, he gripped his hair. Then a warm hand touched his shoulder. William faced his silent sentinel.

"Sam?"

Had his brother comforted him without being prompted?

William jumped to his feet and grasped Samuel's shoulders. "Sam?" Samuel's eyes were as calm as ever. "What should I do?"

He blinked. "Do what you must."

William nodded. Nel didn't determine how useful he was. He was the one who'd saved Vic in the first place. He grabbed Samuel's wrist, and they ran.

The aftertaste of rotten swamp water made Vic desperate for a drink. Her head pounded. If her eyes stayed shut, she wouldn't have to see what situation she'd woken in. She could feel a cold stone floor, but she could only smell the stale swamp on her. Her legs and arms were bound tightly, and her legs tingled as blood struggled to get through. Vic cracked one eye open. In the dim light, she couldn't see or hear anyone in the room with her. Without moving, she scanned the room. The cell came into blurry view. Kai lay on the floor, trussed up next to her.

Vic rolled onto her back with a groan. Why had they tied them up if they were going to leave them in a cell?

"Finally awake?" Kai shifted to face her.

Vic tried to twist her feet to get some blood flow. "A great nap." She rolled to face him. "I don't suppose you have a knife they didn't find?"

"In my boot, but I needed to wait for you to get it."

"I guess I'll just have to save your ass." They shuffled

across the dirty stone floor so Vic could reach his boot. "Which one?"

"My left. It's in the outer layer."

Vic paused. "Why did you need a knife so well hidden?"

She felt along his boot, and her fingers passed a flattened seam along his foot.

"I'm not sure. My sister gave it to me for my birthday, and it became more of a lucky charm. I needed my larger blades, and I couldn't carry it. I didn't want her to think she got me something I couldn't use in battle."

Vic carefully put her fingers in his boot. She didn't want to cut open her fingers. "If we live through this, I'll give your sister all the strawberries in Verrin."

"Me too."

The covered blade finally slid out of his boot. Her stiff fingers struggled to get the cover off while Kai shuffled back down so his first ropes would be at her hands. With the blade free, she cut the rope around his arms. The first rope snapped open, freeing Kai's hands. He slid down, and she freed his torso.

Kai took the knife from her and swiftly cut through her rope. She welcomed the pain as blood rushed back into her hands and arms. He cut through the ropes binding her legs and then his.

They stretched out their limbs, then faced the iron bars.

"Now what?" Vic asked. She'd already gone through this once. Was it only this morning she'd left the cell?

"Unfortunately, I think all we can do is wait. I didn't know these cells were here, so I don't think anyone else knows either."

"Last time, I had to pretend to be a radiant to leave." She

swallowed. "I think this time they might bring in William's father. I think it'll work out better for them if I don't disappear." Kai's hand gripped hers as she continued. "And you ..."

"Will be left here." He scanned the walls and bars as if assessing his new home.

"Kai ... I can't become ... that ..." She couldn't claim to know what a radiant thought, but it seemed worse than death. Vic eyed the knife and pleaded with him with her expression.

He gripped the knife in his other hand. "No, you can't ask that of me."

"If you make the cut deep enough, they won't be able to stop the bleeding." Shame filled her for asking this of him. "Would you want to become a mindless human? My body will be alive, but my mind will be gone? They'll use me against my family." She gripped his hand tighter. "I know this is asking a lot—"

"Asking a lot? You're asking me to slit your throat. Asking me to live with that memory while I rot down here."

Vic hugged herself. "You might get out, but if they bring a radiant down here to purify me, I'll let you decide ... after. I want you to know my wishes before I can't tell you them anymore."

Kai let out a shaky breath. "I can't promise you, Sparks. I'm sorry. I'll try, but I can't promise."

"I understand." She was giving up. There were no other words for it. Xiona wouldn't make a mistake this time. Vic would fight until they sucked her soul from her body, but even a fool could see this was the end. "If you get out and your family is safe"—she took a deep breath—"will you help my sister?"

"Please don't give up so easily." He glared at the blade. "I wish I'd stayed tied up instead of talking about this. It isn't over yet."

"For me it is." Her blood pumped through her ears. Images of the turned radiant flashed in her mind. Their empty eyes and smiles. Was it so bad to die rather than become that?

His shoulders slumped, and with those words, she defeated him. She reached for him, but the sliding sound of stone forced her to turn. A flash of white cloth appeared in the doorway, and she whimpered. Without a thought, she snatched the knife out of Kai's hand. Her heart beat frantically as she turned away before Kai could stop her. The cold blade calmed her down, and she took a deep breath.

"Sorry." She pressed it against her skin.

A body tackled her from behind. She writhed against him. "I can't! I can't become one of them!"

Warm hands cupped her face and forced her to look into a pair of startled blue eyes.

"William?"

"What do you think you're doing? Trying to kill yourself without putting up a fight?" His grip tightened on her face. "What made you give up so quickly? There's still hope."

His heavy body pressed her into the stone floor. Vic grew limp and let the knife clatter to the floor. "Hope? My sister wouldn't come with me. My Order is led by a murderer, and my city is as corrupt as the blight we fear." She'd fought to get her sister to follow her, but she'd been wasting her time. "How much more pointless can my life get?"

William shifted off her and pulled her up. "You told me I didn't have a right to decide what was right for my brother.

What gave you the right to decide what's right for your sister?"

Samuel stood in the cell's gateway.

Vic sighed. "That's low, throwing my words back at me." She grinned crookedly. "I didn't want her to leave me." A warm tear tracked down her cheek. She'd left her home and fought to be a reaper, only to hold her sister back. Her sister was right: she didn't trust her. But could her sister see what was happening? "We both thought we were saving the other. Blight take us and our stubbornness."

Kai put his arm around her. "This whole time, you only had your sister in mind. I think she knew that."

"I still feel uneasy about Haven. It wasn't what Tristan said, but how he said it. Am I overreacting because I'll miss my sister?"

Kai tilted his head. "We've only scratched the surface of what's wrong in Verrin." He sounded tired. They all wanted to protect their families, but it was proving impossible.

William nodded. "Why don't we look into it, then? I'll help you."

"Thank you." Vic glanced between the brothers. "What are you doing here?"

"I'd like to know that too." Kai stood back quietly, and he picked up the knife Vic had dropped. He stored the knife away, and he didn't meet Vic's gaze.

"We should leave. Dei is here, and they're attacking Nyx."

"What?" Kai didn't wait. He burst out of the cell and ran up the set of stairs.

"You couldn't have led with that?" Vic ran after Kai. "We really didn't have time for all the chatting!" she called behind her.

"I didn't know you'd be down here trying to stab your-self!" William shouted after her.

She assumed he'd keep up. What was Dei doing? They didn't know that only a few reapers were turning humans into mogs. Dei might kill innocent reapers. She'd lost sight of Kai, but she heard the clash of battle before seeing the carnage. The hall was filled with the shouts of black-clad reapers as they rushed past. No one noticed her as they ran. She couldn't stand around without a weapon.

"What are you going to do?" William asked.

"We have to stop this fight. Most Nyx reapers don't know what's going on." She stared at him. "You couldn't wear anything besides white?"

"I might be the only safe one. I don't think they'll aim at me."

"I don't think they'll care if they kill you since you shouldn't be here." Didn't he understand how much magic users hated the radiant? Now she'd need to protect the brothers.

William's jaw tightened. "I'm the only one who knew how to get in the cells. You're welcome."

Vic shook her head and went toward Xiona's office. She doubted Xiona would trust Bomrosy again with Vic's scythe. She ducked past the fighting. She needed to find Nel and explain. The Nyx reapers had no reason to listen to her. Kai was the only one who could stop this on the Nyx side.

She reached Xiona's office, and the door hung loosely on its hinges. Dei had gotten here first. Vic hoped that Xiona had gotten taken before she could hide her scythe. Vic darted into the room, William still following. "You know it won't be easy for me to protect you."

"Says the person I saved twice," William muttered.

Vic left him alone. Who was she to tell him where to go? If he wanted to get stabbed, that was his choice. "Maybe you should tell Samuel to wait for you."

Vic rushed through the office and let out a happy yelp when she spotted her weapon. Kai's weapon stood next to it. The fool had run off without a weapon. She grabbed them both.

"I tried, but he won't listen."

Vic didn't have time to understand what that meant for a radiant. She needed to find Kai before he got himself killed. "I need to get to Nel. Did you see her?"

"Most of the reapers are out in the courtyard."

Vic ran out of the office. Her boots pounded against the stone floor. She held a folded scythe in each hand. She slipped on the ground and saw red smears of what could only be blood. Vic gritted her teeth and ran. The bitter scent of copper mixed in the air as she made her way to the courtyard. Most of the reapers stayed engaged in their own battles in the hall. Maybe only ten battles at most. She forced herself to keep moving past bodies on the ground. What was Nel thinking? She'd claimed she didn't want a war, yet here she was attacking. Vic's blood pounded in her ears. She'd known that trusting Nel was foolish, but she admired how Nel looked after her reapers. Was this a power play, or did she really want to stop Xiona?

"Vic, help!" a Nyx reaper called out to her.

As Vic ran by, she slammed her folded scythe against the Dei reaper's legs. He fell down with a thud. Before the other reaper could kill them, Vic raised the scythe and thwacked it against the Dei reaper's head. She looked at the Nyx reaper. "Let's not get a high body count if we don't have to."

She raised her brows at her. Who was Vic that the reaper would listen?

Vic sighed and continued to jog. She had no power here. She guided her weird radiant parade out the main doors. She froze at the sight of reapers fighting. Dei outnumbered them since Nyx only recruited one reaper every quarter and their numbers were in the eighties. Hundreds of black-clad bodies fought in the stone courtyard. Clangs and shouts echoed in the courtyard. In the dim light, only a brief glance at a brand could tell friend from foe.

"Do you see Kai?"

"No, but I see Nel." William pointed to the right, at Xiona and Nel locked in battle.

"I don't suppose I can convince you to stay here?" She didn't want him to get hurt. This wasn't his fight.

William looked out over the battle. "I think I might be safer with someone who knows me from Nyx."

He had a point. "Don't get killed, light lover."

"Wasn't planning on it." William reached back to grab Samuel's arm.

Vic stayed close to the edge of the battle as she took off toward Nel. It might be too late to do anything. These two Orders wouldn't forget this attack. If all of Nyx had been at fault, she wouldn't have been so fast to stop this, but it was her fault for going to the Dei commander. Nel had sounded like she wouldn't take any action, but now here she was, killing blameless reapers. Vic bit the inside of her cheek as she dodged fighting reapers. When she could, she tried to knock them out. At most, they'd have a headache, but at least they'd still be alive.

A tall blond male stepped in her path. "Ah, the founder bitch."

It was the man from the trials, Yaris. He had the black X of Dei on his pale neck.

"Nice to see you again. Please move, I'm going to Nel."

He smirked. "I'm sure you are, Nyx bitch."

She glared. "Okay, I'm a bitch, but you need to move. I know Nel, and I need to get to her." Couldn't he just understand?

"Go around. He won't listen," William whispered.

"You think?" Vic pushed to the side, but Yaris stepped in front of her and lowered his scythe.

"I think it's time to see who the best reaper is."

Vic wanted to scream in frustration, but she tossed Kai's scythe to William instead. Then she flicked opened her weapon. "Fine, but you're wasting my time over a personal grudge."

Yaris didn't respond and swung his scythe in a massive motion aimed at her neck. Vic met it with her weapon and stepped aside so his scythe slid down hers, his blade locking with hers. She pulled with her entire body, whipping his scythe out of his hands.

"Grab it, Will."

She didn't turn to see if William listened and swung her blade, aiming it at Yaris's chest.

"Wow, you've proved yourself," Vic sneered. That battle had only taken a second.

He stepped forward, and Vic pressed the blade against his chest. It cut through his black shirt.

"Don't push me, Yaris. Leave while you can. Why don't you come back after you've trained for a few years?"

He left, but not before yanking his scythe out of William's hands.

Vic refocused on the fight as Nel hit the ground. Blood

spurt from her mouth as she rolled onto her side. Vic bowled through the battle, not caring if she got hurt. Xiona stood over Nel with her scythe raised. Vic wouldn't make it in time.

All she could do was watch as Xiona ran Nel through with her blade. Then, from the side, Kai charged out of a throng of bodies toward Xiona. He still didn't have a weapon, but Vic saw the flash of a blade as he attacked her. He was going after her with his tiny knife.

"Blight take him!" Vic pumped her legs to get to him.

One of Xiona's reapers came after Kai and pushed him aside, but Vic saw Xiona flinch as she recovered from the surprise of his attack.

Vic jumped between Xiona and Kai. She hoped William would get Kai his scythe.

"How many times do I need to get rid of you?" Xiona flicked her scythe, and blood spattered the ground from her blade.

Vic braced her feet. "Probably just one more time."

Xiona laughed. "Fine, then. I'll trust your word."

They eyed each other, then their scythes clashed. Vic's arms vibrated from the blows. Xiona wouldn't fall for her tricks like Yaris had. Vic remained on the defensive as Xiona closed in, waiting for Vic to leave an opening. Xiona used the end of her scythe as much as the blade, something Vic's trainer had drilled into her.

Xiona's blade flashed in front of her, and Vic stepped back to avoid it. She couldn't look behind her, but she could hear Kai fighting the other reapers.

The wood smacked over and over. Xiona's eyes gleamed. She thought she'd already won. Then Vic faltered on a crack in the stone ground. Vic tried to dodge the fall of the wooden handle, but it thudded against her arm. The bone snapped, and Vic shouted as she pushed herself back to avoid more blows.

She held her scythe in her left hand, but her swings had become clumsy. Xiona's blade rose, and Vic knew she couldn't stop it. She stepped back again, but white cloth caught the corner of her vision. Samuel stood next to her, gazing at the fight before him. Vic shouted in surprise. Xiona would not divert her blow; she would hit Samuel. Vic pounced, dropping her scythe. It clattered to the ground. She grabbed him with her left arm and pulled him down to the stone ground.

The blade missed them, but Xiona stood over them. She sneered at Samuel. "A bit of cleanup is due." Smeared blood covered her scythe.

With horror, Vic saw her thrust her blade at Samuel's neck. Had Xiona lost her mind? Samuel was helpless. Why kill him first? With her bare hand, Vic blocked the blade and gripped it in her left hand. She gasped as it cut through her flesh. Her blood ran hot down her arm.

Behind Xiona, William glowed white, looking like a spirit. Vic kicked at Xiona's legs to push her toward William. Xiona stumbled back. Vic released the blade.

It was a horrible choice, but she needed to be stopped, and Vic had no more body parts to sacrifice. "Stop her, Will!"

William stood still, his wide gaze telling her he didn't have a weapon. Vic held up her bloody left hand. His mouth opened, and he raised his hand in a surreal moment.

Xiona had recovered, but William gripped the back of her neck. It only took a moment for the anger in Xiona's eyes to be replaced with a strange calm. Xiona's scythe dropped to the ground, and she smiled peacefully while the war raged around her.

Vic's mouth dropped open. Xiona's follower screamed at William and charged. Kai ran him through with his blade, done with his other battle. Vic shuffled to standing. A ring of dead bodies surrounded them.

23

VIC

The clang of reaper scythes drew Vic out of her trance. She ran toward Nel and fell to her knees at the commander's side. Her right arm dangled uselessly at her side.

Nel held her hands over the open wound, and Vic placed her hand over the leader's.

"So this isn't looking great," Vic muttered. She could feel the warm blood over Nel's cold hands.

Nel coughed, and more blood bubbled out of her mouth. Vic thought she saw the commander smile.

While Vic held her hand over the wound, she scanned the surrounding battle. Reapers retained their own healers, but she couldn't see anyone pulling aside the injured. "I thought you didn't care what Xiona did? Not all of Nyx was bad."

If Nel understood her, she gave no signal. Her eyes faded and lost focus. The gray color dulled until life left them completely. Vic closed her eyelids and choked back a sob. This shouldn't have happened.

Hands pulled her away from Nel's body and wrapped around her. Her nose filled with the scent of clean linen. She folded into William and let herself grieve, then took an unsteady breath and backed away. William's white clothes had smears of blood down the front.

"Kai?"

"He went to find a healer." He took in the body of the Dei leader. "The battle has died down, and all the healers are trying to manage."

"Commander!" the shout sounded over the cries of the wounded. Becks plowed through the fallen reapers and knelt at Nel's side. She glared at Vic. "This is your fault."

"You don't hold back, do you?" But Becks was right. She's the one who'd asked Nel to stop Nyx. All these bodies were her responsibility.

Becks rose and faced Vic. She drew her blood-stained scythe. Vic heard William stand next to her. A nice thought, but he couldn't purify everyone. That idea made her uncomfortable.

Vic folded her scythe with a loud snap. She raised her arms to her sides. "I think we lost enough reapers today."

Bodies clothed in black filled her vision. The courtyard of Nyx had been turned into a graveyard.

A muscle in Becks's jaw jumped. "We only came to get Xiona, but all the stupid reapers attacked on Xiona's call. We tried not to kill them." Becks took in the fallen around her. "We came to help you and your commander." Grief replaced the anger in her voice.

Vic didn't know what to say. She already blamed herself for all this.

Becks folded her scythe and put it in her harness. She picked up their fallen leader and signaled for the Dei reapers to gather the wounded. Then they ran out into the night, leaving their dead. Vic knew that if they stayed, it would only lead to more fighting until they explained that they'd only been trying to stop Xiona. Then, hopefully, the Nyx reapers would burn the Dei reapers with honor.

William stayed next to her. Kai didn't come back. "W-we need to help the wounded."

He went to the nearest bodies to check for signs of life. Samuel and Xiona followed him like ghosts.

"Ah, you might want to tell Xiona to go somewhere ... away ..." If the reapers saw their leader in that state, they would kill William. Vic shifted her gaze away from the leader's blank face. No more silent calculating, only the happy gaze of a radiant.

He whispered to the ex-commander, and she ran off in the dark. Vic hoped no one had seen what had happened. She checked the reaper nearest her for a pulse. With Xiona gone, they'd accomplished their goal. Kai would be the commander now. The thought didn't fill her with relief but weariness.

"You need to get your arm treated first. Also, the bleeding should be stopped."

"Oh." Vic stared down at her broken arm. She couldn't feel any pain. Her left hand was still gashed open and dribbling blood all over the ground. Her brain felt foggy.

William guided her to the healers set up in the dining room. The long tables had been pushed to the side and makeshift cots now covered the space. Vic flinched as the healer sanitized, sewed up, and bandaged her left hand.

The healer gave her something for the pain while she wrapped Vic's right arm in low-grade imbued bandages. "We need to save the others for life and death situations. In a few days, we'll have more bandages."

Vic nodded, and the healer set her arm. William held her as she convulsed in pain. When it was over, she lay still, sweat dripping down her face. William cleaned her up.

"Stay here and I'll help with the bodies."

Vic shook her head and wobbled to her feet. "I can still walk. I'll go until I pass out."

William let her be foolish. He might understand her more than she thought. His expression softened, and he followed her outside to the scene of the battle. They wandered among the bodies to find the wounded and left the dead for now.

A woman reaper gave off a death rattle, and with the help of another reaper, Vic carefully picked her up and swiftly took her to the main hall. They found an empty cot, and a reaper ran forward with imbued bandages. They would try to keep the reaper alive while healers were busy with other injured.

The reaper looked over the injured woman and sighed. "We're running out of imbued bandages. I've been ordered to ration them."

"Follow your orders. If the ration runs out, it runs out. Don't feel guilty for doing your job." How had she become a counselor to this random reaper? She didn't want that job. Deciding who got to live or die and who got more magic to heal? They all got an equal amount, and if they lived, they lived. Her arm throbbed painfully, reminding her she was lucky she hadn't needed higher-grade bandages.

Vic turned to go look for more reapers. The task gave her the single-mindedness she needed to keep going. Otherwise, she would sit on the ground and not move.

During the night, she passed William a few times. He stuck out in his white uniform, stained with blood. He always scanned her to make sure she was okay. With his Samuel shadow silently following him, the reapers never questioned him as he brought in the wounded.

Vic laid the dead together along a side wall. She didn't want to count the bodies. Too many from both sides had died, but more from Dei. Once the wounded situation stabilized, they would burn the dead.

Slow and steady, they sorted through the dead and wounded. Vic didn't know most of them. Only a few weeks had passed since she'd joined Nyx. She swallowed and realized she didn't know the people in her squad.

The sun rose, and the blight glowed a vivid yellow. The courtyard now only contained the dead. Crimson blood stained the stone, turning a rusty brown as it dried.

"Is this our fault?" Kai's voice cut through the silence.

Vic hugged herself. "I think we're supposed to blame Xiona." She turned to face him. His face was pale in the morning sun. "I'm having trouble doing that."

"I have to speak to them. I don't know what to say." His clear gaze focused on Vic. "I'm starting my leadership with lies."

"You can tell them what she was doing. From there, I don't know what to do about GicCorp."

"We need to tell them."

"Then what?" Vic stepped over a drying puddle of blood. "We fight the whole city? What happens without GicCorp? We'll become mogs."

Kai ran his hands over his head. "I know. I guess we need to look into GicCorp. I'm getting the sense that we don't know everything, starting with the vitals."

A painful pressure filled Vic's chest as she thought of Emilia. Now that her sister resided behind the stone wall, what would she do if they uncovered more information about the vitals that wasn't good? No one knew how the magic was purified. Once the imb entered, they connected to the magic and couldn't leave it. "They aren't telling us something, and now my sister's involved."

Kai placed his warm hand on her shoulder. "We'll find out what's going on and help your sister."

"Commander?" A reaper appeared next to them. "Everyone would like to talk to you." He gave Vic the side-eye.

"Understood." He gestured to Vic. "Let's go."

Vic followed them to the dining area, now medic ward. Healers wandered among the wounded, but their urgency had slowed. Those who weren't seriously wounded stood to the side, their gaze on Kai and Vic as they entered.

Their gazes felt harsh. Vic knew they wondered why Dei had attacked, and they might want to launch a counterattack. She didn't know what the ramifications of this battle would be. The lack of city officers was disturbing. Why weren't they here? Had no one told them?

Kai continued to the front of the room and stopped, taking a moment to scan the reapers. His stance only portrayed confidence in his new role as leader.

His clear voice echoed in the room as he said, "This attack on Nyx was unexpected. I know we're all angry over what happened to our fellow reapers." Grim silence greeted him as they listened. "There was a discovery a few weeks ago, and I've been caught in the middle of an economic game played by Xiona. Most of you are innocent, and when you saw your leader under attack, you acted with loyalty and honor."

Kai paused. "I'm sorry they left you in the dark, and I'm sorry that because I wanted to keep my family safe, I didn't stand up to Xiona until I had a plan. So I'm going to let you know what happened. This is why Dei attacked us."

The reapers shifted as they listened. Vic didn't know how they would react.

"I found her and six others cutting gicorbs out of people in the city."

An angry roar filled the room.

Kai raised his hand, and they fell silent. "You know what this means. When I confronted her about it, she claimed she did it to boost our numbers and create more blight collection for Nyx."

Vic backed up against the wall and slid down. Disappointment filled her. He couldn't out GicCorp yet, but seeing the anger on the reapers' faces, she wanted them to know the truth.

"I believe no amount of money is worth more than human life. Our purpose is to collect blight to protect people, not to advance our rank." Kai took one more look around the room. "If you don't believe this, we'll need to have a talk. Dei found out what Xiona was doing, and they attempted to stop her." He sighed. "I don't agree with how they went about it. We lost many good reapers who didn't understand. For that, I'm sorry, and I will work to clear our name and ensure nothing like this happens again."

A storm of reaper voices rose as Kai finished. He was immediately surrounded, and Vic slipped out the door. She was a new reaper. It was better that they didn't know about her involvement in what had happened. A blood-stained William greeted her outside.

"You look like a mess."

The usually pristine William straightened his cuffs. Vic would have found that funny if they hadn't been hauling dead bodies.

"I suppose black covers the blood better."

She grabbed his wrist, and her left hand smarted from the motion. "Let's go get cleaned up."

Vic guided him to Kai's room. She let him shower, then handed him some of Kai's clothing. He hesitated to take the black garments.

"Would you rather put on your blood-stained white clothes, light lover?"

His expression fell as he took the clothes. "I don't think I should wear white anymore."

He'd forced the change on two people now. Words of comfort didn't enter her mind. Everyone's beliefs had been shattered in only a few days. "Why don't you and Samuel stay here until we can get something figured out?"

He nodded, and she went to wash the blood off her skin.

Vic let the warm water pound against her head as she stared at the wall. Her wounded arm and hand made cleaning herself difficult, but she got all the blood down the drain.

Xiona was no longer in charge of Nyx. This didn't feel like a victory. Dread filled her that this was only the beginning of their battle.

❧ 24 ❧

WILLIAM

He looked odd in black, maybe because his tanned skin looked pale. He lifted his hands, but there were no cuffs to straighten. They'd borrowed more of Kai's clothing for Samuel. William took his clothes to the area for burning.

The reapers who weren't seriously wounded worked in a well-organized rhythm as they put together pyres. A few glanced his way and gave him and Samuel looks. Some nodded to him, maybe in recognition of his helping with the wounded last night.

William didn't want to stay. He was an outsider. He trailed up the steps to find Vic's room. He knocked quietly.

"Come in."

He opened the door, and her back was to him as she toweled her hair. The morning light came through the window and hit her hair just right, making it look like burning flames. Without asking, he sat down in the only chair. Samuel stood behind him until William gestured for him to sit on the bed. A gray cat jumped in his lap, and he absentmindedly stroked the fur. The cat purred and made his hand vibrate.

"What's the plan, light lover?" She tried to sound teasing, but William could hear the tiredness in her voice.

What was the plan? "Is the swamp still an option?"

"Probably not."

The cat jumped down from his lap. To William's surprise, the cat snuggled into his brother, and Samuel pet the cat with a smile on his face.

"What do you want to do?" Vic asked.

"I don't know." He hated that he'd become a beggar in a single day. "I suppose I could find a wand." He slowly twirled the ring on his hand. "I don't want to purify anyone until ... until I find out more about what my father is doing." He didn't want to use magic either. Why did it have to be one or the other?

Vic frowned. "What exactly is he doing?"

William explained that he thought his father was purifying the unwilling.

"Blight and stone," Vic swore. "Just what we need. More people to prey on in the city. Don't they realize that they'll soon run out of people to control?"

"I don't think that's a problem for my father as much as it will be a problem for GicCorp." His father didn't want magic anymore. If GicCorp found out, there would be problems.

Vic rubbed her forehead. "I'm so happy to live in such wonderful times. We get to be mogs, radiant, or homeless and starving." She let out a manic laugh.

"Do you think your father or any of the other founders would help?"

"Maybe, unless they're in on it. Who knows anymore?" Vic plopped into her chair.

William brushed the cat hair off his borrowed pants. "I guess it's time to dig."

"I think so."

"We may find something worse."

"I wouldn't expect anything less." Vic stretched out her legs. "Do you need help finding a place?"

"Is your old apartment for rent?"

She gave him another grin that made his heart pound. "I think Kai has a better option. But you may want to get a wand. I have a feeling credits will be sparse."

"How far I've fallen." What was he without the rules and structure of a radiant?

"Us magic users will do that to you." Vic winked.

He smiled. It was strange to smile after all that had happened, but his chest felt lighter around her. "I was bound to be corrupted."

Vic stood, and he grabbed his brother to follow the fire girl out the door to his new life.

Vic's stomach turned at the smell of burning human flesh. Too many reapers from both Nyx and Dei burned today. Kai quieted talks of revenge. Everyone waited for officers to flood the building, but they never came. The burning of reapers was a private affair, mostly because a reaper ravaged by a mog was no sight a family member wanted to see. Kai would be tasked with telling families that their loved ones were dead.

News of the reaper battle hadn't reached the newspapers either. Gray ashes fluttered down and coated the reapers' black clothing. Becks from Dei stood off to the side, along with a few from her Order. Despite a few looks, Vic didn't think they were in danger of a fight. Not on a burning day.

Reapers faced death every day. No one had thought it would come from other reapers. The embers died down, and the Dei reapers left. They would sweep the ashes, and then a farmer would pick them up and take them to mix into the soil. Would they mention that the quantity was greater than normal?

Vic's gaze followed the Dei reapers to the gate. In the quieting smoke, she made out a tall figure. Tristan Nordic made his way toward her, and Vic clenched her fists at her sides. She took a slow breath. He appeared in front of her, and somehow, the ashes of the reapers had avoided his clothing.

"Nice to see you alive and well, Victoria." His hands rested on his lapels. "I hope you don't plan on playing any more pranks on your family. Your father was quite hurt by that radiant display."

Her fingernails dug into her hands, and the healing wound on her palm smarted. "I'll try to control myself." She took it that Tristan was letting her get away with the story —for now.

"What did you want, Nordic?" Kai asked, his arms crossed over his chest. Vic couldn't read his face, but it was as though he'd expected Tristan here today.

"I think it's best if we talk in your brand-new office, commander." He put his arm out to his side, signaling for Kai to lead the way. "And your little partner can join you." His stare zeroed in on Vic.

Kai didn't respond but turned to walk to Xiona's old office. He held open the door for them and shut it after Tristan had entered behind Vic. Tristan sat down and faced Kai's desk. He folded his hands over his knees and waited for Kai and Vic to sit.

Vic stayed to the side of her chair, with Tristan in her line of sight.

Once Kai sat down, Tristan talked. "I'll get to the point. We need not lie to each other here."

Vic gripped the edge of the chair to give her palms a break. Her stitches pulled at her skin.

"I gave Xiona a choice between making mogs or losing all funding from GicCorp," Tristan calmly said. "You should know that what reapers collect from credits isn't enough to survive on. Even if you pulled down multiple mogs a day, you'd still struggle to feed your people in the way you're used to. Also, let's not mention the deal you get for food purchases. We contained the information about your little civil war with Dei. You'll find there is nothing in the city we don't know about." Tristan sat back in his chair. She wanted to slap the relaxed expression off his face. His mood would fit a tea party better than this situation.

He continued, "We're surrounded by swamp and trapped in a city, and my family holds all the power. You can either get in line or have your little rebellion." With clarity, Vic knew that the reapers meant nothing to him. They would be controlled or wiped out.

"We could tell everyone what you're doing," Vic said, testing the waters to see how Tristan would respond.

He chuckled. "Go for it, Victoria. I'm sure everyone will believe you. The spoiled founder persona doesn't benefit you. It would be a shame to pull another one of your pranks."

"All the Nyx reapers know what you're doing."

"Do they? Or do they think it was Xiona?" His face remained a perfect mask. He already knew everything.

A muscle in Kai's cheek jumped. The reapers were only beginning to trust him. It would be a disaster if he admitted he'd lied.

Tristan studied his nails. "You might be successful in getting the truth out to a few people, but honestly, what power do you have?" His eyes gleamed. "You better play it safe and keep your thoughts to yourself until you have a better hand to play."

Vic shifted in the chair. "Our choices are to continue to make mogs or lose GicCorp money?"

"I always knew you were a smart one." Tristan stood and brushed off imaginary ash from his jacket. "I'll take your answer now."

Kai pushed himself up from his chair. "I think you already know my choice."

Tristan's eyes dulled. "You're a fool, but I knew you would be. These people you protect won't support you."

"That's their choice, then," Vic replied.

"Dear Victoria, have you heard from your sister since the ceremony? She's doing so well as a vital. You should be proud to have a hero for a sister. She's the reason you can charge and not become a mog. Isn't it wonderful?" Tristan's tone dripped with honey.

Vic lunged at him, and in a moment, his wand appeared. A force like a wall hit her and threw her back. She lay on the ground, shocked. What had he done? He didn't imbue anything.

Tristan placed his wand back in his jacket, his dark expression calm. "You have no idea what you're dealing with, little heir. Stay behind these walls and try to survive without support."

With that statement, he left them.

Vic pulled herself up and used the wall to support herself. Her right arm throbbed from the blow.

"What in the blight was that magic?" Kai asked.

The cold wall helped Vic stop shaking. "I don't know." She faced Kai. "I need to get my sister out of there. I know she wants to save me, but I don't think the vitals are there to purify the magic."

Kai pulled her to him, and she listened to his steady heartbeat. "We'll get her back."

Vic nodded against his chest.

Emilia, what did we do? Vic asked herself.

"I need to see what we have in storage. We'll need to ration our supplies."

"To think I wanted to join an Order so I wouldn't have to starve."

They sadly smiled at each other, and Kai left her alone.

Vic wandered out into the courtyard.

Vic walked past reapers sweeping up the ash. Her feet took her out of the Order. The sound of the canal echoed in her head. The scythe bumped against her back.

It didn't matter how long she walked. She let her mind empty. The wall of glass rose in front of her. It gleamed in the sun. Vic pushed open the gate, and her feet stepped into the courtyard. The same glass fountain greeted her.

Vic hugged her chest as the ache grew inside her. The empty home surrounded her like a coffin welcoming her into the afterlife. Her vision burned, but she climbed the steps to her sister's room.

She pushed the door open. A beautiful figure made of glass greeted her. Anger, shame, and defeat raged inside her as she saw herself and Emilia immortalized.

"Why? Why didn't you follow me?"

"You know why." Her father's voice greeted her.

Vic focused on him. She hadn't seen him in the room. "Do you think vitals are really keeping us all alive?"

"There are things that I hoped I wouldn't have to tell you."

"You need to make a choice, Father." Whatever his plan, he needed to let her in if he didn't want to lose her.

"I know." He was acting differently. Or was it normal?

"I will get her back."

"Good."

Vic stood in silence with her father, their eyes filled with the two sisters who had tried but failed to protect each other.

ALSO BY MARI DIETZ

FOUNDERS SERIES

Reaper's Order

Radiant's Honor November 2020

Magic's Curse Spring 2021

THANK YOU

If you found any enjoyment from this book please consider leaving a review. For every review I get, a puppy gets snuggles.

But in all seriousness, thank you!

ACKNOWLEDGMENTS

It feels surreal to publish my first book. It's funny to think that this series wasn't going to be my first. I had a lot to learn, and I decided to go with a shorter series before taking on a longer project.

The best part of this series is that it wasn't even on my radar. I saw this beautiful pre-made cover at Ravenborn Covers on Facebook and thought, *Why do you need a reaper cover? That isn't even in your five-year plan.* But I couldn't get this cover out of my mind, so I took a chance and messaged her. Then I came up with a story to match the cover.

The world of Verrin and the characters that populate it came to life. So, many thanks to Ravenborn for the amazing cover for this book and the next two.

I'd also like to thank my wonderful editor. My grammar is a bit of a chaotic mess. She put so much time into this book, and even though it isn't her job to teach me how to self-edit, I find myself catching more of my mistakes... until I form a new habit. Thank you so much, Elizabeth (arrowheadediting.com), for all the hard work you put into helping me make my dreams come true.

Also, to my amazing Alpha readers, thank you. A huge shout out to those who put up with the messy drafts and point out errors.

Angela, Nicollee, Mary, Sarah, Grace, Helen, Bryan, and even my mom—without you, I would have had too much self-doubt to finish. Thank you for your honest feedback. It really helped make this book the best it could be.

A few years ago, I wouldn't have thought this was possible. When you write, you feel like you're isolated. I have my ups and downs, but thanks to my video chats, I don't feel so alone. Thank you Katie, Tanner, Chris, Mary, Jessica, Justin, and Bobbie for pushing me. It helps knowing I'm not alone in the struggle of writing.

To the wonderful Fire Hazards that help me get unstuck and to the Women Warriors that make me challenge myself and not take the easy plot path, without you, I wouldn't have gotten this far. I'm so excited to keep growing with you and strive to craft better stories.

To be a bit silly, I have to thank my number-one writing buddies, Fabio, Yona, Casanova, and Pixel. Whenever I feel discouraged, my sweet dogs are there to let me snuggle them.

And, to Stacy Rourk, The Blurb Doctor for helping me fine tune my blurb.

Last of all, I'd like to thank you, the reader. Maybe you picked up this book because of the awesome cover or maybe someone recommended it to you. Thank you for letting me share this world with you, and I hope you stay until the end of the journey with me.

Thank you all so much. I am extremely blessed. This is only the beginning.

ABOUT THE AUTHOR

Mari Dietz wrote her first poem about crickets when she didn't even know how to write. Her mom typed it up for her on an old typewriter. From then on, she was a goner to the written word. Over the years, she fell in love with the world of fantasy and thought maybe one day she could write something too.

She took a few side roads and got a major in Theater and English. Then she somehow ended up teaching in South Korea for three years. Now back in the middle of nowhere, she teaches Creative Writing and writes her own books in her "spare time," when not distracted by lesson plans, anime, or K-dramas.

Four rescue dogs give her the privilege of living with them, and they keep her sane-ish.

This is her debut novel and series. If you want to contact Mari, feel free to connect on:

Twitter
Facebook
FacebookGroup
Website
Amazon
Instagram
She can't wait to hear from you!

facebook.com/maridietzauthor
twitter.com/marildietz
instagram.com/maridietz